WHAT'S IT
gonna take

USA TODAY BESTSELLING AUTHOR

LACEY BLACK

Lacey Black

What's It Gonna Take
Burgers and Brew Crüe, book 5

Cover Design by Melissa Gill Designs
Photographer Wander Aguiar
Model James Clippinger

Editing by Kara Hildebrand

Proofreading by Sandra Shipman, Joanne Thompson, and Karen Hrdlicka

Format by Brenda Wright, Formatting Done Wright

IBSN-13: 978-1-951829-30-8

Lacey Black

Reagan

"I quit," I belt out the moment my ass hits the pub chair.

My cousin, Madelyn, blinks at me from across the table. "What?"

I sigh deeply and reach for the glass of water already sitting at the table, fully aware it's probably hers. "Yep. I quit. I didn't even give notice."

"Wow, okay," Madelyn states, watching me gulp down her water and absently rubbing the small swell of her stomach. "Tell me everything."

I glance down and smile, loving the way pregnancy looks on my most favorite person in the world. My cousin Madelyn has only been a part of my life for the last few years, but it's as if she's always been by my side. Our mothers are sisters but were never close. In fact, our childhood was as different as night and day. Madelyn grew up in New York, rubbing elbows with the elite, while I've worked entry-level jobs and lived in Small Town, USA my entire life.

"Well, I was the only teller who applied for the branch receptionist position, and Archer decided to give it to some newbie tartlet with perky double D's and blond extensions." I can feel my heart rate spiking just thinking about it.

"He's such an asshole," Madelyn mumbles, waving to someone behind me, but I don't turn to see who. I'm still too fired up over my afternoon confrontation, and the resulting quitting of my job, to be polite to whoever is nearby.

"He is. Capital ass, capital hole," I proclaim. "That's why I quit. Ever since he took over as bank manager last year, he's been pushing it with the employees, even more so than he did before," I add.

Back when Madelyn moved to town, Archer pressed me for her number, begging for me to introduce them. They went on one date, which didn't go well for him. Actually, that date was the night my cousin met her now-husband and father of her unborn baby, Jameson.

He co-owns this restaurant and bar, Burgers and Brew, with three of his friends. It's the best place to grab lunch, dinner, or just unwind with a cold drink after a long day of work. They also own the brewery next door, which makes my favorite beer, All American Crüe. They've been distributing regionally throughout Ohio until about a year ago, when they were picked up by a major grocery chain. You can now find several varieties of Crüe Brew in fifteen states throughout the Midwest and eastern United States.

"I'm not saying Shellie with an I E isn't qualified to man the phones and greet customers who walk in, but I'm pretty sure her bra size is bigger than her IQ, and there's no way she deserves to get that position over me, especially since she's only been there three weeks," I state, probably a little too loudly, but I'm beyond caring at this point.

I've worked my butt off at Stewart Grove Trust and Savings, starting as a drive-up cashier before moving to the lobby side. I love people, have always enjoyed chatting and helping customers with their banking needs, but I'll be honest, money is dirty. You can only clean your hands so many times before your fingers start looking like raisins, dry and cracked from too much hand sanitizer. I've had to buy stock in fruity lotion.

That's why I wanted the new position. I could still talk to the customers without having to touch money all day. It was the perfect job for me.

Until it was given to twenty-one-year-old Shellie *with an I E*.

"So...you quit. What are you going to do now?" my cousin asks, worry marring her beautiful features.

I shrug. "No idea. Probably lose my apartment, my car, and be living on the streets in less than two months." My laugh is humorless.

Where's the alcohol?

Just as I turn to find a server or bartender or hell, even a janitor who can get me a beer, my face practically jams into the armpit of a man. A tall man. Sexy one too, who smells woodsy and clean and makes my blood hum through my veins.

He also knows he causes this reaction, which is why he does it. Garreth Taylor has nothing better to do than to tease me. He has worked as the assistant manager of Burgers and Brew for about four years, so our paths have crossed on several occasions. Especially since we have girls' night here most Tuesday nights.

"If you wanted to get closer to me, I can think of other places you can stick your face, love. Unless you have a thing for armpits. Is it a kink?"

I sigh and pull my head back so I can look up into gorgeous smiling eyes the color of rich, dark chocolate. "Why is your armpit near my face?"

He ignores my question. "I mean, I'm all for exploring whatever kinky side you have. Wanna tie me up? I'm game. Whips and a ball gag? I'm willing to try it once. All you have to do is say the word."

I roll my eyes dramatically and turn back to face Madelyn, doing everything I can to ignore the dull ache of desire that starts between my thighs. Garreth has one hand positioned on the back of my pub chair and the other on the tabletop, and the way he leans in and toward me makes me all too aware of his close proximity.

"I was just getting ready to flag someone down to get me a drink, since no one has come to our table yet," I retort, even though that's not completely true. I've only sat down a few minutes ago, and Madelyn already has something to drink.

Garreth smiles a heart-stopping grin. One that makes my stomach flutter with the release of a hundred butterflies. "Well, look no further, love. The man you've been looking for is right here."

I can still smell him.

I school my features and plaster on my best *you're-annoying-me* face, even though my heart feels like it's going to tap dance out of my chest. Usually, this is when I feel incredibly guilty for finding him so damn attractive, but I can't help it. The man flirts shamelessly with me, always doing everything in his power to cause a reaction. "I have a boyfriend," I remind him for the umpteenth time.

Ever since I met the man, he's been nothing but a huge flirt. Always with that big, cocky smile and that perfectly proportioned, handsome face that women drool over. And the hair. A shaggy blond head of hair that your fingers just beg to dive into and pull. Every time I remind him of my significant other, it seems to only spur him on further.

But I will also say, in the time I've known Garreth, he's never taken it too far. It's always that bold teasing I've come to expect anytime he's near. He's never made me feel uncomfortable or like he's overstepping when he does it. If anything, he makes me smile, even though I won't let him see it. No, a smile would only encourage his flirting more.

"You wound me," he replies dramatically, bringing his hands to cover his heart.

Unable to hold back my chuckle, I shake my head at his antics. "How about a beer?"

"Anything for you," he croons, setting a napkin down in front of me. He doesn't have to ask what kind I want. He already knows. I order the exact same drink every Tuesday.

"Sorry we're late," BJ announces as she approaches the table, Mallory hot on her heels. "This one had a boob emergency."

Garreth steps back so he's not blocking the chair beside me, allowing BJ to easily slip onto the seat, but he doesn't go far. He moves directly behind where I sit, his fingers brushing against me as he holds the back. "Ladies, welcome. I was just getting ready to grab drinks. What are you having?"

"Regular margarita, on the rocks with salt," Mallory orders, taking one of the remaining seats.

"Beer. A big one," BJ states before she yawns. BJ's married to Isaac, one of the owners of the restaurant and bar.

"Coming right up," Garreth replies before heading for the bar.

"They're busy tonight," Mallory notes, her eyes automatically moving to the bar, as if she's looking for her husband behind it, even though he's home tonight with the kids. She's married to Walker, the man who runs this side of the business and keeps the alcohol flowing. They've been married five years and have three kids. Lizzie is eight, Duncan is four and a half, and Waylon is almost two.

"They are," BJ confirms. "Did you notice Garreth didn't even blink when I mentioned your boobs?"

Madelyn giggles. "That's because he's used to you talking about them."

"Very true. My boobs always seem to be the focus of conversation at least once during the course of the night," Mallory confirms.

"So what happened tonight?" I ask, trying to keep my eyes focused on my friends and not on the sexy assistant manager who's helping behind the bar.

"My bra strap broke."

"And her boobs were practically flying all over the place," BJ adds. "Walker was happy."

"He's always happy when my boobs make an appearance."

"Sorry, sorry I'm late!" Lyndee cries, practically running to our table and flopping onto the remaining chair. "Elliott had a diaper explosion right before I was set to walk out the door." Elliott is her and Jasper's two-year-old son. Jasper is one of the other co-owners, the wizard in the kitchen. "What did I miss?"

"Mallory's boobs fell out and Reagan apparently quit her job," my cousin announces, causing all eyes to turn to me.

"You did?" BJ asks with wide eyes.

"Do you have something else lined up?" Mallory inquires.

"Was it because Archer Stewart is an asshole?" Lyndee hedges innocently.

"Part of the reason, yes," I confirm, glancing around for my beer.

As if knowing I'm eyeing him, Garreth looks up. He's setting two beers on a tray, doing it easily and without spilling a drop, all while maintaining our gaze. Someone else sets the margarita down beside the glasses, and he picks them all up and carries them our way. "Ladies, your first round," he says, setting drinks down around the table before looking at Lyndee. "Wine?" When she confirms with a nod, he adds, "Your server tonight is Max, and he should be here in a few minutes," before turning to grab Lyndee's drink.

"Thanks, Garreth," Mallory hollers before chugging some of her margarita.

"Anything for you, ladies," he replies with a big grin and a wink before heading back to help at the bar.

"He's been a godsend," BJ announces, even though everyone at the table already knows it. They've all discussed it in great lengths several times, appreciating the fact their husbands can trust their business to someone else, giving them all a little more free time to be with their families.

"I heard we had a diaper problem." Lyndee turns to see her husband approaching our table.

"It was more of an explosion, and it was nasty," she confirms, giving him a hard kiss on the lips. "Dustin was gagging and refused to help clean it up."

"Can't say I'm not glad I wasn't there for that," he teases, tapping her on the nose as he gazes lovingly down at her.

"Yeah, you're always gone when the really bad ones happen," she quips, sticking her tongue out at him.

He laughs. "I can't stay too long but wanted to say hello." Jasper bends down and steals another kiss. "Love you."

"Love you too. I'll come see you before we leave," she announces, earning a nod from her sexy husband before he walks away to return to the kitchen.

"You two are so cute," Mallory says, already slurping up more alcohol, "but I want to hear more about Reagan's job."

Sighing, I take a long drink of my beer before launching into the same short spiel about Archer giving the job to someone else, even though I'm better suited. Plus, I've put in over four years at that job, far more than Miss Perky D's.

"So, what now?" BJ asks.

I shrug. "I'm not sure. I'll find something. I always land on my feet," I insist, dreading the whole application and interview process in my immediate future.

"You can always work here. Isaac was saying they're short a bartender, which is probably why Garreth has been helping," BJ informs as the man himself approaches carrying Lyndee's wine.

"Max is still handling another table, so let me get your orders into the chef," he states, flashing a grin that seems to make everyone swoon just a little. I bet everywhere this man goes, there's a trail of wet panties left in his wake.

Everyone starts hollering out their orders, and I watch in complete fascination as he nods with each one, not bothering to write them down. He never does. Every time he's waited on us, he remembers what we ask for and delivers the plates perfectly. I can see why all the employees love working for him.

"Umm…Reagan? Isn't that Justin?" my cousin asks, drawing my attention away from the hot assistant manager.

"What? Where?" Turning toward the front entrance, I find my boyfriend, Justin, and his assistant, Tia, enter the bar. Weird. "He said he was working late tonight, since I was doing girls' night."

Then, he throws his arm over her shoulder and draws her into his side.

Okay. Very weird.

And very friendly.

"Uhh…" BJ says as Tia laughs at something my boyfriend says.

Justin takes his hand and wraps it around her hip, pulling her petite body against his chest. His tongue then falls into her mouth. Yep. That's the only way to describe it. Like an out of body experience, I sit here and watch my boyfriend's tongue do an impression of this sickening mating ritual bit I read about in a sci-fi romance book I accidentally bought years ago. Tia seems to love it, her mouth wrapping around my boyfriend's tongue and sucking.

Gross!

"What the hell is going on, Reag?" Madelyn whispers as we all stare at the show.

I'm up and moving before I can consider what I'm going to say. What does one say when confronting their boyfriend, who's tongue-fucking his assistant in the middle of a busy bar? "Justin, what the hell?" I demand the moment I reach his side.

He looks at me, startled and confused. "Hey, Reagan." He sounds nervous.

Good.

Fucker.

"Uhh, yeah. *Hey.*" I prop my hands on my hips, waiting patiently for someone to tell me what in the world is going on. You know, like Ashton Kutcher. I'm pretty certain he's about to jump out from behind the bar and yell, "Punk'd!"

When that doesn't happen, I glare a little harder at my boyfriend, who has the audacity to shift and hide behind Tia.

Loser.

"Did you, uh… Well, I sent a text."

"A text?" I ask, fully aware we've now drawn eyes from all over the bar.

"Yeah." He swallows hard. "About us," he adds, guilt written all over his face. "Didn't you get it?"

My mouth drops open as realization sets in. "You broke up with me…in a text?"

He lifts his shoulder, as if it's no big deal. "Well, yeah. You were busy with your girls' night. I didn't want to bother you," he insists, glancing across the room to the table where my friends sit.

"And you thought bringing your assistant and making out with her in the place you knew we were coming for dinner was the way to not *bother* me?"

Again, he shrugs. "I guess. Listen, we're gonna have dinner, okay?" Justin says, turning pleading eyes to Tia, as if she can somehow get him out of this awkward situation.

"Yeah, sure. Sorry to interrupt." As I get ready to turn and walk away, I holler, "Oh, and Justin? I hope you get the clap and every erection you have for the rest of your life ends with you pissing fire." And because I can't stop myself, I turn to Tia. "I hope you don't mind three-minutes' worth of—" I hold up my pinky to demonstrate exactly what she's in for.

Then, with my head held high, I turn and walk back to my table, dozens of sets of eyes trailing me the entire way. There's a lump the size of Texas in my throat, but I will those emotions away, begging them to just hold off until I'm alone before they fly. I will not cry over a jerk like Justin in public.

I will not.

Especially with Garreth Taylor watching.

Garreth

My blood is boiling.

What kind of douche canoe sends a text to break up with a woman, and then shows up at the same place said woman you just broke up with is eating dinner?

Justin fucking Morales, that's who.

I want to punch him in his smug, dirtbag face, but I won't because my employers frown upon it. Well, maybe not Jameson as much as the others, especially when he hears what happened to his wife's cousin. He'd probably jump to the head of the line to knock out a few teeth.

I remember growing up with Jameson and Walker. They definitely weren't afraid to get into parking lot scuffles. We didn't hang in the same circles, but I never had any issues with them. I was just more focused on getting good grades, playing baseball, and getting into college.

After college, I stayed in Cleveland, but not in the field to utilize my engineering degree. I actually discovered I enjoyed the restaurant industry. I worked as a dishwasher, bartender, and server through much of my post-high school years at a little place near campus called Tiny's Tavern. It was always packed on Friday and Saturday nights, even with their limited bar-food menu.

14

When I graduated, I started searching for a job as an IT consultant, but after interviewing at several different companies, I realized it wasn't what I really wanted to do. I enjoyed my job at Tiny's, so I threw away four years' worth of college education and found a job as an evening assistant manager at a restaurant. From there, I grew, eventually managing one of the biggest restaurants in Cleveland.

Reagan approaches where I stand, eavesdropping on her confrontation and not ashamed in the least. Her eyes are cast down at first, and when they finally meet mine, I can see her embarrassment and anger swirling together like a tornado. Part of me wants to reach out and pull her against my chest, vowing to kick his ass for hurting her, but I know she won't appreciate that right now.

Instead, I go to the one place I know will get a reaction out of her. "I'm so turned on right now," I mutter, throwing her a wink and a smile.

Just like that, the shock and rage reflecting in her stunning eyes falls away and is replaced by laughter. "Oh my God," she sputters through her giggle fit. "What is wrong with you?"

See? This right here. I'd rather see her happy and laughing instead of what that asshole made her feel like. When she smiles, there's this light that surrounds her. It's vibrant and makes me feel like I won a million dollars or something equally as badass.

"You wound me, love." I place a hand over my heart and sigh dramatically.

Reagan rolls her eyes, much as I'd expect her to. "You're nuts."

I sober and step closer, greedily breathing in her sweet scent. "Do you want me to drop a drink in his lap? Or maybe step on his patty before I serve it? I'd do it in a heartbeat, for you," I tell her, only half-joking.

Reagan gives me a sad smile, and Jesus, I don't like it. "I do appreciate the offer, but I don't think that's necessary. Please don't make any health code violations on my behalf," she replies with the faintest grin on her pretty lips.

"If you change your mind, send me a signal, okay? Maybe blow me a kiss from across the room or twerk. Twerking's always good."

Her face completely relaxes as she laughs and shakes her head. "You're terrible. I'm going to head back to my friends," she says, reaching out and squeezing my arm. Little bolts of lightning streak through my veins and land firmly in my balls. It's hard to just stand here and watch her walk away. "Oh, Garreth?"

Glancing up, I meet her gaze. "Yes?"

"Thank you. For making me smile." She rewards me with another small smile.

My throat is tight with emotion. "Anytime."

Reagan rejoins her party, immediately jumping into an animated telling of what happened over with Justin. As much as I'd love to go over there, I can't. I have a job to do, which right now, is serving the ex. Even if I'd rather kick his ass out or just flat-out refuse to serve him, that's not my job, and I always strive to do the best job I can.

Dammit.

By the time we close, I'm exhausted and ready to kick off my boots. They're horribly uncomfortable to work in at a place like this, where I'm on my feet for hours on end, but I've learned to just deal with it. Sneakers look too casual for my liking, and I'm not required to wear dress clothes like the previous place I managed, so boots it is. Plus, I just feel more comfortable in them and jeans.

I flip off the lighted open sign and lock the front door. The entrance over at the restaurant was locked shortly after nine and that area is roped off to keep patrons from going over there. Usually, I help the servers clean the restaurant side, but tonight, I just wasn't able to. The bar was busy enough I had to help Max and Dalton. Max is in training and is still learning how to be a little more efficient with his time and pace, but I have high hopes for the young man.

I jump behind the bar and start stocking the coolers before Jameson can. That's usually the first job he helps with, but I haven't seen him since he popped over to kiss his wife and check on the girls at dinner earlier this evening. When he does finally make his appearance from the brewery next door, his wife and her cousin are hot on his heels.

"Sorry. They were filling me in on what happened with Justin earlier in the evening, and I lost track of time," Jameson says, grabbing bottles of beer and sliding them into the cooler.

I recall having to put on my best professional face to take care of Justin and Tia. No, I didn't spill his drink on him or step on his hamburger patty, but when I mentioned what happened to Jasper, he might have *accidentally* added a little extra pepper to his steak fries. The douche spent his entire dinner wiping his brow and chugging liquid, which definitely gave me a little satisfaction where Reagan is concerned. "No problem. We have it handled."

"How's Max doing?"

I shrug and glance behind me, making sure he's not standing right there. "He's doing all right. He's still slow, which is why I spent the night helping on this side, but he's getting it."

Jameson nods. "It doesn't help Dirk didn't show up again," he states, shaking his head.

"No, definitely not. It's his second late call-off in as many weeks. I'm going to ask him to come in early before his next shift to find out why. I hate to just fire the guy, because he does have all that baby mama drama going on, but at the same time, he needs to know we're counting on him to work his shifts."

"Let us know how it goes," he says, referring to him and his partners. I usually answer to Isaac, or Numbers as everyone calls him, but I still work closely with the others. I'm in on the hiring process, along with either Numbers or Walker, depending on what position they're interviewing for. I oversee the training for the restaurant and bar, while Jasper takes care of the kitchen.

At first, I was a little concerned about working for so many men. I mean, the whole too many rock stars and not enough roadies was a legitimate concern, but once I started, I realized I had nothing to worry about. Each of the four owners has their own area of expertise, and it really works for them. I'm incredibly grateful to be back in my hometown and working here. They're phenomenal bosses.

Laughter pulls my attention away from my task. It's a sound I'd recognize anywhere. Turning, I find Reagan and Madelyn sitting at the far end of the bar, staring down at a phone screen, big smiles on their faces. She looks so much happier now than earlier, despite the fact it's past ten. Usually, Reagan leaves with the others during girls' nights, but not tonight. I suppose her not having a job to go to tomorrow morning has something to do with it.

"So, when you gonna tell Reagan you've got a crush on her? Want me to pass a note in study hall?"

The question startles me, my eyes ripping from Reagan to Jameson. "What?"

The asshole smirks at me. "Fine, pretend you don't know what I'm talking about. You've been sweet on Reagan for as long as I can remember."

"Sweet on her? What is this 1955?" I ask with a chuckle, deflecting.

"Try and change the subject all you want, but it doesn't change the fact it's true. Everyone sees it."

Panic bubbles in my gut, mostly because I thought I'd done a better job at hiding my attraction to Reagan. "Everyone?" I ask, sounding surprisingly casual.

Jameson shrugs his broad shoulders. "Well, I do. And Numbers. I think Jasper too, come to think of it. Not sure about Walker though. He's only working two nights a week, so he doesn't get to see you drool all over Reagan like the rest of us."

"I...don't drool over her," I retort lamely.

"Do. Bad. I mean, don't get me wrong, none of the staff have said anything about it, so it's probably not obvious to everyone, but I can definitely see it." He glances over at his wife, the faintest smile playing on his lips. "I'm an expert at sitting back and watching."

I busy myself with emptying the case in front of me before closing the cooler to grab more. Jameson is hot on my heels, carrying three cases to my two, and before I know it, the cooler is completely stocked.

Jasper is standing at the end of the bar with the ladies, so while Jameson heads over to talk to them, I busy myself behind the bar with the register, closing it out. Max goes to clean tables and set barstools on top of them, while Dalton washes all the dirty glasses. The entire nightly process definitely goes much faster and smoother with extra hands.

When I have the tips distributed, I hand each guy their stack of bills. I don't keep any from the tip jar. I get paid handsomely to do my job, and even though I help a lot in the bar and restaurant, those tips are for the ones who make a smaller wage and receive the tips as supplement. "Thanks, Garreth," Dalton says before clocking out on the tablet and heading for the back door.

"Hey, sorry to have to pull you in to help me with the tables," Max says, an apologetic look on his face.

"Don't worry about it, man. It takes time when you've never worked in a restaurant before," I reassure him.

"I'll get better and faster. Promise."

I grab his shoulder and give it a squeeze in support. "Don't stress. You're doing really well. You'll pick up the pace as you get more comfortable behind the bar and at the tables."

Max nods and takes off for the exit.

Finally, I'm able to take a deep breath and head to where the small group is gathered. They're the last ones here. Madelyn, Jameson, Jasper, and Reagan sitting together and chatting, and the moment I approach, they pull me into their conversation.

"What do you think about hiring Reagan? Shantel is going on maternity leave next week, and we haven't hired anyone," Jasper says, leaning his elbows on the bar.

I avoid looking over at Reagan, who just so happens to be sitting on the stool closest to me. "We haven't hired anyone because between me and the servers, we thought we'd have it covered for six or eight weeks," I reply, tilting to my right and catching a whiff of her sweet scent.

"True, but it would keep you free to finish training Max," Jasper reasons.

"And she can bounce between restaurant and bar and fill in where needed," Jameson adds, and I swear I can see him trying to hide the faintest hint of a smile on his lips.

"You know what, guys, this is silly. You don't have a position open right now. I told you, I'll apply at the grocery store or the other bank in town. Hell, I bet I could even pick up hours at that new clothing boutique that just opened. I'll be fine," Reagan declares, waving off the conversation regarding her.

"No, I think we could definitely use you," I find myself stating without giving it a second thought. Honestly, I'm not sure it's a great idea. On the nights Reagan is here, I find myself a little...distracted. She's fucking beautiful, and I'm so attracted to her, it makes it hard to do my job when she's near. Having her here may very well cause my professional demise, but she needs a job, and I can't seem to stop myself from wanting it to be here.

With me.

I feel her gaze on me, so I quickly add, "How soon can you start?"

Reagan stares at me with shock-filled eyes. "Well, I guess anytime, considering I quit my job today with no notice," she says with a little chuckle.

The sound makes my balls ache.

"How about tomorrow at three thirty? You can fill out the paperwork, and then work with Shantel from four to nine."

She nods. "That works. Thank you."

I throw her a smile, and not the cocky one I usually use to get her riled up. "Great." When I glance up, I see Jameson grinning a rare smile, and it's full of humor and mischief. I'm just glad he doesn't call me on the fact it's my night off, but I'll be working now to train the new employee.

"All right, let's get out of here. My wife is home waiting on me," Jasper announces, slapping the bar top and heading for the back exit.

I flip off the lights as we go, following behind the rest of the group. Outside, the warm summer still hangs heavy in the air. It's not as humid as it has been, but the night still holds that wet, sticky feel. Tomorrow is probably going to be suffocating, but that's what Midwest summer nights are like in late July.

Jasper throws a quick wave and heads to his sports car. Though, I will say he went from a two-door Mercedes Roadster to a different four-door model. Jameson leads Madelyn toward his classic 1972 Chevy Nova and opens the passenger door for her. It'll be interesting to see what he does with his vehicle once their baby arrives. Chances are he'll keep driving the car he's had since high school and put so much time, money, and energy into. It was a piece of shit when he first got it, but as a former mechanic, he spent a lot of love on his car, turning it into the classic car of any gearhead's wet dream.

Madelyn hugs Reagan before slipping into the passenger seat of the car, and I'm heading her way before I even realize I'm moving. "Are you okay to drive?" I ask the moment I'm standing beside her.

"Oh, yeah. I stopped drinking when I finished my food a few hours ago and switched to water. I'm more than good," she insists, rocking back on her heels as she gazes up at me.

"I can take you home if needed." I don't know why I said that, other than wanting to make sure she gets there safely.

Her grin is slow and makes her hazel eyes sparkle like brilliant golden topaz, the color of my birthstone. "I appreciate the offer, but I'll be fine."

Nodding, I watch as she slips into the front seat of her newer Ford Fusion and turns over the engine. Reagan gives me a little wave, shuts the door, and slowly starts to back out of her parking spot. All I can do is stand here and watch her go, this deep yearning swirling in my stomach. Why do I wish I were taking her home, and not necessarily to her own apartment? I'd be fine with her going back to my place for the night.

With my hands shoved in the pockets of my jeans, I head to my own truck parked at the back of the lot. To go home. Alone.

Crushes suck.

Reagan

Why am I nervous?

This isn't the first time I've started a new job. This is, however, the first time I've started a new job working for a man like Garreth. One I'm completely attracted to, despite the fact I shouldn't be. I never would have done anything with him while dating someone, even if that someone was Justin, but Garreth Taylor is the biggest flirt I've ever met. He can't help it. It's just the way he is, which is why I need to repel him like bug spray.

Too bad the butterflies in my stomach didn't get the memo.

I slip on a pair of somewhat comfortable flats, praying they don't completely kill my feet by the end of the night. They were my favorite pair to wear at the bank, but I had the luxury of sitting most of the time at that job. I have a feeling I'll be on my feet and running most of the evening at Burgers and Brew.

With one last look in the mirror, I grab my purse and head out. The drive from my apartment to the restaurant is short, and before I know it, I'm pulling into the back lot used by employees and street-parking spillover. I'm still fifteen minutes early, but I can't help it. I'm always early everywhere I go. The thought of being late—especially on my first day—gives me anxiety.

Taking a few deep, calming breaths, I slip from my car, make sure it's locked, and walk to the front of the building, since I don't have a key or access code for the back entrance. I choose to go in the bar side, since that's where Garreth was working last night. Inside, the jukebox plays softly and a few patrons are perched on stools at the bar. There's even a small group of men enjoying either a late lunch or an early dinner at one of the tables.

"Hey, Reag," Walker hollers from behind the bar.

"Good afternoon. I'm here to meet Garreth. I'm going to help out for a while," I reply, walking up to the end of the bar where I sat last night with Madelyn.

He nods. "I'm aware. Happy to have you helping. We can definitely use it, not that I'm complaining about how good business has been. Extra hands are much appreciated," he says with a friendly smile.

"There she is."

That voice. I'd recognize it anywhere.

Pasting on my most professional smile, I turn and face Garreth. He's wearing dark jeans and a green polo with the business logo over his left pec. His hair is down, those longer tendrils framing his handsome face, and he's wearing his own smile, one that makes my lady parts quiver. He winks, probably because he can read my mind and knows exactly how he affects me. It's probably written all over my face, like a neon sign declaring "I think about you naked!"

"Ready to get started?" he asks, interrupting my thoughts.

"Yes. Of course," I insist, pushing all thoughts about a naked Garreth out of my head.

He's my new boss.

He's my new boss!

Get it together, Reagan.

Garreth places his hand on my lower back and guides me toward the same pub table in the back our group usually occupies when we're here. When I take a seat, he hands me a stack of employment papers to fill out. "These are pretty basic. We'll provide

24

you with work shirts to wear. You can take them home and wash them first if you'd prefer. What you have on tonight is fine," he says, taking in my fitted white button-down shirt. I didn't really know what to wear, so I went with a nice shirt and my favorite jeans.

"Okay."

"I'll give you time and be back shortly. Holler if you have any questions."

He leaves me alone to fill out the basic application and tax forms. There's also an employee handbook to review and sign on the last page. It's all straight forward and something you have to complete at any job, but I still take my time reviewing the documents before signing anything. That's something my grandparents—especially my grandma—always instilled in me growing up.

A little while later, I'm signing the last paper when Garreth returns. "How's it going?"

"Just finished," I inform, restacking the papers and handing them over.

"Perfect. Shantel just arrived, so let's go see the break room and time clock system, and then I'll introduce you."

I follow Garreth down the back hallway, past the bathrooms. "This is my office," he says, pointing to the closed door. He uses a key to enter and grabs an envelope off the desk. "This key will get you in the back door. There is also your security code. At the end of the night, I'll show you how to use the system."

Nodding, I slip the envelope into my purse and follow him out. We round the corner and continue. "Up those stairs is Numbers' office. We'd go say hello, but he ran home to stay with his kid for a bit while BJ went in to work. Here," he says, waving his hand for me to enter, "is the employee break room. Your locker number is on your envelope. If you want to secure it with a lock, there are some combination locks in the cabinet there, but for the record, we've never had an issue with theft or anyone messing with anyone's stuff. So do what you feel comfortable with, 'kay?"

I nod, slipping my purse into locker number seven, as indicated on my envelope.

Next, he moves over to a large metal cabinet and unlocks the door. Inside, there are stacks of shirts, all with their company logo on them. Short-sleeved polos, long-sleeved ones, crewneck shirts, and T-shirts. "The bartenders wear the tees, and we give the restaurant staff the option of polo or T-shirt. Usually, as the hostess, I'd suggest the polo, but since you're going to help float in the bar too, I'll let you pick."

"Polo works for me. Medium, please," I reply, starting to feel slightly overwhelmed when he hands me a variety of black and gray ones. "Oh, I only need one. I can wash it before my next shift."

He's already shaking his head. "Nope. We always provide our staff with five. If you need more, let me know," he states, closing and locking the cabinet. "Let me show you the kitchen, and then we'll head to the hostess stand."

I don't tell him I've been in the kitchen before. Ever since my cousin started dating, and eventually marrying, one of the owners, I've become somewhat familiar with the staff and happenings at this business. Even more so than everyday knowledge of other people living in this small town.

"I don't see any damn avocado slices!"

The moment we step through the swinging door, I'm bathed in the sounds and smells of a busy kitchen.

"That's a dollar in the jar," a man hollers from the dishwasher, a smug smile on his face.

"Bullshit! Damn isn't a swear word," Jasper bellows at the man, flipping a pair of patties on the grill.

"Maybe not, but bullshit is. Dollar in the jar." The man grabs a jar off the shelf beside him and holds it up. I can't help but notice it's already pretty full.

Garreth chuckles as we approach. "Some people have gambling habits. Jasper here has a cursing problem."

He points his metal spatula at the man next to me. "Don't you start with me too." Then, as if realizing I'm there, his face softens a little as he smiles. "Hey, Reagan. Good to see you again."

"You too, Jasper."

The man walks up, making a big show of removing the lid off the jar and holding it out.

Jasper sighs dramatically before digging his wallet out of his pocket and pulling a five from within. "Here. Consider me four ahead. I have a feeling I'm still going to come out ahead on this deal."

The man laughs, snatching the bill from Jasper's hand and stuffing it in the jar. "Thank you, kind sir. Now, get back to work, or you'll burn your food."

Jasper shakes his head, shoves his wallet back in his pocket, and walks over to the sink to wash his hands. "That smart-ass at the dishwasher is Patrick. Patrick, Reagan. She's going to help us as hostess and float between the bar and the restaurant."

"Good to meet you, Reagan," the polite man says before returning his attention to his job.

"You too," I say, feeling Garreth's hand on my lower back.

"What's with the jar?" I ask when Jasper dries off his hands and goes back to the grill.

"Lyndee's pi-*upset* because Elliott heard me say asshole last weekend. Now it's his new favorite word."

I hide my smile behind my hand, picturing their two-year-old son walking around and yelling asshole.

"It's not that funny, Reagan. Lyndee made me sleep on the couch that night," Jasper states, carefully crafting two burgers on the plates in front of him. As soon as he does, someone else places a stack of homemade steak fries and sprinkles them with their signature seasoning. "Order up!"

"Come on, Reag. Shantel is waiting."

I throw Jasper a wave and follow my new boss out a different set of swinging doors that leads right into the main dining room. Off to my right, I find the servers' station, where they retrieve drinks and other necessities to take care of their tables. We continue walking through the restaurant, toward the front, where a petite redhead is sitting on a stool beside the hostess stand, her belly very swollen with pregnancy.

"Shantel, I'd like you to meet Reagan. Reag, this lovely woman is Shantel. She's going to help train you on the hostess duties."

The pregnant woman gets up and extends her hand. "You used to work at the bank, right?"

"I did. It's a pleasure to officially meet you," I reply, returning the gesture. "I believe your older brother was in my class in school."

"Shane or Spencer?"

"Shane. Spencer was two years younger, right?"

She nods, returning to her seat. "Yes, and I was four years younger than Spence. I'm married to Jackson Angelo. His parents own the travel agency down the road."

"Oh, yes. I know Anne and Hans. She was at the bank just the other day, boasting about her first grandchild arriving soon."

Shantel smiles, glances down, and rubs her belly. "It's a boy, and we're all pretty excited."

"I bet."

"I'll let you two get to it," Garreth says, pulling us back to the reason I'm here. "Shantel, holler if you need anything."

"Will do, Garreth."

He backs up, his gaze holding mine just a little longer than appropriate and sending goosebumps across my skin. When he turns around, I can't help but steal a quick glance at his ass, which looks pretty amazing in a pair of blue jeans, I might add.

With a sigh, I return my eyes to the woman who's going to train me, ignoring the knowing smirk on her face. "Okay. Let's do this."

"Reagan, can you clear off the last table?" Kellen asks from behind the bar without looking up from the drink he's making. "Max went on break, and I have a few more drinks to make."

I'm already heading that way. "Absolutely."

Tonight has been an eye-opener. This place is busy, despite it being the middle of the week. The restaurant filled up just after five and stayed that way until nearly seven o'clock. I picked up their seating system pretty easily and was able to give Shantel the opportunity to rest her feet while I seated guests. After that, I moved over to the bar side to help, since there weren't as many people coming through the main entrance. The bar has been hopping since, keeping Max, Kellen, and even Garreth busy.

I reach the table and start stacking cups and plates to take them to the kitchen. Just as I grab the used napkins in the center of the table, a large, warm hand does the same, causing our fingers to collide. "Sorry," I quickly say as my eyes look up and meet Garreth's rich brown ones.

He takes the napkins and the stack of dirty plates in his hand, leaving me with the cups. "How's your first night going? You seemed to be doing well on the other side."

I follow behind him as we move through the bar to the kitchen and place the used stuff in the bin to be washed. Patrick is loading up the dishwasher again, shaking his head. "That's the last of it," Garreth announces.

"Good deal. I'll get these all washed and put away," Patrick states, reaching for the dirty dishes.

We're moving back out the door moments later. "Usually our dishwasher buses tables, but sometimes they get backed up in the kitchen, so servers will jump in and help, especially if we need the table. If that happens, flag me down so I can get the table cleared."

"I don't mind helping with that. I mean, that's why I'm here, right?"

He stares at me for a few long seconds before finally nodding. "It is." Clearing his throat, he adds, "Come up to the bar and I'll show you how to add drinks to an existing tab."

That's how we spend the next hour and a half, until it's time to lock the door. I admit, I'm exhausted, overwhelmed, and ready to get off my feet. I received a short dinner break with a free meal, as well as a break to put my feet up for a few minutes. I also realized I'm going to need to purchase new shoes if I'm going to make it an entire seven-plus hour shift on my feet.

I wince a bit and lift my foot, trying to alleviate some of the discomfort.

"You okay?" Kellen asks.

I startle, not realizing I was just standing here, staring off into space. "Oh, yeah. Sorry, just zoned out for a second," I reply with an awkward chuckle, grabbing the wet, soapy cloth to make sure all of the tables and chairs are wiped down before I flip the stools over and hang them off the bar and pub tables.

"Come on," he says, following me around to the front of the bar and slapping the first stool we come to. "Sit."

Confusion must be written all over my face. "Excuse me?"

"Your feet. They must be killing you in those things. You'll learn real quick-like around here, some shoes are made for comfort, some for style. A few shifts in the wrong shoe, and you'll instantly be ready to flip to the other category," he says, slapping the stool once more. "Up you go."

Unsure what's happening, I slowly take a seat on the stool. When I look down, I see the boots on his feet. "You're telling me those work boots are the most comfortable things to wear in a bar?"

"Hell no. Gel inserts help. Maybe you can try them," he suggests.

My eyes zero in on my slip-ons. "Probably not an option. There isn't much room to add an insert."

Kellen props his boot on the footrest of my chair and taps his upper thigh. "Come on. First night foot rub. It's a tradition."

I bark out a laugh. "You're going to massage my feet? Do you do that for everyone who works here?"

He fakes offense, dramatically placing his hand over his heart, and I shake my head at his antics. "You wound me. Of course I do. I'm a nice guy."

"Nice guys better get behind the bar and finish their shift."

We both glance over and find Garreth standing there, his arms crossed over his chest. There's a look there I've never seen before. No, that's not true. It's the same look he wore last night after the whole Justin and Tia fiasco.

"Busted," Kellen mumbles. "Sorry, boss. The lady was complaining about her feet hurting, so I was going to give them a little rub."

"Rub feet on your own time, McGregor."

Kellen salutes Garreth. "Aye, aye, Captain. Sorry, Reag. Looks like the foot massage will have to be later tonight. If you give me your number, I'll—"

"Back to work," Garreth interrupts, stepping beside me as I scramble from the stool.

"I'm so sorry," I start, but stop when he holds up his hand. His eyes are softer now, the hard edges I saw moments ago replaced with the laugh lines I've become accustomed to seeing.

"It's fine, honestly. We all sit when needed. Go ahead and have a seat while I finish putting up the stools," he insists, grabbing the one beside me, swinging it around and setting it on top of the bar.

"No, I'll help." I grab the one next to where he stands and try flipping it. Of course, it doesn't go nearly as smooth as when he did it, but I refuse to look like a weakling in front of my boss. My very *sexy* boss, who smells amazing, despite the fact he's been working all night. I smell like grilled meat, deep fried potatoes, and beer, but Garreth smells all woodsy and fresh, like he just frolicked in a pine forest on a sunny, spring day.

His arm brushes mine as he reaches for the stool I'm jockeying. Electricity courses through my veins, and it takes every ounce of restraint I possess to keep from swaying his way.

Yeah, this may not be the brightest idea I've had. Yes, I need a job, but working alongside Garreth Taylor might be the hardest feat I've ever done. Sure, because he's my temporary boss, but mostly because he's the last type of guy I should be attracted to. I mean, I thought I had found a decent one before with Justin and look how that turned out. I'm not sure I can trust my own decision-making abilities right now.

One thing is for certain, nothing will ever come from this crush I seem to suddenly have on the flirty bar manager.

No way in hell.

Garreth

My eyes return to her again. I can't seem to stop them from seeking her out over and over again.

When I left the kitchen and returned to the bar to help get everything closed down, I was shocked to see Reagan sitting on a barstool, Kellen smiling down at her with that glint in his eye only a man with interest can have. Fuck me, I wanted to walk right over there, throw her over my shoulder, and take her away from him.

Even if I know that particular fantasy will never happen.

I'm now her boss, and that complicates things. Sure, there's no rule here about dating staff—especially after Walker married Mallory—but it's not a practice I often engage in. In fact, it's never happened. I never wanted to put myself in a position where another employee could accuse me of favoritism. I've prided myself on being fair to all employees, but now with Reagan working here, it's difficult.

Because I want her.

Bad.

Once the barstools are all hanging from the bar, I send her to gather what's left of the tabletop condiments. Basically, she's now as far away from Kellen at the bar as possible. As subtly as possible, I watch her place the salt and pepper shakers on a tray and carefully carry them to the kitchen, where they'll be filled by the kitchen staff in the morning and replaced on the tables before we open.

"Everything okay, boss?"

I look over my shoulder and find Kellen standing there, a knowing grin on his face. "Yeah, fine. Why?" I ask, pushing Reagan as far from my mind as possible.

"You just look a little...distracted. That's all." Again, he flashes a smug smile that heckles my nerves.

"Nope, not distracted at all. I just have a job to do. We *all* do," I retort.

Clearly understanding the meaning behind my statement, Kellen laughs. The fucker actually laughs at me. "Copy that, boss."

Reagan returns from dropping off the shakers and jumps in to finish hanging the stools at the pub tables. As hard as I try, I can't stop seeking her out, watching her while she works. Worse, I've had to make sure I don't flirt with her the way I usually do, which has probably been the most difficult feat of the night. Flirting tends to come to me naturally, but with Reagan, I can't help myself. The way her cheeks flush and she looks away, pretending my comments don't affect her, is what wet dreams are made of. She has this innocence about her, yet is a spitfire I find wildly attractive.

Over the years, I've found plenty of women attractive. Dated a few too. Not that many since I returned home to Stewart Grove four years ago, but there have been a couple. We never made it past a few months of casual dating, however. In fact, I haven't really had that deep connection and desire to truly get to know a woman since my ex-wife. Not until I met Reagan. I don't even really know her, but she feels different than the others I've hung out with or dated.

Not that Reagan and I are dating.

Or ever will.

"I think we're good, boss," Kellen announces, interrupting my thoughts.

"All right. Go ahead and clock out." Turning, I find Reagan standing at the end of the bar, uncertainty written all over her gorgeous face. "I'll show you how to use the keypad and lock up," I tell her.

"I can do it," Kellen offers, but I quickly shut him down.

"I got it." Somehow, I'm able to keep the bite out of my tone.

Kellen chuckles and heads for the back exit, Max hot on his heels. When I hear the door shut, I turn to Reagan. "Come on over here, and I'll show you how to clock out. You can also use the one in the break room, but we keep a second tablet with the payroll system behind the bar for convenience."

Reagan nods, following my instructions as she clocks out from her first shift. "There," she says, giving me a proud, yet relieved grin.

"Great job tonight," I tell her, feeling wildly relieved myself. "How did it go?"

She leans back against the bar, her shoulders relaxing as she sighs. "Good. I never expected to be this tired and sore. You guys are rock stars for doing this night after night," she comments.

I glance down at her feet, noticing again the shoes she chose to wear and recalling the scene I walked in on a little while ago. "Come here," I state, reaching out my hand.

She hesitates for a second, her eyes glancing down at my extended hand, before she places hers in mine. A shot of electricity shoots up my hand as our palms touch. Warmth spreads through my veins.

I lead her around to the front of the bar, and with my unoccupied hand, I toss the stool in the air, flipping it over and setting it down on the floor. "Wow, that was impressive," she states, a hint of awe in her voice.

"Lots of practice," I reply, tapping the seat.

"What?" she asks.

"Sit."

When she doesn't move fast enough, I release her hand and grab her hips, gently lifting and placing her on top of the stool. She squeaks in surprise, her delicate little hands reaching out and gripping my upper arms. Our gazes meet, and it takes every ounce of self-control I can muster to not kiss her.

As if reading my thoughts, her tongue slips out and licks her bottom lip as she looks up at me. There's a hint of nervousness in her hazel eyes, along with a touch of wonder and encouragement.

Fuck, does she have any idea how sexy she is?

To keep from kissing her, I gently lift her right leg, placing her foot on my thigh. I can feel her eyes on me as I remove the little black shoe and the thin bootie sock I didn't even realize she had on. "What are you doing?" she whispers.

My answer is to hold her foot in my hands and pressing my thumbs into the arch. Her groan in pleasure fills the room and lands squarely in my balls. My cock is hard, pressing firmly against the zipper of my jeans. It's uncomfortable and begging to be adjusted, but I ignore it. The last thing I want to do is draw attention to the reaction she causes in my groin.

"Holy shit," she mumbles as I continue to knead her foot. "I should be grossed out that you're touching my sweaty feet, but I can't seem to find the need to care right now."

I snort a laugh, gently lifting her foot and going to work on her sore, tired muscles. Her eyes flutter closed, that sexy mouth of hers falling open in ecstasy. I can't help but wonder if this is what she'd look like in bed, when I'm sliding between her thighs. Her nipples pebble against her shirt, and my mouth goes completely dry. Is she as turned on right now as I am, or is that just a reaction to the foot rub?

Needing to redirect my dirty mind, I clear my throat and lock my gaze on her feet. Of course, that doesn't really help either. Her toenails are painted a bright pink and her toes are long and lean and for some crazy reason, I even find those sexy.

"You should probably find a different pair of shoes to wear," I suggest, looking over to the left and counting to five in my head.

Her eyes slowly open and focus on me. "I've already come to that conclusion." She looks down at my boots. "Those don't look comfy either."

"They aren't," I reply with a chuckle.

"Men are weird," she mumbles. I shift her foot, taking the ball of her foot in my palm and rolling my fingers across it. "Holy shit, that's amazing. A girl could get used to this."

A man too…

I switch to the other foot and shower it with the same attention as the first, doing everything I can to turn my body enough to conceal what's going on in my pants. The last thing I want is to freak her out or have a sexual harassment suit thrown at me because I can't stop myself from getting hard when she's near.

"You can wear athletic shoes," I suggest, finishing up the second massage. "Or some of the servers in the restaurant rave about those slip-on shoes you get at the mall. They're supposed to be the most comfortable shoes you'll ever wear."

She gives me a small smile. "Thanks."

"I'm sure any of the others could give you recommendations," I offer, finally releasing her second foot and taking a step back.

The slight grin on her face never wavers. "I wasn't talking about the shoes."

Ahhh.

She meant the foot massage.

I want to propose to do it every time she works, but that's probably crossing the line too. I don't offer the other employees, so why would I offer her?

You know why…

"We should probably finish closing up," I say, turning my back and sucking in a deep breath. Being near her, having my hands on her—even just her feet—does something to me, and I'm not just referring to the problem I have in my pants.

Reagan slips back on her socks and shoes and jumps off the stool, quickly returning it to its place on the counter. She follows behind me as I shut off the lights, leaving on only one strip behind the bar and the ones in the hallway. We stop in the break room and retrieve her things, while I poke my head in the kitchen to make sure it's shut down too. Though, I don't need to do it. Jasper and the other kitchen employees always make sure it's done.

Finally, we walk to the back exit. "You probably won't be the final employee to leave, but just in case, this is how you set the alarm." I demonstrate, inputting my personal code into the system, and clicking enter. Once the beeping starts, I add, "You have one minute to exit and secure the door, which automatically locks when you leave. We also ask you to double-check it though." When we step outside and the door closes, I pull the handle to verify it's locked.

As we slowly make our way to where she's parked, I ask, "I guess we never really went over your schedule. Are you okay to work Friday and Saturday night this week?"

We stop beside her car, and she turns to face me. "Of course. Four o'clock?"

"Yes." I shove my hands in my pockets to keep from reaching out.

"Great. I'll see you then." Reagan doesn't move, at least not right away, but eventually turns and opens the driver's door and slips inside.

I reach out and close it, making sure she's secured inside before taking a step back. She turns over the engine and buckles her belt before throwing her car in reverse. I wave lamely and watch as she goes, wishing I could have invited her back to my place, but knowing it's the right thing to do to let her go.

With a loud sigh, I head to my truck and climb inside, anxious to head home. I'm not sure why though. There's nothing there but silence and loneliness. For the first time since I moved back to Stewart Grove, I wish I were going home to someone.

I wish that someone was Reagan.

"Mom?" I holler as I step through the screened door at the side of the house.

"In the kitchen," comes her reply immediately.

After kicking off my shoes, I move through the laundry room and into the large, spacious kitchen of the house I grew up in. My mom is standing at the island counter, cutting vegetables for something that smells familiar. "Are you making soup? In the middle of summer?" I ask, placing a kiss on the side of her head.

"Of course, I am. Soup is perfectly acceptable any time of the year, Garreth."

"I beg to differ. It's a thousand degrees outside," I counter, taking a seat on one of the stools at the island.

Mom rolls her eyes with a smile on her face. "That's fake news."

I chuckle and reach for a carrot slice, careful not to lose a finger in the process. "Where's Dad?"

"Golfing with George."

"How is Dr. Harvey?" I ask, referring to my father's oldest friend.

"Same, mostly, though he started dating that lovely woman who manages the hotel," Mom informs. George's wife, Helena, passed away nearly five years ago from cancer. He had just taken a short leave of absence from his practice as a surgeon when she was diagnosed. He was able to spend about nine months at her side, caring for her until she passed. Growing up, Dr. Harvey and Helena were like a second set of parents to me, so losing her was incredibly difficult. It's part of the reason I jumped at the offer to come back to Stewart Grove and help manage Burgers and Brew.

I was ready to be close to my family again.

"Happy to hear that. Helena would want him to be happy," I state, ignoring the small lump that forms in my throat.

Mom's eyes fill with tears. "That's what we said. He was torn for a while, worrying it was too soon." She grabs a paper towel and blots at her eyes. "Enough about that. How's everything with you?"

"Pretty good," I reply, stealing another chunk of carrot.

"Work?"

My mind flashes to Reagan and the fact I'm working with her now.

"What was that face?"

I look up, my mom's eyes dancing with humor and excitement. "There was no face."

"Oh, there was definitely a face," she declares with a knowing smirk. I've never been able to get away with anything where she's concerned.

As if made of stone, I keep my face as straight and unaffected as possible.

"But since you insist there was no face, I have someone I think you'd be interested in," she says as she finishes chopping the carrots, an innocent grin on her lips.

"Of course you do," I mutter, earning me a pointed look.

"You need to get back out there. You've been home a few years, and you haven't exactly dated."

"And how would you know that?" I ask, humor laced in my question. Mostly because I already know the answer.

Mom rolls her eyes. "Oh, please. Don't play dumb, Garreth. It's very unbecoming. You know this town is too small to get away with anything. That's why you shouldn't be surprised I know all about you and Sharon What's Her Name back in high school."

A deep rumble erupts from my gut. "That doesn't surprise me. I'm certain Old Man Hankey was praying about what he saw in church the next morning."

"My point," Mom starts, holding out her finger, "is that's the last time I've heard good gossip about you in this town. That's not normal, and probably not healthy either. You're thirty-seven."

"I'm aware of my age," I tease, trying to keep things light when I feel the heaviness of this conversation starting to weigh down on me.

"*My point*," she repeats, "is it's time to date. Find a nice girl to settle down with. Give your old mom grandbabies while she's still young enough to enjoy them."

An image of Reagan flashes in my mind, but I quickly try to push it away. The last time I had the picture of a woman and happily ever after in my head, I ended up broke, divorced, and with all my underwear shredded.

Needing to redirect my thoughts, I reply, "You're not old."

Mom sighs and stares at me with that look she perfected when I was about five. It's the one that lets me know I said or did the wrong thing. "That's not the point. Do you want Dorita's number?"

"Dorita? Dorita Hamilton?"

"Yes."

I'm already shaking my head. Of course I know who Dorita is. Even though she's nearly ten years my junior, she's a preschool teacher and a preacher's daughter. I've seen her around, but never in the restaurant, because she doesn't believe in alcohol. I'm not a huge drinker myself, but why on earth my mom thinks we'd be a good fit is beyond me.

"Uhh, no, that's okay."

"She's a lovely woman."

I nod in confirmation. "Yes, she is, but I don't think we have too much in common." Besides the fact I'm not exactly the clean-cut type you bring home to mom, with my longer hair and late hours at the bar, but I also haven't been to church in nearly a decade.

Standing up, I walk around to where she stands. "Sorry, Mom, but you're just going to have to deal with whatever delinquent Jezebel I bring home," I tease, popping one last carrot into my mouth before kissing her cheek.

"I wouldn't even care about that, as long as you bring someone home every once in a while. Well, preferably someone who doesn't steal my good china. You know how I like to bring out the good stuff for special occasions. What would I do if I was missing a spoon or a teacup?"

"I make no promises. Tell Dad I said hello," I holler, heading for the side door.

"Do you want some soup?"

"Sure. Throw it in the freezer and I'll grab it in December," I reply, earning the laugh I was going for, which makes me grin from ear to ear.

My mom is the fucking best, with a sense of humor that makes her the life of any party.

Just as I slip inside my truck, my phone chimes with a text.

Jasper: Sunday afternoon cookout at my place. Be there. Four o'clock.

Jasper: And don't bother telling me you have to work. We've already changed the schedule to give you the night off.

Shaking my head, I fire off a response.

Me: I suppose I'll see you then. What should I bring?

Jasper: Did you just insult the chef by offering to bring food?

Me: Of course not. I was gonna offer strippers or a keg for keg stands.

Jasper: As long as the strippers leave at bedtime. Last time, Elliott threw a fit when he had to miss the end of the show because of bed.

A deep chuckle slips from my mouth. This is why I love working for these guys.

Me: Deal.

I set my phone in the console and pull out of the driveway, heading to work. I have fifteen minutes before I'm expected to be there, but more importantly, I have less than an hour to prepare myself for another night working with Reagan. Something tells me, I'm in for another long, hard night.

Pun intended.

Reagan

A thrill of excitement sweeps through me as I clock in on Saturday night. Even though I know I'm going to be busy, my feet probably in agony by the end of the evening, there's still a buzz of anticipation in the air.

Mostly because I know Garreth is here.

Last night, I was able to steal subtle glances at him off and on, and with each one, I seem to find myself liking him even more. He's so charismatic with the customers, efficient and helpful with the staff, and makes everyone around him comfortable and at ease. The men always seem to have a good time when he's around, and the women? Well, I've witnessed the females physically swoon when Garreth is near. I've heard the stories about Walker and the panties thrown behind the bar. Something tells me Garreth has had his fair share of lingerie tossed his way too.

The one thing I've noticed in my short time working at Burgers and Brew is the fact he seems to *not* be flirting with me. Honestly, I should probably be grateful he's no longer tossing dirty innuendos my way, but for some reason, I'm...well, I'm not. I thought *maybe* I caught a hint of something in his eye when he massaged my feet on Wednesday night, but just as quickly as it appeared, it was gone, leaving me to wonder if I just imagined the whole thing anyway. I can't help but wonder what changed since Tuesday night to all of a sudden warrant him no longer flirting like crazy, and the only thing I can come up with is Justin.

I'm not in a relationship.

Does that mean he was only flirting because I was safe? Because I had a significant other waiting, so there were no chances of me digging my claws into the sexy bar manager? Since he returned to town, I've not so much as heard about him dating, let alone seen him with a woman. Well, besides the ones at the bar. Even then, he never seems to proposition them to his place later that night or invite them to get to know each other better in the near future.

But now I'm blissfully single and the flirting comes to an abrupt halt.

Why?

I head to the front and find the podium empty. It's still a little early for the dinner rush, so there's only a few tables occupied, and the servers seem to have everything handled. Grabbing the cleaner and a rag, I start sanitizing menus from the lunch hour. We clean them before they're handed out to the next patron, and that task usually falls on the hostess.

"Shantel went into labor this morning."

I glance up and find Garreth standing before me, a warm smile on his face that lights up his dark chocolate eyes. "She did?"

He nods. "Shane called me a little bit ago with an update. She's progressing, but slowly. You okay on your own tonight? I'll be nearby, ready to help."

"I'll be fine," I insist, taking a deep breath. Turns out, that's the wrong thing to do, because I catch a whiff of Garreth's woodsy scent, and it goes straight to my lady parts. A shiver sweeps through my body.

Garreth, noticing the reaction because apparently nothing gets by him, steps closer. "You okay?"

I'm lost in the pools of dark brown eyes. "Hmm?"

The corner of his mouth—a very kissable mouth—curls upward. "Are you cold?" He reaches out and lightly touches my arm. "You have goosebumps."

I practically jump out of my skin. "Yes. Cold. That's it," I insist, my voice a little breathy and unnaturally high.

A full-wattage grin spreads across those damn lips. "Well, hopefully, you'll be busy moving soon so you're not so cold." The look on his face tells me he doesn't believe my story, especially since it's summer and a million degrees outside.

"Yeah, hopefully," I reply, my brain still stuck on the word *moving* and wondering exactly how we could be *moving* together.

"Reag?"

"Hmm?" I ask, not even realizing I was staring at his groin at this point.

Oh my God, my brain is sabotaging me.

His lips form a full smile now, and the way my cheeks burn, I know I'm blushing furiously. He steps even closer yet. We're almost chest to chest. I could easily throw my arms around his neck, plaster my front to his, and kiss him, which is a new development. When I was dating Justin, I never really thought about Garreth this way. Sure, he was a gorgeous man with the most amazing eyes I've ever seen, but I didn't see him as anything more than just the hot, flirty guy he is.

Now, I can't stop thinking about him in ways that are too inappropriate for a man who is technically my boss.

"If you need anything, just say the word," he whispers, his warm breath tickling my cheek.

Swallowing hard, I meet his gaze, the invitation for him to join me in a storage room on the tip of my tongue. I'm saved from such humiliation, however, when the door behind me opens and my grandma and a few of her friends walk in.

"Well, well, well, I was hoping I'd run into you," Grandma announces as she offers me a smile. Her eyes quickly bounce between me and Garreth, and I realize it's because we haven't exactly separated yet. We're still standing incredibly close. Too close for a boss and employee.

Jumping back as if I were burned, I turn to face the woman I'm extremely tight with. "Hey, Grandma. How was euchre club?"

"Your grandma cheated," one of her dear friends, Hazel, announces with an ornery smile.

"I did no such thing," Grandma insists, feigning innocence and placing a delicate hand over her heart.

Garreth snorts a laugh. "This seems to be a regular occurrence with you, Estelle," his deep, rich voice croons. I swear, every woman within earshot swoons a little in his direction, including the four elderly ladies in front of us.

"Oh, Garreth, don't you believe everything you've heard," Grandma insists, plastering a wide grin on her face. Then, to my complete shock and dismay, she leans in and loudly whispers, "Unless it's about that time I went skinny-dipping with Harvard Jones back in 1947. That was completely true."

I gasp. "Grandma!"

"What?" she asks innocently. "It was all just a little fun before I met your grandpa."

"Oh my God," I groan, trying to hide my blush behind my hair.

Garreth laughs easily and extends his elbow for my grandma to take. "I hadn't heard that one yet, Estelle, but something tells me you were a gorgeous force to be reckoned with."

"Still is," Hazel chimes in.

"You're a charmer," Grandma states, smiling up at him as if he hung the moon and the stars and placing her delicate hand in the crook of his arm. "You know, you'd be perfect for my Reagan. Are you still single?"

Garreth barks out a laugh. "Yes, I believe Miss Hazel is correct. You are a force." He winks at her, and I swear I hear my grandma sigh. "Let me show you ladies to your seats," he says, leading the group away from the hostess stand.

I quickly grab four menus and fall in line behind them, wishing I were anywhere else than listening to my grandma list my good qualities and why I'd make a wonderful wife. I'm surprised she doesn't have a printed PowerPoint presentation prepared for times like these.

I should probably keep that thought to myself, or she's liable to run home and print out something.

When I reach the table, incredibly disappointed the floor didn't open up and swallow me whole, I place the menus in front of each of the four chairs and step back, unable to get away from the torture that is my grandma.

"My Madelyn married one of your bosses, so I can't set you up with her," Grandma continues as she takes her seat.

"Yes, Jameson. Congratulations on a great-grandbaby," he replies with that always-present smile on his handsome face.

"Thank you! I've already started shopping, you know."

"They don't even know what they're having yet," I say, which only earns me a wave-off.

"I can still buy plenty of gender-neutral baby things, Reagan. It's my first great-grandbaby. I started shopping immediately after Madelyn peed on that stick," she states pointedly. "Besides, this might be my only shot at a great-grandbaby before I die," she adds dramatically.

And the Oscar goes to...

I can't help but roll my eyes. Garreth notices, his facial features dancing with humor. "I think Reagan has plenty of time to find someone who values the amazing, gorgeous woman she is. You'll have another grandbaby in no time, Estelle. Mark my words. Any man would be lucky to be with Reagan. Now, if you'll excuse me, ladies, I'm going to check on a few things in the back. Enjoy your dinner, and I'll tell your server, dessert is on me tonight." He winks and smirks before practically strutting away.

Panties everywhere erupt in flames.

"Wow," Hazel mumbles.

"That man is fine," Agnes adds.

"Mmhmm." This from Dorothy.

"Reagan, you need to lock that man down now. Did you see the way he looked as he walked away? He's got bedroom skills," Grandma states boldly.

My jaw falls, just as her dinner mates chime in with various forms of "Oh, yes" and "Definitely."

Grandma looks up at me and decides to throw salt on my humiliation wound. "You know, a good smirk is a sign of stellar oral skills."

"And, I'm out of here. Your server will be with you in a moment," I blurt out, practically running from the table.

Since my first night of working at Burgers and Brew, honestly, I've thought about Garreth's oral skills. It was featured in a dream two nights ago that left me wet, aching, and panting when I woke, causing me to slip a hand inside my panties to alleviate the burn. But I do not—and I repeat—do *not* need to hear those words coming from my grandmother's mouth.

Ever.

Again.

My face flames so hot with mortification it physically hurts. Grandma Estelle has always had a loose tongue, but these last few years, ever since my cousin Madelyn moved back to town, she's been a little too much so. She used to embarrass Madelyn all the time about Jameson, so why am I not surprised she's turned her amateur matchmaking eyes on me.

The evening dinner rush starts earlier than I expected on a Saturday, and before I know it, every table is filled and there's a small group of patrons waiting for a seat. Garreth comes over and checks on me, as well as stops by my grandma's table for a visit. As promised, he has dessert delivered, and doesn't appear to be rushing them out the door to accommodate those waiting.

I, on the other hand, am worried they're taking up a table too long. The foursome has been chatting, slowly eating their food, and enjoying themselves for well over an hour. I can't help but fret, wondering if I should encourage them to finish up.

Garreth heads my way, saying hello to every table he passes. The moment he reaches the hostess stand, I say, "I'm sorry they're still here. I can ask them to wrap it up."

He gives me a surprised look. "Don't you dare. They're fine."

"But they've been here a long time," I argue quietly, hoping none of the customers standing around hear.

He steps in closer, keeping his voice down. "Reag, they're fine, really. Booth number seven and table number fifteen are about to leave. That'll accommodate the two parties waiting. There's no need to rush off Estelle and her friends."

Absently, I nibble on my bottom lip and glance around his broad shoulder to where my grandma's group sits. "I guess. I just feel bad people are waiting for a table, you know?"

"Yeah, I get it, but it's part of the industry. We seat who we can the moment we can do it. No one wants it to happen, but it does."

Taking a deep breath, I feel myself relax a little, thanks to his reassurance. "You're right."

"Of course I am," he quips with a wink.

I can't stop the eyeroll. "Actually, I do suppose it's your fault they're still here. You're the one who insisted on dessert."

Garreth chuckles low and raspy, my eyes dropping to where his arms cross over his chest. "That is true, but who am I to deny my adoring fans?"

"You're so full of yourself," I add, even though he's right. My grandma and her friends—much like everyone else, I'm discovering—adore him.

"That I am." Someone catches his attention near the kitchen. "I gotta run and check on something. You're okay up here?"

I quickly nod. "Of course."

"Good." He takes a step back and smiles as he adds, "Holler if you need me."

Then he's gone, heading off to do what he does best, while I'm left standing here, watching the way his blue jeans mold to his perfect ass as he walks. I'm pretty sure I hear a collective sigh of appreciation from no less than three women nearby.

"Wipe your drool, Reagan."

I blink and turn, facing my grandma. "How was dessert?" I ask, pasting on my best smile.

"Oh, it was marvelous," she confirms, her eyes following Garreth as he moves toward the bar side of the building. "And the view wasn't so bad either."

"Eye candy. That's what my granddaughter calls good-looking men," Hazel chimes in.

"You ladies are trouble," I announce, shaking my head at their antics.

"We're old, Reagan. Not dead. Please tell that handsome man who bought us dessert how much we appreciate it," Grandma says, leaning in and placing a kiss on my cheek.

"I will."

"Come have lunch with me soon. I need to hear all about you and that Justin fellow. Imagine my surprise that I heard about the breakup at the beauty salon on Thursday."

"Thursday? Wow, the Stewart Grove gossip tree must be slowing down," I tease. Considering it happened Tuesday night, I fully expected Grandma to hear by sunup the next morning.

I walk over to the door and hold it open while Grandma and her friends leave, only to have two more tables worth of patrons follow me in. That's how the rest of my Saturday night goes. We stay hopping busy until it's time to shut down the restaurant side. I don't even have time to think about the sexy manager who usually monopolizes way too much of my thoughts.

Ha!

Good thing my name's not Pinocchio.

"Last call!" Walker hollers to the packed room. It's the first weekend I've worked with him, and I can see why everyone loves him. He's charismatic and energetic behind the bar, and the fact I know he's a family man only adds to his appeal.

I bus empties off tables just to keep myself busy until close. "Excuse me, are you the new girl?"

The familiar voice is like nails on a chalkboard. I turn around and find Amie Donnelly standing there, her boobs practically popping out of her tank top.

"Amie," I greet, careful not to make it too icy.

She narrows her eyes. "I'm sorry, do I know you?"

Bitch.

"We went to school together," I deadpan, not at all surprised she has no idea who I am. It's not like Stewart Grove is a big city. We're teetering at the eight-thousand mark on our last census, and there was about one hundred and twenty-five kids in our graduating class. We're not talking Chicago here. Plus, there's the fact she used to be fuck-buddies, or whatever it is you'd call it, with Jameson, who's married to my cousin Madelyn. I know she knows who Madelyn is, and considering we're together all the time, I can't imagine Amie really having no clue who I am.

She stares at me for a solid five seconds before shrugging. "Anyway, I need you to give this to Garreth." She practically pushes a slip of paper in my hand, her blood-red nail scratching my palm.

"Excuse me?" I ask, dumbfounded.

"It's my number."

I can't help but look over to the bar, where Garreth is helping serve the last wave of alcohol. He smiles at a few customers and takes their money, shoving cash into the tip jar, before moving on to the next person in line. Turning back to where she stands, I blurt out, "Aren't you married?"

Amie rolls her eyes dramatically. "So? I have needs."

"And your unsuspecting husband is out of town a lot?" I mutter my question, turning back to finish cleaning the table, the napkin with her phone number palmed in my hand.

"Who are you, the marriage police?"

Sighing, I glance over my shoulder to the woman with a reputation a mile long. She's a piece of work, but she's also a paying customer. So even though I'd rather tell her to take a long hike off a short cliff, I flash her a smile as fake as her boobs and say, "Sure thing, Amie."

She rolls her eyes. "Whatever. Just give him my number. He's expecting it." With that, she tosses her blond hair over her shoulder and turns away, disappearing into the masses.

When my tray is full and I have a random menu pinched between my upper arm and my side, I carefully head to the kitchen, trying not to drop anything. Just as I get ready to push through the swinging door, a hand gently grabs my arm. I startle, but fortunately, don't drop a thing, considering Garreth is there and reaches for the tray.

"Wow, nice reflexes," I say when I know the glasses are safe.

"It's one of my many skills," he quips, flashing me that sexy smile I can't get enough of. "Need a hand?"

I look down at the tray and the fact he's already holding it. "Looks like I've already got two extra."

"Sorry I scared you," he says, balancing the tray and walking into the kitchen with me.

"It's fine," I insist, setting everything down on the counter to be run through the dishwasher. "Thanks for saving these."

He shrugs, crossing his arms over his chest and looking positively edible in the process. "You only needed help because I distracted you and caused you to almost spill them."

I nod, adjusting my hold on the menu. When I do, I realize I still have the napkin in my hand. "Oh, I almost forgot. This is for you."

He arches an eyebrow and takes the balled-up napkin. "What's this?"

"Amie Donnelly's phone number."

His dark eyes flash to me. "Seriously?" he asks without so much as moving his hand.

"Yep. Apparently, you're expecting it." There's a little venom in my statement, but we're not going to discuss why.

Garreth shakes his head and turns, tossing the napkin in the trash without even looking at it. "Not interested."

Together, we return to the hallway, and I can't help but be surprised. "No? Isn't every man interested?" I ask, part sarcastic and part honest. I've heard a lot of men—single and not so single ones—have all fallen prey to Amie's charms.

"No," he states, stopping in the middle of the hall and facing me, his face full of a fire I wasn't expecting. "Not my type."

"Oh." My throat feels dry and scratchy, his woodsy scent wrapping around me like a blanket, familiar and warm. "What is your type?"

Shut up, Reagan!

Garreth just stares at me, the faintest smile on his full lips. "I seem to find myself drawn to darker hair lately, and I'm partial to hazel eyes these days."

My heart stops.

Is he saying what I think he's saying?

Before I can ask this burning question, he taps me on the tip of my nose and says, "Better get back out there. We have a bar to close down." He winks, turns, and walks away.

My eyes are glued to his ass the entire way, until he rounds the corner and is no longer in my sight. I lean against the wall, trying to calm my erratic heartbeat. "Smooth, Reagan. You act like a schoolgirl with a crush."

What's a girl to do?

Garreth

I stop in my office to take a deep breath and adjust my hard cock in my pants. What is it about this woman? She has had me tied in knots since the first moment I laid eyes on her.

Admittedly, I've known plenty of beautiful women in my life. Hell, I was married to one, but even then, none hold a candle to Reagan Turner. She's not only pretty, but smart, witty, and cares deeply for her family and friends. She's everything I didn't even know I was missing from my life.

After a few minutes, I get my raging libido under control and return to the main bar area. The crowd is already starting to thin, and Walker and his team are busy starting to close down. He's got Kallie and Max behind the bar with him tonight, and while we usually only have two bartenders, we're making sure Max is ready and where he needs to be before he's really thrown to the wolves.

My eyes automatically seek out Reagan, who is finishing cleaning tables. I want to jump in and help her, but I'm afraid if I get too close again, I'll initiate that kiss I was thinking about in the hallway.

Damn, did I want to kiss her. Probably more than I've ever wanted to kiss her before, and that's saying something, because I've thought of nothing but for more than almost four years. But she's now an employee, albeit temporarily. I can't go around kissing those I work with, and more specifically, those who are directly under me.

Boy, would I love having her beneath me...

Clearing my throat, I force myself to look away from Reagan and help with what needs to be done. However, as it is on nights where all four owners are here, it doesn't take long to finish for the night. Numbers grabs the broom and sweeps up the major messes, even if we have a cleaning crew that'll come in before we open in the morning. Jameson and Walker stock the coolers and liquor shelves, while Jasper helps Reagan hang stools. I close out the register, while Kallie washes the remaining bar glasses and Max washes down the bar and surrounding areas. Before I know it, we're all set to head home.

"Hey, Reagan, do you work tomorrow?" I hear Jasper ask as I approach with her part of the tips.

"Nope."

I stay close, so I can hear their conversation, but not close enough they know I'm eavesdropping.

"We're having some friends over for a cookout. Lyndee asked me to extend an invitation to you. Anytime around four," he tells her, and my heart rate kicks up a few extra beats with excitement.

"Oh, thank you. I don't think I have anything going on. I'd love to come. What can I bring?"

"Nothing. See you there," Jasper says, finishing the stools before heading over to where his partners stand at the bar.

I try not to smile outwardly, but it's incredibly difficult, especially when I'm anxious to see her outside of work. Outside of the boss/employee relationship. Outside of spending work hours with her. No, I still don't see anything happening with Reagan, but if I get to spend time with her in the company of friends, I consider that an added bonus.

I just have to be on my best behavior.

I park on the street behind Walker and Mallory's SUV and grab the bowl sitting on the passenger seat. I know I wasn't supposed to bring anything, but I was raised better than that. Even if it's something as simple as a bottle of wine, you never go to a gathering or dinner empty-handed.

The moment I step out of my truck, I can hear laughter and kids yelling from the backyard. I'm smiling as I follow the sidewalk around the side of the house, release the latch on the gate, and step inside, making sure it's securely locked when I'm done.

"Garreth!" Lizzie hollers, running straight from the sprinkler's line of fire toward me. She launches her wet body straight at my chest, but I manage to catch her without dropping her or the bowl in my hand.

"You're soaked!" I bellow as her little arms wrap around my neck.

"Gar!" Duncan yells, hot on his sister's tail. He wraps himself around my leg, ensuring my khaki shorts are also now a darker shade of wet. Right behind him is Rorik, Numbers and BJ's son, who wraps himself around my other leg.

"Hey, Dunc-man. Ror," I greet. "Where are the terrors?" I ask, referring to Waylon and Elliott.

"Eating the trees," Duncan announces before turning and taking off for the sprinkler, his partner in crime, Rorik, one step behind.

I look at Lizzie curiously. "Eating the trees?"

"They keep trying to eat the bark," she informs me with a shrug.

"Interesting."

"Daddy keeps telling him to stop, and that makes Elliott laugh. Jasper yelled at Daddy because his boy is teaching Elliott all the bad stuff."

"He's teaching my boy all sorts of naughty things, Lizard," Jasper teases, kissing Lizzie on the cheek before I put her down on the ground. She giggles and waves before turning and running for the sprinkler, wet blond curls flying all over the place.

"Thanks for inviting me," I say, taking in the Lizzie-sized wet marks on my shirt. The good news is it's ninety degrees outside, so it won't be wet for long.

"I see you defied my orders and brought food anyway," Jasper grumbles, taking the bowl from my hand.

"It's fruit salad. I was thinking of the kids."

"You're such a good uncle," Jasper sings in a tone letting me know he's teasing me.

I chuckle, shoving my hands in my pockets. "What can I say? I like the kids better than the adults."

"That's because you have the same mentality," Walker jokes, joining us at the far edge of the property and carrying two beers. "Here."

Reaching for the bottle, I pop the top off and take a long pull of the brew. "Thanks."

"Where's mine?" Jasper snipes.

"In your cooler over on the patio," Walker replies with a shrug, grinning at his friend as he sips his own beer.

"Asshole," he mutters, making sure there aren't little ears to hear.

"Let me take that, Garreth, since my husband forgot his manners."

I turn to see Lyndee hand Jasper a beer as she gives him a knowing smile. "*Someone* loves me," Jasper mutters, narrowing his eyes at Walker.

"She's the only one," Jameson proclaims, stepping up to our group.

The lone female in the bunch rolls her eyes. "You guys are ridiculous. Welcome, Garreth. You didn't have to bring anything, but I appreciate it."

"It's just a fruit salad," I insist, suddenly feeling a little lame for bringing a dish to share.

Her brown eyes brighten. "That sounds wonderful, thank you. I'm sure everyone will love it. Elliott is on a huge oranges kick right now."

"That's because he thinks they're a dessert, like cookies, and desserts are better than the main course." Jasper narrows his eyes playfully at his wife, who just smiles back sweetly. I can see the love between the chef and his baker wife.

"I didn't teach him that."

Jasper barks out a laugh. "Bullshit."

"Bullshit!" Waylon hollers, running past our group and repeating it no less than four more times.

Walker turns a menacing glare to our host. "Thanks."

Jasper just laughs. "Serves you right for teaching my kid the word bastard. He actually called his grandma that the other day. I mentally cursed you out the entire time my mom chewed my ass for using foul language."

That only makes Walker and the rest of us laugh harder.

"I'm going to take this over to the table and leave you men to bicker over the state of your friendship," Lyndee announces, reaching over and squeezing her husband's arm before walking away.

"Jesus, it's hot out here," Numbers states, wiping sweat off his brow.

"Yeah, but the kids are happy," Walker says, causing all of us to collectively turn and watch the cluster of little ones play in the water. Walker's three, Numbers' son, as well as Jasper's boy, are all playing together under the large shade tree. Even though they range from eight to two, you can tell they're a close group, just like their parents.

"The girls are already drinking," Numbers observes.

I glance over at the ladies all sitting together beneath a big shade umbrella on the patio. They're laughing at something, all eyes watching the kids, as they sip drinks that look fruity. Well, everyone but Madelyn. She's drinking bottled water.

My eyes automatically focus on Reagan. She's in a light blue tank top with little shorts that draw your eyes to her tanned legs. Her long hair is pulled up high on her head, and she's sporting a pair of flip-flops on her feet. Between her casual appearance and the broad smile on her face, she looks more relaxed than I've seen in a while.

I like it.

"I've already decided I'm only having two beers before dinner and then switching to water so I can drive home. Ever since Mal had Waylon, she has about a three-drink limit. Anything more than that, and she professes her love to everyone she sees and wants to buy the kids ponies for Christmas," Walker says, a faint smile on his lips as he watches his wife.

"I have to stop by the bar tonight and close, so I'm not drinking after this one," Numbers says, holding up his bottle.

"I can go in and cover close," I insist, hating one of the owners has to go back in, especially when they've all given so much to the business already.

"No, I volunteered to give you a night off with all of us. That never happens, since one of us is usually there," Numbers insists.

He's not wrong. On my nights off, one of the others is there to close, and while I'm enjoying spending time with the guys and their families outside of work, I feel guilty for not being there.

"Stop it," Jameson chastises.

"What?"

He gives me a knowing glance. "You're feeling bad because you're not there and Numbers is going back in. Well, stop. When we discussed having this cookout, we all agreed we wanted you here. It's your night off. Enjoy it." He holds up his beer bottle and taps mine with a clink.

Jameson is usually a man of few words, but he hit the nail on the head with that one. We all know each other pretty well, but he's always been the most observant one. Silent and watchful. That's the best way to describe Jameson Tankersley.

"I'm going to light the grill. Go make yourself at home," Jasper announces, squeezing my shoulder as he walks by.

My eyes instantly seek her out once more, as if entirely on their own, but she's no longer sitting at the table with the other ladies. Glancing around the yard, I don't see her playing with the kids, which tells me she probably slipped in the house.

That's where I go.

"Hey, ladies," I greet as I walk by, heading to the back door.

"Hi, Garreth," Mallory says at the same time BJ hollers a quick, "Hey!" before telling Rorik to stop trying to karate-chop Duncan. Madelyn waves, a small grin on her lips, and I can't help but notice the humor dancing in her eyes as she glances to the door, where her cousin most likely went a few minutes ago.

Before I reach the door, I turn to Jasper, who is lighting a massive grill. "Mind if I use your bathroom?"

"You don't have to ask," he states, his attention focused on lighting the six gas burners.

I slip inside the gorgeous house, soaking up a few seconds of sweet air-conditioned reprieve, and head toward the half-bath just down the hall. The door is closed and a sliver of light spills from beneath the door. I lean against the wall, waiting, so I'm the first thing she sees when she steps out.

The door lock releases, the knob turns, and the light goes out. Then, just as Reagan is stepping across the threshold, I see arms flailing and she's stumbling forward, straight into my chest.

"Jesus, love. If you wanted to get close to me, you're always welcome. No need to throw yourself at me," I quip, adjusting my arms to keep her from falling all the way.

The sound of her sigh makes me smile. "You're so full of yourself. My flip-flop just broke, genius."

I want to protest as she rights herself and stands before me, her gaze locked on mine. Her eyes are slightly narrow, as the cutest blush creeps up her cheeks. It's the same blush I've become accustomed to since we met, and I've flirted with her shamelessly whenever she's near. Honestly, I've missed the fuck out of this blush, and now that we're not in the work setting, I want to see nothing but this look on her face.

"You don't have to make excuses. You're not the first woman to fall at my feet," I tease, still holding her against my chest.

She rolls her eyes so dramatically, it's comical. "I'm sure the trail of fawning women is extensive, but I'm not in that group. I tripped and fell when my flip-flop caught."

Unable to help myself, I reply, "Fell from heaven, I see." It's over the top, for sure, and earns me the reaction I was going for.

Reagan bursts out laughing and swats me on my chest, standing to her full height, which is still several inches shorter than my six-two frame. "You're unbelievable."

"Thank you," I reply with a grin.

She shakes her head, that sexy smile still spread across her kissable mouth. "That wasn't a compliment."

"Says you."

Reagan takes a small step back and glances around. "I'm sorry, you're probably needing me to move so you can use the restroom."

"Actually, I came in to see you."

Her eyebrows draw together in confusion. "Me? Why?"

I take a step closer, needing her sweet scent to wrap around me once more. "Well, I wanted to say hello, for one. Two, I just wanted to see you. And three? Well, it had been a while since you fell at my feet in adoration, so I wanted to make sure that happened before you went through withdrawals."

She sighs once more and closes her eyes. "You're impossible."

"Impossibly good-looking, from what I've gathered."

She barks out a laugh, the smile still trailing across her lips. Until she looks down and notices her messed up flip-flop. "This is what I get for buying shoes from the dollar store."

I follow her line of sight and see the problem. The rubber strip that connects the top strap to the bottom, which runs between your big toe and your second toe, ripped from the bottom. "Hmm," I mumble, bending down and slipping the broken shoe off her foot. "Yeah, I don't think it's salvageable."

"No, usually not. They're cheapies anyway. I have a pair of sandals in my car. I'll just run out and grab them," she says, reaching for the unusable flip-flop in my hand.

"Come on," I state, turning around and squatting down.

"Excuse me?" she asks.

Glancing over my shoulder, I find her eyes locked on my ass. "There's time for ogling later, love. Let's go get your shoes."

Wide eyes fly up to meet mine. She opens her mouth, clearly ready to argue, but snaps it shut. "I'm perfectly capable of running to my car to get my own shoes."

"Of course you are, but I'm offering you a lift." I squat down again, getting low so she can jump on.

"A lift?" The humor is evident in her question.

"Yep. We're talking a Grade A piggyback ride here, so hop on, sweets. Times a wastin'."

"Garreth, my car is like ten feet away."

"Yeah, but you'd have to walk across hot gravel and blacktop that's been baking under the sun all day, so you might as well take advantage of the lift."

She sighs. "I'm going to regret this," she mutters before stepping up behind me, placing her hands on my shoulders, and hopping on.

My hands go back, her ass fitting so perfectly in my palms. My dick? Oh, he's clearly on board with my current position, and all I can do is pray my semi-erection isn't completely noticeable to everyone else when we walk outside.

"Ready, my dear?"

"Giddy up, horsey," she quips, drawing a huge grin on my face.

I stand up and head for the back door. If I'm going to have Reagan on my back, I'm definitely taking the long way around to her car, not caring we'll be parading in front of our friends. At this point, it's all about drawing out my time with her.

This contact.

The bad part is, these little moments may never be enough.

Reagan

He walks right out the back door. Right past our employers. Even though I'm on his back and can't see his face, I can feel the smug smirk he's no doubt wearing.

I can also feel everyone's eyes as we move with determination across the patio and toward the side gate. "My shoe broke," I state lamely, reminiscent of when Baby said "I carried a watermelon" in the movie *Dirty Dancing.*

"Sure," BJ sings, followed by snickers.

"Me next!" Rorik hollers, jumping through the sprinkler and running in our direction.

"You're next, buddy," Garreth announces, pushing through the gate before the four-year-old can catch up.

I try to ignore the feel of his hands on my ass, but there's no way I'm able to. Why? Because he has really *big* hands, and the inappropriate side of my brain keeps focusing on the fact. You know what they say about big hands, right?

Yeah, me too.

Garreth heads straight to my car and stops in the grass beside the curb. He seems hesitant before slowly lowering me down to the ground. Those big hands slide across the globes of my ass until they have no choice but to let go.

He spins around and faces me. "Next time, we'll try reverse cowgirl." Then, he flashes me that cocky smirk and waggles his eyebrows suggestively.

A bark of laughter spills from my lips as I consider his absurd statement. "I don't think that's possible."

Leaning in just ever so slightly, he whispers, "Oh, it's possible. Challenging, I'll give you that, but possible. We'll try it sometime."

I shake my head, unable to dislodge the grin from my face, and reach for the door handle. I'm so grateful I still have a change of clothes in here, complete with sandals. Otherwise, I'd have to go barefoot for the rest of the night or borrow shoes from Lyndee, who's several inches shorter than my five-nine height. I bet there's no way she wears a size ten shoe.

The moment I slip my sandals on my feet and toss my broken cheap pieces of crap in my car, Garreth's right in front of me again. "Ready?"

"For?" I ask.

He turns and squats in front of me. "Your ride back."

"Yeah, sorry, bucko. You'll have to find someone else to try your reverse cowgirl bit," I retort, even though my lady parts are screaming in protest.

He tsks and shakes his head. "There would never be a partner as fiery as you, sunshine."

Warmth swooshes through my veins at his compliment, but I don't comment. I have no idea what's happening here. He's like the old Garreth, the one I grew accustomed to dealing with before I was working at Burgers and Brew. Flirty and fun. Nothing like the man I spent the last week with.

We slowly make our way back to where the cookout is happening. I can feel the heat of his body radiating from him like a furnace, and it has nothing to do with the temperature outside. Garreth is tall and lean, with hard muscles and a killer smile, and when he walks beside me, his arm casually brushing against mine, his nearness short-circuits my brain.

"'Bout to send out a search party," Jameson mutters as we step through the gate, the faintest smirk on his face.

"Dinner's done, if you two are finished playing around," Jasper chastises, but I catch the hint of humor in his words.

"I'm next!" Rorik announces, running toward where Garreth stands.

Garreth squats, getting down to Rorik's level. "The food's ready now, buddy, but how about afterward, if you clean your plate, you'll get the first piggyback ride."

BJ and Isaac's four-year-old son nods his head. "I can do that."

"Me too!" Duncan hollers, followed almost immediately by his little brother, "Me too too!"

Garreth just laughs. "Yes, you all too. Everyone can have a ride, but you have to eat all your food."

My heart melts a little. I've seen him with the kids before, but there's something different about today. Maybe it's the way he's been so easygoing and teasing me that makes his interaction with the kids like catnip to my lady bits.

"Cajun chicken breasts with smoked Gouda cheese," Jasper announces, pointing to a large platter, "and some plain boring chicken for the kids and pregnant women."

"Women?" Mallory catches it first, turning and pinning the rest of the ladies with a look.

Everyone looks around, waiting for someone to say something. Eventually, it's Lyndee who says, "Fine, yes, it's me! I just found out and I'm already sick. I need plain chicken because the thought of anything spicy makes me want to vomit." She throws her arms up in the air dramatically.

"But...you were drinking?" BJ asks hesitantly, her eyes full of concern.

"I made a non-alcoholic one for me when you weren't looking," Lyndee states with a sheepish grin.

Suddenly, everyone's moving, enveloping Lyndee and Jasper in hugs. Even the kids get all excited and have no clue why. When it's my turn to offer congratulations, I squeeze my friend a little harder than normal and inhale her sweet, sugary scent. She always smells like she stepped out of the bakery, and often we can spot a dusting of flour somewhere on her person or frosting in her hair.

"I'm so happy for you," I whisper, grateful this small group of amazing women brought me into their inner circle a few years ago. They definitely didn't have to, but they accepted me as a friend, with or without Madelyn in tow.

"Thank you," she sniffles, dabbing at her eyes with her shirt. "Now, who else is going to get knocked up too? I liked having a friend to do this with last time," she adds, referring to her pregnancy with Elliott at the same time Mallory was pregnant with Waylon. "This time, Madelyn and I need a third. We'll be like a gang."

"Not it!" Mallory hollers, taking a hearty drink of her alcohol.

"Wait, let's talk about this, Mal," Walker says, heading in her direction.

She dodges his kisses when he pulls her against his chest. "Nope, not happening."

"But you look amazing pregnant," he whines, then completely sobers. "We can still practice, right?" He waggles his eyebrows suggestively and does something with his hips that makes me turn my head fast.

"Yes, you big goof," she replies.

"And we're not taking it completely off the table?" he asks, his question so full of hope.

Mallory sighs. "It's not off the table," she concedes, a knowing smirk on her lips.

I never thought I'd see Walker so smitten by his father role, but he's the best, most doting dad I know. Growing up, and then when they opened the bar, he dated a lot—and by that, I mean slept around—and never talked about settling down. My, how the tides have turned for him and his friends.

"Well, that leaves BJ," Lyndee says, and all eyes turn in her direction.

"You're going to have to wait until after the tattoo convention we're going to in January. I don't want to be pregnant in Vegas that week. We're using it as our late honeymoon," BJ says, referring to the large convention she was asked to present at in the beginning of next year.

As if on cue, everyone slowly turns to face me. "No. No, no, no. Get that out of your heads right now," I insist, bringing my margarita up to my lips and chugging. "I just broke up with my boyfriend, remember? I got dumped by text message."

"Who says you need a boyfriend? Just some fast swimmers," Lyndee reasons, but my attention is no longer on her. Instead, I glance at Garreth and don't miss the flash of anger that crosses his features.

"Reagan isn't having some random dude's baby," he counters with a little extra insistence.

"Yeah, you're right. I'm sorry," Lyndee replies, as if finally realizing what she was suggesting. "Let's get the kids' plates," she adds, turning her attention to rounding up Elliott and the rest of the littles to help them make plates.

Jameson is staring down Garreth, who seems to be doing everything in his power not to look up at him. When he finally does, Jameson smirks at him, which surprises me a little. Even though he's been with my cousin for a few years, and I've gotten to know him a lot better, he doesn't always let his emotions show.

What in the world was that about?

Everyone jumps in to make plates for the kids, so I try to hang back out of the way under the awning. It's hot today, but at least it's a dry heat, so if you're under some shade, it doesn't feel as terrible.

I take in the chaos surrounding five kids and their parents, and I can't help the pang of longing that leaps in my chest. I always thought I'd be a mother by now. You know, married with at least two by the time I was thirty-one. The perfect house with the big backyard filled with kids toys and a dog.

But over the years, I started to watch that dream slip further and further from my fingertips. Even while I was dating Justin, something told me he wasn't "the one." Sure, we got along great, but work always came first for him.

And apparently, his secretary too.

Funny how things change, isn't it?

One minute I was working a job I really enjoyed and had a boyfriend, and the next, I'm single, working at a restaurant and bar, and surprisingly, loving this new path. I get to be in front of people, which was my favorite part of working at the bank, and feel like I'm truly contributing to the success of a local business, even if it's just by greeting people pleasantly and clearing off tables when needed.

Believe it or not, if you'd have asked me a week ago if I thought I'd be happy with this change, I'd have probably said hell no, but I am. More content in a short amount of time than I thought possible.

"What's that smile for?"

I startle, not realizing Garreth is now standing directly beside me.

"Just taking it all in," I reply, chuckling when Rorik reaches over and steals a grape off Elliott's plate.

"Organized chaos. That's what I've always called this." There's definitely a hint of humor in his voice, which makes me turn and look his way. His lips hold a smile, and his rich-chocolate eyes shine with contentment. Before I can say anything or really note how relaxed and happy he looks, he takes me by the hand and leads me to the food table. "Let's eat, Reagan."

I try to ignore the electricity that zings through my veins, but I'm unable to. Every time this man touches me, it's like fireworks. Exciting, bright, and full of heat. It's so captivating, I don't want him to let me go.

Unfortunately, he does, as he reaches over and grabs two plates. "Here."

I pile food on my plate, not really paying attention to what it is. I'm hypnotized by the warmth permeating from his skin, the movement of his hands as he gets his own food, and the scent of his clean soap. Just standing next to him is like an aphrodisiac, heady and intoxicating.

"Try this," Garreth says, taking something off a platter and setting it with my food.

"What is it?" I ask, taking in the concoction.

"It's grilled pineapple salsa on toasted bruschetta bread, and it's fucking amazing. Jasper made it a few weeks back for Gigi's retirement, and I almost ate the entire platter. It's the best combination of sweet and spice and will leave you craving more." There's no missing the way his eyes drop to my lips. As if his scrutiny cues the motion, I lick my bottom lip. I'm not sure if it was because of the food he described or the way he said it, but all I know is there's a hum of awareness between my thighs so strong, I wonder if anyone else can feel the current.

"Thanks," I mutter quickly, taking a step back. I desperately need to put a little space between myself and Garreth, especially because his demeanor is the exact opposite of what I've grown accustomed to recently at work.

With more food than I'll ever eat, I hurry to the table I was sitting at with the ladies before, grateful to see a fresh pitcher of margaritas. The kids are sitting at a small kid-sized table right beside us, but the men seem to be congregating beneath the big tree in lawn chairs.

"What was that?"

It takes me a few seconds to realize Madelyn's question is directed at me. I look up, finding all four sets of eyes like little laser beams directed at my face. "What?"

"That!" BJ whisper-yells, pointing to where the food tables are. "You two were practically dry-humping by the fruit salad."

My mouth drops open and I can't help but glance around to see who might have heard. Fortunately, the kids are all occupied with their food, and the men seem to be more concerned about the state of Jasper's landscaping, since they're pointing to a row of evergreens and chuckling. Taking a deep breath, I lean forward and keep my voice down. "I don't know what's going on. He's super flirty today."

Madelyn pulls a confused face. "He's always super flirty with you."

Before she even finishes her statement, I'm already shaking my head. "No, actually, he's not. He's been...different this last week," I say, for lack of a better word.

"What do you mean?" Mallory asks, glancing over to the kids' table.

"Well, last Tuesday, he was his same ol' self, but then on Wednesday, he was distant. More of the same demeanor Friday and Saturday, but then back to flirty Garreth today. He's giving me whiplash," I confess.

"Wait, aren't those the nights you worked?" BJ asks.

I nod, taking a bite of the grilled pineapple salsa thing he set on my plate, and I have to admit, it's amazing. The pineapple is sweet, but the little pieces of jalapenos and onion give it an extra kick of flavor. "Oh my God, he's right. This is so good," I mutter, taking another big bite.

"So, let me get this straight. He's flirty when you're at the restaurant with us, but not when you're there to work?" Mallory asks.

Again, I nod. "Yeah, but he's like that with everyone."

"Uhh, no he's not," Lyndee insists.

"He is. I've seen him."

BJ leans forward, her voice low. "But he's really not. He's super friendly and fun, and the guests love him, but I've only ever seen him flirt like that with you, Reagan."

"It's true. When he comes over to our table, he always stands beside you. I've even busted him leaning in and sniffing your hair," Madelyn adds.

A blush creeps up my neck. "What?"

"Oh, it's true. That man likes you," Mallory insists between bites of chicken.

"He's been watching you since the moment he got here, Reagan." This from Lyndee.

Casually, I glance over to where the guys are sitting and confirm what she said. His rich brown eyes are focused on me, even though he's talking to Walker about something. "Holy shit," I whisper, whipping my head back around to face the ladies. "Why is he acting so aloof at work then?"

Madelyn chuckles. "Because he's trying to stay professional, silly. He doesn't want to cross that line with you as your superior."

Mallory points a piece of chicken at me from across the table. "There is no rule that states you can't date though."

"Of course not. Otherwise, you and Walker would have broken that rule the moment he laid eyes on you," BJ says. "Listen, Reagan, I think his biggest hang-up is that you work for him."

I consider her words and note the nodding in agreement from the others.

Before, when I was dating Justin, it all seemed so harmless. He flirted but never crossed the line. Now, I'm not dating anyone, but I'm working for him. If he's trying to be professional, that might be a bigger hang-up than me dating someone. "What do I do?"

"I think you need to talk to him," Madelyn states. "Tell him you like him. You do like him, right?"

I take another casual glance to my side and find his eyes on me once more. Our gazes hold for several seconds, his features hold a softness I can't quite describe. Maybe a touch of longing mixed with sadness.

"Yes," I whisper, giving him an easy smile. I turn back to the table and confirm, "Yes, I do like him."

"Then talk to him. Tell him you do and see what he says. If the work thing is that big of an issue with him, then at least you know what stands in your way," Madelyn says, just as Waylon comes up to the table.

"I done!" he bellows eagerly, holding up his plate of food and dropping whatever's left on the ground.

"I see that, Way," Mallory says, taking the now-empty plate from her two-year-old's hands.

"I got it, babe. You finish eating," Walker says, picking up the food and tossing it on the plate before scooping up his youngest in one quick motion. "Come on, little man. Let's go wash the oranges off your face."

"No wash!" he yells, twisting in his dad's arm, but not getting anywhere.

"He's so sexy when he's in dad mode," Mallory states, watching her husband walk away. Once they're inside, she turns back and says, "Ladies, I'm going to be pregnant again by the end of the year. I can't deny him anything, and he's too irresistible."

We all giggle in unison.

One by one, the kids all come up to our table with some version of a finished plate, and with each one, the dads jump in to help. I can't help but notice how lucky my friends are. They all found great guys to spend the rest of their lives with.

Then my eyes seek out the one man I find myself growing more attracted to every day. It's funny how things change. One minute, he's a friend who makes you laugh, and the next, all you do is picture him naked and wonder if the big hands, big feet thing is really true.

Grabbing my margarita, I sit back and openly gawk at him from across the yard. He's giving the boys the piggyback rides he promised, and I'm not sure whose smile is bigger—his or the kids he's parading around the yard.

I've been single less than a week, but for some reason, I feel drawn to him. He's good-looking, but not the type I'm usually attracted to. Garreth's longer hair and scruffy jaw is proof of that. Now I'm curious. Is it harmless flirting or is there more to it? Does Garreth really like me, or is his endless flirting just part of his personality?

I'm not sure, but I think I'm going to find out.

Garreth

She's beautiful.

Sitting under the setting sun, surrounded by her friends, she's kicked back in a lounge seat with a drink in her hand. She's had a few since dinner, not that I'm counting. Mostly, I'm just watching the way she licks the salt off the rim of the glass and then traces that little tongue over her lips, but I can tell the tequila is getting to her.

She's getting giggly, and I like it.

"The bossman keeps giving me the look. I think it's time to get the kids to bed," Mallory says with a slight slur to her speech.

"No, he's giving you the I want to do dirty things to you look," BJ insists, slurping what's left of her drink.

"I miss drinking," Lyndee mutters.

Jasper steps over to where she's sitting and kisses the crown of her head. "Sweets, it's been like four days."

"I know," she sighs. "It's been a long four days."

The girls all giggle, which brings a smile to my face once more. They all look so relaxed, so happy, and when I glance around at the guys, who are now rounding up tired, dirty kids, I can't help but notice how content they appear too. If you would have told me back in high school I'd be working for Walker, Jameson, and a couple of their friends at their bar and restaurant, I'd have laughed in your face. Growing up, I didn't picture them in their current roles as business owners, husbands, and fathers, but man does it fit them well.

It even makes me a little envious.

I thought I had that once.

I pictured the wife, kids, house, and dog, but apparently, she didn't. At least not with me. Sure, it was a blow to the ego, but I'm glad I found out before we both invested any more time in a relationship that was going nowhere. Now, she's happily married to an investment banker with two kids, and I'm here, watching the woman I have a massive crush on lick salt off her lips.

Funny how the winds change.

"Leave the chairs. I'll get them in the morning," Jasper says when I start stacking his lawn chairs together.

"I don't mind helping, and besides, it'll take two minutes and be done," I insist, continuing to finish the task.

"You can tell he's a bar manager," Numbers states with a chuckle. "He's closing your yard down."

I don't comment, mostly because what he said isn't wrong. Why not just do it now, so you have less work to clean up in the morning?

As soon as I stack the last chair, I hear Jameson say, "You ready to go?"

Turning around, I find him looking at Reagan. "Yep," she replies, grabbing her purse.

"I can take you home." The words are out of my mouth before I can even consider them. Both Jameson and Reagan turn to face me, and while her face holds a question, he's giving me a knowing smirk. "I mean, you and Madelyn live in the opposite direction," I add before either can reply.

"But you live that way," Jameson replies, pointing to the north, in the direction of his old house. The one I rent.

"Yeah, but it's still closer than you. It'll take me thirty seconds," I counter. The truth is, Stewart Grove is small enough, even if Jameson and Madelyn take Reagan home, it wouldn't add that much time to their commute, but I want to take her home.

Reagan offers me a small smile. "Actually, that would be great," she insists, turning to Jameson. "Then you can make sure my cousin gets home and in bed quicker."

The big guy stares at me for several long seconds, and I do everything I can not to squirm under his scrutiny. There's something powerful, and maybe a tad bit intimidating, in his eyes, as if he's trying to make sure he trusts me with his wife's cousin.

"Thanks for the offer," Reagan says to Jameson, going up on her tiptoes and kissing his cheek.

"Text Madelyn when you get home," he replies, earning an eye roll.

"I'm not going off with a serial killer. This is Garreth."

His face softens a bit as he looks down at her. "I know. Just want to make sure you get home safe."

"We'll be fine," she insists, heading my way. "Ready?"

I nod, leading her over to where Lyndee stands with my bowl.

"I think we ate most of it. Thanks, again, for bringing it," she says, going up on her tiptoes and kissing my cheek.

"No problem," I reply. "Thanks for inviting me."

"Aren't you coming with us?" Madelyn asks Reagan when she sees her with me.

"No, Garreth offered to take me home. It's closer."

Madelyn gives her a knowing smile. "That makes sense." There's definitely a teasing tone in her words.

"Don't be cheeky," Reagan whispers as she hugs her cousin.

Madelyn just continues to smile. "Me? Never."

After saying goodbye to everyone, including the kids, we head for my truck. "I can help you get your car tomorrow," I offer as I open my passenger door.

"I'm not worried about it. I'm off tomorrow, so I can walk over and get it. It's not far." Reagan climbs up in the seat and reaches for the seat belt.

"I'll drive you," I insist, feeling a wave of protectiveness wash over me.

The truth is, it's really not that far for her to walk, but there's no reason for it. I'm perfectly capable of bringing her here before work. Plus, it'll give me more one-on-one time.

It's a win-win.

After closing her door, I take a few deep breaths and climb into the driver's seat. Instantly, I'm hit in the face by her sweet scent, and I start to reconsider my decision to drive her home. Being in this enclosed space, even for just a few minutes, might be the ultimate test of my willpower.

When I pull away from the curb, I honk at the others, all climbing into their vehicles, and head in the direction of her apartment. She lives off Hanson Drive, not too far from here, so I proceed that way, keeping my speed at the appropriate twenty-five miles per hour in town. I'm sure it has nothing to do with my desire to draw out our short time together.

"Can I ask you something?"

I glance over and find Reagan's gaze intently watching me. "Of course."

She doesn't say anything for a few seconds, but when she finally does, I'm caught completely off guard. "Why don't you flirt with me when we're at work?"

It takes me a solid five seconds to even formulate a response. "Because I don't want to jeopardize our working relationship."

When she doesn't respond, I look her way once more, finding those alluring hazel eyes still watching me. "What about outside of work?"

This entire conversation has me so off-kilter, I can't come up with my usual witty reply. Sure, I've met a handful of forward women, especially working at the bar, but I've never seen this side of Reagan before. It's...different, and frankly, fucking hot.

I turn the corner onto Hanson Drive and press my foot down a little harder on the accelerator, needing to get to her apartment fast. If we're going to have this conversation, I'd rather not have it while I'm sidetracked with driving.

The moment I pull into her lot, I find the closest spot and park. I keep the ignition running so we have air, release my seat belt, and adjust myself in the seat so I'm angled her way. "Outside of work. Well, that's a tricky question." I'm deflecting. I know it.

"Actually, it's not. You flirt with me a lot and have since I've known you, so you clearly enjoy it. What I guess I'm wanting to know is if it's just something you do because you can't help it or if you do it because...well, for other reasons." Now she seems a bit more hesitant, as if perhaps the bravado she started with is starting to slip.

"Other reasons?" I ask, arching my eyebrows upward in question.

Reagan sighs. "Yes, other reasons."

"Like what?" I prod, hoping she's getting at what I think she's getting at. No, I wasn't expecting her to call me out on it, but now that she is, I'd like to see where this conversation goes.

"You know, just...reasons."

"Come on, sunshine. Give me one. One reason."

She rolls her eyes and sighs again, but I see the moment her boldness slips back into place like a protective shield. She's going to say it, and I have a feeling, once she does, everything will change. Reagan squares her shoulders, and says, "Reasons like you're attracted to me."

"Yes," I confirm immediately.

"You are?"

"Definitely. I've had a crush on you pretty much since I moved back to town," I confirm.

Now it's Reagan who seems flabbergasted. "Really? Why didn't you ask me out?"

I shrug, throwing my elbow up on the back of the seat. "Well, when I moved home, I was focused on getting myself established with my new job and getting situated in a new house. Then, when I felt like my feet were firmly on the ground again, you were dating that one guy. What was his name? Dale?"

"Dave."

"Yes, the car salesman," I say, remembering how horribly jealous I felt the first time they came to the restaurant for dinner—and every time after that, to be honest. I had to intentionally stay away from their table so I wouldn't try to stab him with a fork. Fortunately, that lasted less than a year, but then she seemed so down for a while after their breakup. I made sure to step up my flirting game, because even if the smile wasn't exactly for me, it made me happy to see one on her gorgeous face again. I felt like I was helping, even for only a little while.

"And then?" she urges, begging me to go on.

"Well, then there was Peter the wiener, who earned that nickname fair and square when he came in and ordered the hotdog off the menu at a gourmet hamburger restaurant, and then finally Justin, who almost got punched in the junk last week because he had the balls to break up with you in a text."

She gives me the softest smile that makes my heart race. "I can really pick 'em, can't I?"

"We've all had our share of regrettable relationships," I reply, noticing how she's adjusting herself in her seat and moving closer.

"That sounds like a story, but we'll wait another day to dive into it." She gets on her knees, puts the console armrest up, and moves beside me. "So, you've had a crush on me for four years?"

It's hard to swallow over the lump of anxiety lodged in my throat. "Yeah."

"Hmm." She's moving again, this time, practically crawling on my lap. I have to force myself not to reach for her, but I think it best to let her take the lead. Placing her hands on my chest, she whispers, "Were you ever going to do anything about it?"

"Probably not. You're a little out of my league," I confess.

That catches her by surprise. Her mouth falls open, forming a perfect little circle, and all I can think about is all the dirty things I'd do to and with that sexy mouth of hers.

Reagan moves again, climbing onto my lap and straddling my legs. She's got to be uncomfortable with a steering wheel in her back, but if she is, she doesn't say. She flexes her fingers against my chest, scoring her nails through my T-shirt and driving me fucking wild. "Do you know what I think?" she whispers, leaning in enough for her warm breath to tease my cheek.

"I don't, but I'm pretty anxious to find out what it is," I tell her, doing everything I can not to rock my hips and grind my cock against the apex of her legs.

Her lips hover over mine as she says, "I think, not only are we in the same league, we're playing on the same ballfield," she rolls her hips and slides herself across my very hard cock, "with the same bat."

I groan, finally letting myself touch her. I grip her hips as she gently moves, driving me absolutely wild with desire. "Reagan." Her name is both a plea and a curse on my lips.

"Do you want me, Garreth?"

I close my eyes, knowing there's no way I can fight it. Not her. When I open them and meet her lust-filled gaze, I give her the only answer I can. "Yes."

"Good, because I want you too," she states, pressing her lips against mine.

It takes my brain a second to catch up, but when it does, I'm all in. I deepen the kiss, coaxing her mouth open with my tongue and sliding it inside to taste her. She's pure heaven on earth as her own tongue glides against mine for the first time.

Her hands move, her fingers diving into my hair and scraping my scalp. I've grown it out these last few years, mostly as a way to say fuck you to my ex-wife, but I never expected to love my long hair as much as I do right now, with her fingers tangled in it.

"I've been thinking about your hair," she mutters, her mouth now hovering just over mine. "I wondered if it was as soft as it looked, and what it would feel like to run my fingers through it."

"And?" I ask, that single question sounding a little pained.

"It is every bit as soft as I imagined, and I really like touching it," she confesses, giving the strands in her hand a slight tug. My cock jumps in anticipation.

"I happen to be a fan right now myself, sweetness."

Her lips curl upward, and I can't hold back my need to kiss her once more. Her mouth is a beautiful sin. I know I shouldn't want it, but I'm too weak to fight the desire. I have no idea how long we sit in my truck and make out like teenagers, but by the time we come up for air, the windows are steamed over and I'm so amped up, I can barely see straight.

"Garreth?"

"Hmm?" I ask, sliding my nose down the column of her neck and inhaling the sweet scent of her skin.

"Will you come inside with me?"

I pull back, a little surprised by her request. Her eyes are dark pools of desire that do nothing but fuel the already raging inferno inside me. "You've been drinking," I reply gently, my palm cupping her cheek.

Unmistakable hurt flashes through her eyes. "You don't want to?"

Needing to touch her, needing to make her understand, I take the sides of her head in my hands and hold her gaze. "My hesitancy has nothing to do with wanting you, Reagan. I want to go inside with you more than I've ever wanted anything before in my life, but I just don't want you to regret this in the morning."

Her features soften as she grins. "I could never regret you, Garreth. And I haven't had as many as you think. I nursed my last two drinks until the ice was melted and they were watered down. I just kept sipping because I thought I needed the liquid courage to ask you about the flirting. I know exactly what I'm doing and who I'm doing it with, and I really want you to come upstairs with me." She swallows hard as she adds, "But only if you want to."

I'm already gone for this woman. What is it about her I can't fight or deny? Her sweetness is complemented perfectly by her sassy side, but I'm also a huge fan of this mix of vulnerability and boldness I've seen tonight. Every piece of herself she shows me makes me like her even more than before.

I'm afraid after tonight I won't ever get enough of her.

Holding her gaze, I let every ounce of desire I've been trying to keep tamped down shine through. "I want you."

So fucking bad it hurts, but I leave that part out.

She flashes me a quick smile. "This doesn't change anything between us," she insists, and even though I know she's referring to our friendship, I know she's one-hundred-percent wrong.

This changes everything.

Once I go up there, I'll want more. I'll crave Reagan like never before, even if we just go back to being friends.

I'll just have to prove to her we're more than friends.

I'll show her we can be something great.

Something real.

She's mine and doesn't even know it yet.

Reagan

There's a slight tremble of urgency to my fingers as I link mine with his and lead him toward the front entrance of my apartment building. I've never brought a man here with the intention of sleeping with him. Not someone I wasn't dating, anyway. But the thought of not inviting Garreth feels like an even bigger crime than the prospect of casual sex.

We take the elevator up to my fourth-floor apartment, his strong woodsy scent enveloping me every step of the way. When we reach my door, I pull my keys from my small purse and try to slip one inside the knob. Of course, this is when my hand shakes enough to cause me to fumble the key. Before I can try again, Garreth reaches out and wraps his big, warm hand around mine and helps guide the key into the hole.

The door creaks open like a loud foghorn in the night, probably catching the attention of every neighbor on this floor. I've never noticed my door squeaking like this before, but tonight, it's like a blaring advertisement of my naughty intentions.

Inside, I close and lock the door before turning and facing him. He's leaning against the wall, watching my every move, the thrill of anticipation surrounding us.

Clearing my throat, I ask, "Would you like a drink?"

He takes a step forward, his eyes burning hotter than the mid-afternoon sun. "Do *you* want to get a drink?"

I shake my head.

"I don't need a drink, love," he whispers, pulling me closer.

Garreth runs his hands up my arms and around to my back, drawing me to his chest. His kiss is insistent, yet gentle as I open my mouth for him once more. This man can kiss, that's for sure. Each one leaves me desperate for more.

I dig my nails into the flesh just hidden beneath the sleeve of his T-shirt, causing a growl to erupt from deep in his throat. "I don't know what it is, but the bite of your nails on my skin drives me fucking wild," he says, breaking the kiss for only a second before diving back in for more.

His hands begin to roam, sliding down my back and cupping my ass. He pulls me firmly against him again, and like a monkey, I start to climb. He lifts, and my legs automatically wrap around his waist.

I worry I'm too heavy. I'm a taller girl, standing at five nine, with long legs, but surprisingly, it's not too awkward or difficult to lock my ankles behind his back. And he doesn't appear to be straining to hold me up, if the way his mouth plunders mine is any indication.

Garreth spins around, pinning my back to the door with a thud. My knees fall open as he grinds his erection exactly where I need him. I rip my mouth away from his, my head hitting the hard door as his mouth descends on my neck. He sucks hard, nipping and licking the delicate flesh. I wonder if he can feel the erratic pound of my heartbeat beneath his lips.

"Fuck, you taste so sweet. I want to lick every square inch of your body," he states, his fingers tightening against my ass as he rocks forward.

"I'd be okay with that," I whisper, leaning back to give him better access to my collarbone.

"All in good time, love. I'm in no hurry." With that, he spins on his heels and turns in the direction of my bedroom. "I'm assuming this is the right way."

"Second door on the right," I reply without removing my mouth from his neck. Day-old scruff prickles my lips, and the thought of that very burn sliding across my thighs has me clenching them.

"What was that?" he asks, crossing the threshold for my bedroom.

"I was just thinking about whisker burn," I confess quietly.

He pulls back slightly and meets my gaze. "Yeah? Any particular part you were thinking of?"

I can feel heat creep up my neck and stain my cheeks as I nod.

"Well, don't get shy on me now, love," he says, huskily. His eyes burn black with desire as he stares intently. "Tell me. Where are you picturing this whisker burn?"

I press my chest against his, my elbows sitting on his shoulders. Leaning to the side, I get close to his ear and whisper, "My thighs."

Garreth groans, spinning us around and gently laying me down on my bed. "Show me," he instructs, sitting back on his knees between my legs.

"Here," I say, drawing a line from just above the side of my knee, slowly angling it upward until I reach the top of my thigh where my shorts sit. "And here."

"Hmm," he replies, his eyes glued to each movement of my finger. "I see." He shifts to lying on his stomach, his head now positioned at the apex of my legs. "So, you're thinking you need a little whisker burn...here." He drops his mouth and kisses across my inner thigh, dragging his cheek across the sensitive flesh as he goes.

"There. Yes. That's...nice."

Why is it suddenly so hard to breathe?

"I agree, but I think we'll get a better picture if we remove these shorts," he says, reaching up and unfastening the button. The drag of the zipper echoes through the room as he slides it down. I lift and shimmy as my shorts are pulled down my hips, my legs moved and adjusted until the shorts are completely off, tossed over his shoulder. "That's better already," he mutters before lowering his mouth.

The first connection of his tongue against my panties is like touching an electric fence. I jolt, red-hot lust charging through my veins, reckless and wild as it races through my body and lands firmly between my legs. I was wet before, but that was nothing compared to this new surge of desire.

"This is better than my dreams."

The statement surprises me, mostly because he said it so quietly, I almost didn't hear it. Before I can utter a word, he's pushing aside the cotton and wrapping his lips around my clit. What happens next can only be described as mind-blowing.

My body arches off the bed, or as much as it can with him positioned between my legs. Garreth alternates between licking my clit and applying gentle suction with his mouth, driving me straight toward the edge of insanity. My hips automatically move, desperately seeking more friction, more pleasure, more...

Just more of everything.

The short amount of time it takes to bring me to orgasm is embarrassing, but I can't help it. It's been a while since anyone's gone down on me. Justin wasn't a fan and would often complain about the taste. It didn't matter I was a big fan of oral, giving and receiving. He wasn't into it, so it didn't happen.

But this...this is...wow.

I cry out as my release washes over me. Wave after wave of pleasure ripples through my body as my hips rock and move entirely on their own accord. My fingers are tangled in his hair, something new I'm apparently quite fond of, as I try to anchor myself to the bed.

To him.

To this amazing feeling he stirs to life within me.

Garreth moves once more, his mouth descending onto mine as he covers me from head to toe with his body. I taste myself on his tongue, and it only seems to add more fuel to the already burning fire between us. My hands are hurried as I pull at his T-shirt, doing everything I can to get closer to bare skin.

He reaches behind his neck and pulls it over his head in one swift motion before dropping back down and pressing me into the mattress. My legs wrap around his hips, bringing his very large—very *large*—cock in line with the very place I ache for him.

"I could live the rest of my life strictly off your taste, love. It's fucking fantastic," he says, sliding his tongue into my mouth.

I hum my agreement, sucking his tongue deep into my mouth, much like I'd do if it were his cock.

"Jesus, Reagan," he groans, flexing his hips and grinding against me.

"We're wearing entirely too much clothing," I insist, scoring my nails down his sides and reaching for his belt.

Garreth jumps and laughs, his right hand snatching my left one. "That wasn't very nice."

I give him a wide, innocent smile. "What, this?" I ask, scraping the nails on my right hand across his side and making him jump once more.

"Bloody hell, woman. Stop that," he counters, trying to catch my other hand before I can do it again.

A giggle spills from my lips as he grabs my other hand and holds them above my head. He hovers over me, gazing down at me with so much heat, the charged air practically crackles. Suddenly, all of the humor and fun melts away. In its place is an intensity that leaves me breathless.

He lowers his mouth, his lips a bit more urgent than before. My back arches, eager to feel the weight of his body pressing down on me. "Please," I beg against his mouth.

Garreth pulls back slightly and asks, "You sure?"

"Definitely."

As if realizing it's actually going to happen—and now—he climbs off me and removes his shorts and boxer briefs at the same time, leaving himself completely naked. My mouth waters at the sight of his cock. It's hard, long, and thick, with beads of moisture seeping from the tip.

I really want that in my mouth.

Garreth snorts. "Afraid no can do, sweetheart. You wrap those sexy lips around my dick, and it'll all be over before we even get started." My eyes widen, mostly because I didn't realize I said that out loud, which makes him snicker. "Yes, you said that aloud. Now, what do you say we finish getting you naked, yeah?"

I don't think I can agree any quicker. Sitting up, he reaches for my shirt, very gradually lifting it up my torso. He's doing it so slowly, I almost reach up and help him, until I see the look in his eyes. It's part desire, part wonder, as if he's carefully unwrapping a present and drawing out the suspense.

Once my shirt is removed, he gazes down at my bra. "I've never been a flowers guy, but I can get on board with this," he states, referring to the small white flowers adorning the soft yellow satin.

"It's not sexy," I counter, wishing I had worn one of the lace push-up bras I have buried in the back of my underwear drawer.

"Are you kidding me?" he asks, his voice hoarse. "I've never seen anything sexier."

Finding every ounce of confidence I can, I reach between my breasts and release the front clasp, keeping my eyes trained on his face the entire time. I watch his eyes flare the moment the satin falls away. His lips part and a big rush of warm breath puffs from his mouth as he runs his hand down his face. "Christ, love."

I reach down and slip a finger under the elastic of the panties and start to shimmy them down my hips. I'll probably have to throw them out anyway, considering they're slightly stretched out of shape, but I don't care. It's a fairly inexpensive price for an epic oral orgasm.

Suddenly, an important detail hits me square in the face. "Garreth? I don't have any condoms." My eyes widen with panic, especially because we're mere moments away from needing said protection.

He pauses, as if considering his options. Then, he quickly reaches over the side of the bed for his shorts, digging his wallet from the back pocket. He fishes through it and smiles. "Got one. I don't know how long it's been in here," he starts, flipping it over and sighing in relief. "We're good. Not expired." He makes quick work at sheathing his erection and gazes down at me. "You have legs for days," he observes, running his rough hand down my outer thigh as he takes his position between them. His touch makes me shiver with anticipation.

Garreth covers me with his body, his cock nudging at my entrance, begging for admittance. I hitch my foot up over his hip, widening my legs. Placing his hands beside my head, he holds my gaze as he gently pushes forward. I feel the stretch immediately and gasp. He pauses when he's only halfway inside me, letting me adjust to his size, but I can tell he's struggling. His face is tight, his eyes darker than I've ever seen them before, and I'm not sure he's breathing.

"You can move," I insist, reaching down and grabbing his ass.

All things holy, his ass. It's perfection.

"I think I need a minute," he bites out.

"Okay," I whisper. "But don't take too long."

He offers me a tight smile, but still doesn't move, so I take matters into my own hands. I hold my grip on his ass and push down at the same time I roll my hips upward. The motion causes him to thrust forward, filling me completely. It's almost painful, to be honest, but pleasure quickly replaces the sting.

"That's one way to speed things up," he quips, smiling down at me.

"Yeah, well, you were taking too long."

He pulls back, leaving just the tip, and rocks forward once more. "We can't have that," he replies, pausing long enough to reach for my hands and holding them above my head once more.

"I like touching you."

"I like you touching me too, but something tells me I need to limit your ability to touch me if I'm going to maintain some semblance of control here."

Lifting my chin and chest, I whisper, "What's it gonna take to see you lose control?" To punctuate my point, I rock my hips and groan, loving the way his cock slides so easily inside me.

He bites out a curse. "That. That'll do it."

Then, he starts to move.

Finally.

Garreth sets a punishing pace, his hips thrusting as he drives me into the bed. He plays my body like a violin, and he's the maestro. My nipples tingle as they brush against the coarse hair on his chest repeatedly, and even though I know I came just a few short minutes ago, I'm certain I will again. How could I not with a man this dominant, this possessive, this fucking good in bed.

He shifts his weight without breaking stride, still holding my hands over my head, but with only one hand this time. He cups my cheek before running his hand down my neck to my breasts. "Fuck, you are so damn beautiful," he grunts out, pinching and rolling my left nipple between his rough fingers.

I cry out, pleasure shooting through my body like an explosion.

"Hmm, I think you like that," he murmurs, tweaking my super sensitive nipple once more. "What about this?" he asks just before bending down and sucking that same nipple into his hot, wet mouth.

"Oh God," I mutter, closing my eyes as waves of ecstasy ripple through me.

"Yes, you definitely like that, don't you?" His big hand trails down my torso, his touch burning my skin. "You blush the most beautiful shade of pink when you're excited. Right here." He moves his hand between my breasts as he drives his cock inside me. "That's it, love. Let go. I want to feel your pussy squeezing my cock," he demands.

His words cause a chain reaction. My orgasm starts slow as he pumps his hips, and I can feel my internal muscles clamp around his thick cock. He groans, and just the sound of his own pleasure makes my nipples pebble so hard, they hurt.

"Fuck, yes, Reagan," he mutters, and the sound of my name on his lips as he comes is my complete undoing.

I yell his name as waves of release wash over me like an ocean wave on crystal white sand. It's beautiful, powerful, and consuming, and I pray it never ends.

When Garreth finally stops moving, his body falls onto mine, leaving us both spent and breathless. He tries to shift his weight to the side, but I hold on to him with my legs, keeping him exactly where he is. "Just stay right here for a minute," I say softly, turning my head and kissing his shoulder.

His hand moves to cup my neck, his touch much gentler this time. He releases my hands, slowly dragging his fingers down my arms with a content sigh, as if he's savoring and reveling in the moment. "If I start to squish you, tell me," he grumbles, his face planted in the pillow.

"You okay?" I ask, running my fingers over his sweaty, hot skin.

"I think I died for a minute, but I'll be okay."

I snort a laugh, loving this playfulness. I've never experienced someone so chatty before in bed, someone who told me exactly what he was thinking and how much he loved what was happening. After Justin, the loud grunter, I think I prefer this version better. Garreth is exactly what I didn't realize I was missing from sex.

Including multiple orgasms.

Yeah, I think I'll keep him for a while.

How long is yet to be determined, but if there's more sex like this involved, I might not ever be ready to let him go.

Ten

Garreth

I wasn't kidding. I think I died.

Died and gone to heaven.

I know I'm too heavy to be lying on her for too much longer, but not only do I *not* want to move, I'm not sure I can. My limbs are numb, my body so exhausted from the most intense orgasm I've ever had, I just want to lie here for a while longer and just breathe.

Especially with Reagan tucked comfortably beneath me.

Her body fits so perfectly against mine, like she was designed specifically for me. Plus, I can't get enough of this forward side of her. She's passionate and dynamic, taking what she wants, and I've been thanking the stars above she wanted me.

At least for tonight.

No, I won't think like that. I may not know what the future holds for us, but now that I've had one taste of the exquisite Reagan Turner, no way can I just walk away. I've imagined this night for so long, I need more. And not just in bed—though, I wouldn't be opposed to more of that soon—but I want to get to know her. I want to make her smile and spend what little free time I get with her.

More sex would just be the icing on the Reagan cake.

The time has come to move. I need to get rid of the condom and then we need to figure out where we go from here.

94

"I'll be right back," I whisper, kissing the side of her head and rolling away.

"There's a bathroom there," she states, pointing to the open door across the room.

I slip inside the en suite bathroom and flip on the light, closing the door behind me. It's small, but well maintained, painted a cheerful yellow color with navy accents. Reaching down to remove the used condom, I notice it seems...odd. When I slide it off, a small line along the side catches my eye.

I squint down at it, trying to examine the rubber without making a mess. It doesn't look broken, at least not in the way I've heard in guy horror stories over the years. You know, when the fella pulls out and the rubber rips completely, leaving a ring around the root of your cock? Thankfully, that's never happened to me, so I don't know why I'm worried about it now. This doesn't look like a broken condom to me.

Tossing it in the trash, something still niggles in the back of my mind as I wash my hands. I find a washcloth in the cabinet and wet it with warm water, cleaning up the remnants of the mess. I lay the used cloth over the side of the hamper and grab a second, making sure it's wet with warm water too and head for the door.

I pull it open, bathing her semi-dark room in light. "Hey," I start, prepared to tell her about the weird line in the side of the condom, but all thoughts leave my head completely in a flash.

Reagan is lying on her bed, still completely naked, her legs spread as her fingers dance down her abdomen and toward her very wet, swollen pussy. "I was thinking," she says, dragging the tip of her index finger through her wetness.

"Please," I mutter, clearing my throat and leaning against the doorjamb, "don't let me stop you." My cock is already stirring to life.

"I think I'd like a repeat of your earliest performance. I've already forgotten all about the whisker burn." She teases her entrance, the tip of her finger pushing inside.

I'm already moving her way. "We can't have that, now can we?" I ask, climbing onto her bed and taking my position between her thighs. With a quick lick of my lips, I instruct, "Hang on, love. This is going to be one hell of a ride."

"Garreth is a bit of an unusual name. Does it have a special meaning?" she asks, her warm breath tickling my chest. She's been curled against me, her leg thrown over mine as I draw lazy circles on her back with my thumb.

"Actually, it was an accident."

I feel her move and look down, her eyes meeting mine with confusion. "An accident?"

I chuckle. "Yeah, my mom, bless her crazy heart, claims to have been half asleep when asked for the specific details for my birth certificate. Dad was down getting food from the cafeteria, and when the nurses asked her what my name was, she replied, Garreth, slurring the last letter."

"So it was supposed to be Garrett?" she asks, unable to fight the smile.

"Yep. And apparently, she didn't realize the mistake until she got the certified paperwork from the county," I tell her with a chuckle.

"Oh no," she replies, the same delicate little fingers I watched pump in and out of her pussy while I ate it an hour ago, now covering her sweet mouth. The very mouth that wrapped around my cock and stayed there until I came down her throat just after.

"It's okay. I don't mind the unique name. I love to tease her every chance I get, though. My favorite is reminding her I'll never find my name printed on those gas station keychains."

She chuckles and kisses my pec before returning her head to rest against it. "That's not nice."

"She doesn't mind. In fact, she's where I get my teasing sense of humor. I wouldn't do it if I really thought it bothered her," I insist.

"Why didn't she change it?"

"She said it grew on her and liked the idea of it being different than everyone else."

Reagan runs her fingers around my nipple, causing me to jump. "You really are ticklish, aren't you?" Her giggle is the sweetest sound in the world.

"I am," I agree, linking my fingers with hers. Mostly to keep her from tickling me again, but also because I just like the feel of her skin against mine.

"I get what you're saying about the personalized keychains. My name is never there."

I glance down at her, confused. "I thought Reagan was a popular name."

"Well, popular enough," she concedes. "But my mom didn't spell it the most common way. She was a huge fan of President Reagan when she was young, so when she found out I was a girl, she named me Reagan, spelling it the same as his last name."

"Interesting."

After a few minutes of quiet, our linked fingers resting on my chest, she whispers, "What now?"

"Now it seems silly to change our names, tigress. We're both in our thirties," I reply, knowing that's not what she's referring to.

Her response is to stick her fingers into my side and make me jump for the ceiling. "Devil woman!" I holler with a laugh.

When I settle back down, she snuggles into my side once more. "You deserved that. You know I wasn't talking about that."

Sighing, I lean over and run my nose over the crown of her head, inhaling her amazing scent. "I know."

Reagan shifts, turning on her side, so I do the same until we're facing each other. "The working together part is an issue for you, isn't it?"

I take a deep breath, not nearly as surprised as I probably should be at how well she seems to understand me already. "It is. I've never dated someone I work with, because I never wanted it to cause me or the woman I'm seeing issues. Especially if I'm her boss. I know there's no rule against it, but it still worries me. I don't care what anyone else thinks of me, but if it were to cause problems at work, I'd hate that."

"I understand," she says, reaching over and placing her warm palm against my cheek.

"I'd never want our relationship to jeopardize your position at work."

"Or yours."

I shrug. "I'm not worried about me."

Her lips curl in a smile right before she yawns. "What if we keep it out of the workplace?"

I brush hair off her forehead before sliding them back into the thick strands of her light brown hair. "Like we see each other outside of work, but act all professional at the restaurant?"

She nods and bites down on her bottom lip. Her eyes are eager, almost hopeful, and I already know there's no way I'd deny her, even if I wanted to.

"I like the way you think, Miss Turner," I say, pulling her naked body flush against mine. My cock gets all excited at all the bare skin, but I have to squash his dreams of any sort of repeats. We're out of condoms still, and it's really, *really* early in the morning. She needs to sleep. I place my lips against her forehead. "You need to get some sleep."

As if on cue, she yawns again. "Are you staying?"

My heart starts to thunder in my chest. "Do you want me to stay?"

She nods. "Yes."

"There's no place I'd rather be," I state, realizing there's no truer words I could speak.

I hold Reagan against my chest, listening to the sound of her breathing slowly even out as she drifts to sleep. It takes me much longer to succumb to my own exhaustion, because all I want to do is lie here, holding and watching her.

We may not know where we're going, but at least we've got a start. I've never dated someone from work, but something tells me, if anyone can make it work, Reagan and I can. I mean, look at Mallory and Walker. Sure, it's way too soon to be thinking that level of commitment, but the idea is there, planted in my mind and slowly growing roots.

For now, we'll spend more time together outside of the business we both work for and get to know each other.

And hopefully, I'll get to explore her amazing body again and again.

Something tells me I'll never get enough of that.

"You ready?" Numbers asks, popping his head in my office.

"Yep," I reply quickly, getting up from my chair and stretching my back. When did I get to the age where sitting for thirty minutes does a number on your body? Probably about the time I hit thirty-seven. Everything seems to slowly be falling apart the older I get.

I step out of my office, making sure my door is locked behind me, and join the four owners in the bar. Every Monday they have an owners meeting, and ever since I started as their manager, I've joined them.

Jameson and Walker are already there, and the moment I sit down, Jasper appears with the tray of food. "What's on the menu today?" Walker asks, taking the first plate handed.

"Barbecue brisket burger I like to call the Bangin' Bacon Burger," he announces proudly, setting each of the remaining plates on the table. When he gets to me, he sets a small bowl in front of me.

"What's this?" I ask, completely shocked at what I'm seeing.

"Fruit salad. You insulted the chef, now you eat what you get," Jasper retorts, giving me a cocky grin as he slides onto his chair.

I look down at the fruit, my stomach growling as the aromas of beef, pork brisket, crispy bacon, and barbecue sauce filter over from the plate beside me. "This is horseshit."

Walker tosses a fry on top of my fruit mixture. "There. Now quit your bitching."

Someone snickers, I think it's Numbers, but I refuse to look up. I reach for my fork, prepared to go down fighting and eat what is put before me. However, two bites in—and listening to everyone else's overexaggerated moans of gratification—I jump up, pushing the mushy concoction out of the way.

"Where ya going?" Jasper demands.

"To make myself a damn burger. Then across the street to tell your wife how mean you are," I holler just before I turn the corner and storm to the kitchen, the sound of their laughter following me the entire way.

As soon as I step inside, Doug is there, holding up a plate with a hesitant smile. "Sorry, Garreth. He made me do it," the assistant chef says, handing over my plate of food.

"Of course he did," I mutter, taking my fresh burger and heading back to the bar area. I walk right past the usual table we sit at and pull out a chair for the next one.

"What are you doing?" Jameson asks.

"Eating my food in peace," I state, shoveling a handful of fries in my mouth and chewing loudly.

"This is why you fit in so well," Numbers says, shaking his head at our antics.

"Can we get this meeting started? I don't care if he sits at a different table," Jasper adds, smirking at me as he takes a bite of his burger.

"Actually, before we start the meeting, I need to know why my wife's cousin didn't text her to let her know she arrived to her apartment safely last night." I feel four sets of eyes staring into the side of my head. "And why your truck was still there this morning when I drove by."

I turn, pinning the big, tattooed guy with a look. "You know, I never pegged you for the group gossip."

"That was always Jasper," Numbers announces, trying to hide a smile.

"Fuck off. You're getting fruit salad next week."

"Well?" Jameson asks, a single eyebrow arched up in question.

"I took her to retrieve her car this morning," I reply lamely.

"By staying at her apartment?" Walker asks, openly grinning.

"All night, from what I hear," Jasper adds with a smirk.

My eyes narrow at his laughing ones. Realizing they're not going to let this go, I dramatically sigh and toss my napkin on the table. "Listen, whatever happens between Reagan and me is between us, okay? All I can say is it won't affect the job either of us do here. When we're working, I'm still her boss, and there won't be any favoritism where she's concerned. I will treat everyone fairly and equally. I can still do my job."

"We never said you couldn't," Numbers replies diplomatically.

Jasper sits up straight and meets my gaze. "You're a damn good manager, Garr. There was never any doubt to that."

Jameson crosses his arms over his broad chest and squints just a little at me. Even though I've known him practically my entire life, having a man like Jameson's full scrutiny directed at you is never easy. I try not to move under the weight of his stare, especially when he gives nothing away as to what he's thinking. It's unnerving, really, and I wish he'd look away.

"Besides, it's not like I can say anything about you dating an employee. Sometimes, it's the best thing to ever happen to you," Walker quips, grinning from ear to ear as he refers to his wife.

"Yeah, I really don't care, man. Honestly, I was just busting your balls and seeing if I could make you sweat a little. I actually like the idea of you and Reagan," Jameson says, offering a rare smile.

"You asshole," I grumble, tossing a fry at his head, which he easily avoids by ducking.

"All right, so now that we're all caught up on the status of Garreth and Reagan's relationship," Numbers announces before he pauses. Suddenly, he turns to me and lowers his voice. "You did spend the night though, right?"

Everyone laughs as I smile and shake my head. No way am I actually confirming that. I wasn't kidding when I said what happens between us outside of this building is ours alone. I'm not gossiping about what we do behind closed doors.

"Moving on," I state, turning my back to them and diving into my sandwich. It's delicious of course, but no way am I complimenting Jasper right now. Not after the fruit salad bullshit. "I fired Dirk. He missed again."

"He's changing the subject, so that's a yes," Jasper mutters.

"Agreed." This from Walker.

I close my eyes and try to drown out their ribbing, even if I have a slight smile on my face. I can't help it. It automatically happens any time I think about Reagan and our night together. She works tonight at four, and I honestly can't wait to see her. Is it going to be hard not to take her in my arms and kiss her? Hell yes it will be, but I'll manage. I'm more worried about being caught gawking at her from across the room than I am about my lack of control where she's concerned. The guys behind the bar—especially Kellen—will pick up on that immediately.

I can be a total professional. I'm going to have to pretend she's not the most beautiful woman in the world or remember what she looks like when I'm balls deep inside her and she's coming. Yeah, the best thing to do is to not act affected by her presence.

Ha!

Easier said than done, my friend. Easier said than done.

Reagan

Monday night is a welcomed slower pace from the hecticness of Saturday night. In fact, I find myself looking for little things to do to keep me busy, like rewashing menus, helping bus tables, and refilling condiments between customers.

It also gives me more time to observe Garreth.

He's sticking to the bar side of the business tonight because we're short a bartender. Someone called in sick, leaving only one guy on the opposite side, and since their tables are used as often as this side's are, Garreth finds himself taking orders and serving drinks. That's probably for the best, though. Since he's over there, it gives me less time to gawk at him in his navy polo and nicely fitted blue jeans.

"Hey, Reagan, can you grab two waters for table fourteen?" Angie asks, referring to a two-person table across the room that was just seated. She's currently working on refilling drinks and delivering food to a large eight-person table in the middle of the room.

"Of course," I reply, making my way over to the servers' station to pour two glasses of ice water.

As I go, I glance inside the bar, my eyes instantly finding Garreth. He's behind the counter, pouring a tap beer and laughing at something a woman is saying. She's leaning toward him, practically hanging over the bar like a floozy, and all I can do is get table fourteen water.

My hands are a little jerky as I throw ice in the glasses and fill them. I wonder if Miss Too Close over there wants a glass of ice water? I could accidentally drop it in her lap.

Why am I acting like this?

Am I...jealous?

I'm rarely jealous. I don't think I ever got jealous regarding Justin, even as Tia, his new, young assistant, seemed to stare every time I'd visit the office. I do remember getting a little worked up one afternoon when some woman in a bikini was hitting on Dave. We were at the sandbar, all of our boats tied together, when this tipsy woman in a tiny pink bikini kept reaching over and touching Dave's arm. Sure, it bothered me, but I was mostly jealous because her boobs were better than mine.

But the thought of some woman sitting at the bar, openly flirting with Garreth, has my heart racing and angry jealousy bubbling to the surface. No, I'm not exactly angry, but I've definitely moved past annoyed.

I risk a quick glance between the wall and the doorway to see if they're still talking, and when I do, my eyes lock on his dark brown ones. His hands rest on the counter casually, but there's nothing casual about the way he's looking at me. Fire dances in those dark orbs, slowly devouring me from across the room.

The woman is still talking, but Garreth isn't paying any attention. The corner of his mouth turns upward ever so slightly, but just enough I can see it. It feels private, as if that little smile is only for me.

He taps the top of the bar, gives the woman a polite grin, and steps aside to help the next customer. While he makes eye contact with the person in front of him, there's no mistaking his vision keeps filtering over to where I stand.

Clearing my throat, I take both glasses of water to table fourteen. Even as I go, I can feel his gaze like a hot caress, following my every movement. I'm surprised I don't stumble and fall, considering that's the kind of shit-luck that has always seemed to follow me. After setting the water down, Angie hurries over to take their orders, leaving me to head back up to the front of the restaurant.

Thirty minutes later, my bladder is screaming, so I flag down Meredith, the second server working tonight, and motion I'm heading to the back. I slip into the employee break room and find the bathroom already in use. Since I'm to the point of doing the pee-dance, I make the quick decision to use the public restroom around the corner.

Thankfully, there's no one inside to witness my scurry to the nearest stall, and within a few minutes, my bladder is happy and empty. I wash my hands and check my hair quickly, making sure the humidity outside hasn't turned my long locks into an unruly, wavy mess. I'm pleasantly surprised by what I see in the mirror and move toward the door to head back out to the restaurant.

The moment I step into the hallway, a warm hand gently grabs me around the arm and tugs me into the office across the hall. The door shuts, and my back is pressed against the hard wood a second later. Strong arms cage me in as a hot, insistent mouth claims my lips.

A groan fills the room, and it takes me a few seconds to realize it came from me as Garreth sweeps his tongue across the seam of my lips, begging for entrance. My hands dive into his hair, the familiar softness of his hair sliding through my fingers. He kisses like a man possessed, the firmness of his tongue against mine, the power behind his rough lips. His mouth is pure heaven, and I want more.

Unfortunately, that's not on the agenda tonight.

Garreth rips his mouth from mine, his warm breath panting against my cheek. "Fuck, I've been dying to do that all night."

"I thought we weren't going to let this affect us at work," I quip, mentally noting we couldn't even make it one night.

"That was before I realized how hard it was going to be to see you and not be able to touch you." He trails his lips across my cheek to my ear and lightly nips the lobe.

My back arches, my chest pressing against his. "I'm going to have to quit my job, aren't I?" I ask, not entirely kidding.

"Hell no. You're like an addiction. I need to be close to you," he mutters, slipping his big hand up the back of my shirt and grazing his fingertips across my bra clasp.

"But you just said this is hard," I counter, secretly begging him to release the clasp.

"No, *this* is hard," he mutters, pressing his erection into the apex of my legs. "Being near you is like the oxygen I need to breathe."

My heart soars at his sweet words. "You're making it very difficult not to want to strip you naked."

He chuckles low and gravelly, sending sparks of desire straight to my girly bits. He lightly kisses my jaw before returning his mouth to mine. The kiss is much shorter than I want, and before I know it, he's pulling away. "I think we've got this, love, but only if I'm able to steal a few fixes throughout the night."

"You don't think anyone's going to notice we're regularly disappearing at the same time?"

"Probably not. They're not that bright," he quips, smiling widely and making me laugh.

"Stop," I counter, lightly hitting his chest.

"I'm kidding. To be honest, some of them will pick up on it right away, but for the life of me, I can't remember exactly why I cared so much to keep business and pleasure separate," he says, moving his hand to my abdomen and gliding it up.

"Me neither," I whisper. His big hand cups my breast as a soft sigh spills from my lips.

"Damn it," he grumbles, reluctantly removing his hand and standing up straight. "We need to get back out there."

I nod, "You're right. What about that?" I ask, nodding down to where his erection strains against his jeans.

"*That* will just have to wait until later. What are you doing when you get off work?" he asks, taking another step back, putting much-needed space between us.

"I was planning to do a load of laundry, but I could hang around here for a while," I offer. I'm only scheduled until the restaurant closes at nine, but Garreth will be here until close.

"No, don't do that. Then it'll really look suspicious. If you want, I could stop by after we close," he offers. "If it's not too late. I don't want you to have to stay up, just for me."

I shrug off his worry. "It won't be. Besides, I don't work tomorrow. It's girls' night," I say, referring to the one night a week the ladies all get together for dinner.

"Ahh, yes. I hope you're all coming here."

"We are."

"Good. Then I don't have to worry about guys at other places hitting on you," he retorts with a smirk and a wink.

"Uhh, you don't have to worry about that at all. I'm not the one they usually hit on," I reply. Even though I'm the only single one in the group, the guys always go for eccentric BJ or curvy Mallory.

"You're wrong, love. They notice you. For years, I've silently watched you, and I know without a doubt, every man in the room will look your way at least once. Some, all fucking night long. It's amazing I've never punched some guy in the face for staring at your ass," he argues, crossing his arms over his chest.

I almost comment about the woman at the bar flirting with him but decide against it. Frankly, it doesn't matter. I know a big part of their job is to smile and be friendly and approachable. I also realize I trust him. The man has waited years to make a move on me, so it's not likely he's going to jeopardize what we're starting by hitting on someone else.

"Ready?" he asks, reaching for my hand.

I place mine in his automatically, and he pulls me off the door and spins me around. He grabs the doorknob but stops before he twists. "I'm coming over tonight when I get off work." He places a kiss on the side of my neck. "Oh, and this time? I have a whole box of condoms."

Then, he opens the door and moves to the side, so we're not standing too close. I take one step forward and stop in my tracks. Garreth, of course, slams into the back of me, nearly knocking me into the wall of muscle.

"What's wro—" Garreth starts, and stops. "Oh, hey, Tank."

Jameson is standing against the wall directly in front of us, his arms crossed over his broad chest and a look that might scare me a little if I didn't know how much of a big teddy bear he really is. Okay, so teddy bear might be a stretch, but really, he's not as grumpy as he portrays.

We stand there, all staring, some of us not even breathing. I don't know if I should talk first, or do I just wait for Jameson to break the silence? Lord knows that man could probably win a competition to see who can be quiet the longest with someone who can't speak.

Finally, the uncomfortable wait is over.

Jameson offers a rare grin. "Walker owes me twenty bucks." Then, he pushes off the wall and walks away, leaving both of us standing in the hallway, dumbfounded—and maybe a little guilty.

"That went well."

I glance over my shoulder and meet his humor-laced eyes. "You're trouble, Mr. Taylor. Big fat trouble."

He offers me a wolfish grin. "Right back at ya, babe. Right back at ya."

By the time the knock sounds on my front door, it's just after eleven thirty. The load of laundry has been finished and put away, and I've spent the last thirty minutes trying to catch up on my favorite streaming show, but no matter what happens on TV, my concentration is shot. All I can think about is Garreth and what his plans are for when he arrives.

And I know there are plans.

Dirty ones.

He made sure to whisper his intent in my ear the moment I clocked out.

I release the deadbolt lock and pull open the door without looking through the peephole. No one shows up at my apartment this late at night.

Except him.

He slips inside and has me in his arms a moment later. Garreth kicks the door closed and blindly reaches back to lock it as he takes my lips with his in a bruising, demanding kiss. "Fuck, I've missed you."

"It's been less than three hours," I mutter just before his tongue probes my mouth and renders me completely speechless.

"Too long," he confirms. With one quick motion, he grabs my ass and lifts me against his chest. His long strides eat up the floor until he's at the couch, laying me down on it and covering me with his body. "I had every intention of talking to you first."

"Talking's overrated," I retort, reaching for the hem of his polo and ripping it up his torso.

"Isn't it?" He lifts up long enough to remove his shirt before coming back down on me. "I also had every intention of carrying you to bed."

"Why delay the inevitable?" I ask, pausing my frantic hands long enough to meet his gaze. "I've never had sex on this couch."

"Hmm," he replies, "I haven't had sex on this couch either."

I can't help but smile. "We should remedy that."

The sexiest grin spreads across his gorgeous face. "We should."

Clothes start flying. I start to shimmy out of my cotton pajama shorts and top while Garreth pushes his jeans and boxer briefs down his legs. Unfortunately, that's when he realizes he still has on his boots, so while he's occupied with unlacing those, I take the opportunity to grab his cock. His big, thick, incredibly hard cock.

"Jesus, just one touch and you render me a teenager again," he grounds out, fighting to get his boots off and resisting the urge to thrust up in my hand. As soon as they're free, he kicks off his pants and turns, pinning me down on the couch. "I lose all control when I'm with you."

I slide my fingers into his hair and bat my eyelashes. "I happen to thoroughly enjoy it when you lose control."

He slams his mouth down on mine but rips it off just as quickly with a dramatic growl. Reaching over, he pulls a strip of condoms out of the front pocket of his jeans, ripping off the first square. He has himself covered in record time, but instead of moving between my open thighs, he shifts my leg and taps my hip. "Up you go."

I kneel on the couch, facing the wall, and spread my legs. Garreth positions himself behind me, his cock nudging at my entrance. He grips my hips and leans me forward so my chest is resting on the back of the couch, and then he pushes forward.

Our moans of pleasure fill the room as he gently eases all the way in. "Christ, Reagan," he mutters, bringing his mouth down to kiss my shoulder. He's stopped moving, as if he's allowing me time to adjust to the intrusion.

I don't have time for that, however.

I want what I want, and I want it now.

Gripping the back of the seat cushion, I push back against him, feeling his cock slide so deep, I swear he hits my stomach. I groan loudly as his hands tighten on my hips. "Please, Garreth," I whisper, needing more.

His hot breath tickles my back. "I can't fucking deny you anything," he murmurs before placing an open-mouth kiss on my back and sitting back.

Using my hips as leverage, he starts to move, slow at first, then gradually gaining in speed. The only sound is our mixed panting and his skin slapping against mine. It's raw, real, and better than anticipated.

"Reach between your legs, love. Get yourself there. I want to feel you squeeze my cock while you touch yourself."

Doing as instructed, I slip my hand between my thighs and rub a finger across my wet, swollen clit. "Oh God," I moan, pleasure shooting through me.

"Just like that. Keep doing it," he demands, maintaining his hard pace from behind.

Between being stretched and filled by him and the pressure on my clit, my orgasm is already starting to build.

"You're getting close, aren't you? I can feel your muscles getting tight."

"Yes," I groan, rocking my hips back to meet his thrust. "So close."

"Give it to me. Now, Reagan. Come on my cock."

I press hard against my clit and rocket into orbit. I come so hard, it's difficult to breathe and impossible to do anything but float and feel.

He continues to thrust, driving himself toward his own release. I reach back farther and come in contact with his balls. Even though he's moving, I run my finger over the bottom of them, earning me a loud groan. "Fuck, that feels good."

Shifting my hand, I grab a hold of them, cupping his balls in my palm and giving them a gentle squeeze. The result is nothing short of explosive. He roars loudly as his balls draw up tight and he comes with an intensity that leaves me smiling.

When he finally stops rocking and shaking, Garreth falls forward. He slips his hands around my torso and hugs me to his chest. "That was…yeah."

"Mmm," I murmur, unable to form any other response.

"Might I add, you're more than welcome to grab my balls like that again anytime you feel the urge," he adds with a kiss to my neck.

I can't even fight my grin. "Noted." After a minute of catching our breath, I say, "You know, I had a shower when I got home from work, but something tells me I could use another one."

"Hmm, come to think of it, I could probably use a shower myself. I suddenly find myself a little…dirty," he quips.

I turn my head and bite his bicep. "Let's shower together then. We can help each other get clean," I insist.

Garreth pulls back, his cock falling from my body, as he lightly smacks my ass. "And then we can help each other get dirty again."

Twelve

Garreth

The music is pumping through the speakers, and the post-work crowd is out in full force. It's already busy for a Tuesday night, which is fine by me. It'll make the time move faster. Reagan and the owners' wives are coming for their weekly girls' night soon. That means I'll get to see her tonight, even though she's off work and we have nothing planned for later.

"I heard Jenna called in sick again."

I spin around, surprised to find Walker standing there, especially since he's always off on Tuesdays. "She did, but I have it covered," I insist, filling two frosty mugs with draft beer.

"I know you do, but I figured since Reagan's off too and the servers will have to hostess, your time would be best served floating between the sides," Walker states. "Besides, my mom offered to stay with the kids tonight, so both Mal and I could have a break. I'm not passing up the opportunity to come hang out with my wife, even if I'm behind the bar."

I release the breath I didn't realize I was holding. It's been a long time since we've had employee issues, and with having a few new workers, one who called in sick, and another on maternity leave, things have been a little more stressful here than normal. Knowing

Jasper is in the kitchen and Walker is behind the bar goes a long way to ease some of the anxiety I didn't even realize I was feeling.

"Thanks, man," I tell my old friend.

He waves off my appreciation. "Don't thank me. This is my business to run, and if I'm needed, I'm here."

That's one of the things I love most about this place. Not only are the four owners great guys, but they care tremendously about their business, and if ever there's a pinch, they're here in a heartbeat to fill in.

Walker slips behind the bar and gives a chin lift to Dalton, one of the two seasoned bartenders who works evenings, and jumps right in. I know, without a shadow of a doubt, I don't have to worry about this side of the business tonight.

I head over to the restaurant to check on things, noticing more than half the tables full. The servers are busy, but it looks like they're able to keep up with seating customers as they come in. When the door opens and a family of five comes in, I wave off Angie and grab menus. "Good evening, Hoy family. Table for five?"

"Yes, please," Amber says.

"Right this way," I reply, grabbing one of the small cups of crayons we keep for the kids to color on the back of the paper placemats. "Here ya go. Angie will be right with you," I add, setting the crayons down between the two youngest Hoy kids, who immediately get to work on coloring a picture.

I spend the next thirty minutes, chatting with patrons, seating new guests, and helping the servers where I can. When I hear the door open behind me, I'm pleasantly surprised to find my parents standing there.

"Hey, guys," I greet, smiling widely.

"It's your father's night to cook, and since he cremated the pork chops last time, I decided we were going out to eat," Mom announces, turning her cheek to receive a kiss, which I readily give.

"I thought Dad wasn't allowed anywhere near the charcoal grill after the whole ribeye incident," I state, grabbing two menus.

Mom shakes her head. "You'd think I would have learned my lesson after all these years," she says, but I can hear the teasing tone in her voice.

"This way. I have our best table for you." Of course, that's not entirely true. We don't have any seating areas that are better than others. When they designed this business, they put a lot of thought into the layout.

Mom slides into the booth first, and before Dad takes the seat beside her—not across from her—he leans in and whispers, "She thinks I can't cook. I like to think of it as a way of getting out of it when it's my turn."

"Brilliant," I reply, careful to hide my smile as he throws me a wink and sits down. "What can I get you to drink?" I offer, even though I know their server will be here shortly.

"I'd like a margarita," Mom says, making me raise an eyebrow. "What? It's been a long day. I power washed the deck while your dad napped in the hammock. I deserve a margarita."

"And for you?" I ask my dad, who's smiling widely and clearly not even sorry he took a nap this afternoon in the hammock.

"She left off the part about me power washing the entire house before lunch," he replies, reaching over and entwining his fingers with his wife's. "Beer for me. You know the one."

I do. It's what I bring anytime I'm having dinner with them. He's a huge fan of their Night Crüe beer, a dark lager with a hint of ginger. "Coming right up," I reply, heading for Angie, who is delivering a tray of food to a nearby table. "My parents are at twenty. I'm heading to get their drinks."

"Okay, I'll take their order as soon as I finish here," she replies.

Making my way to the bar, I slip behind the hardwood to make the drinks. I always try to take care of customers myself. No reason to stand in line and wait for a bartender to do it when I'm perfectly capable of handling it myself.

"Is that your parents?" Walker asks, pouring a beer as I throw a shot of tequila, Cointreau, and lime juice in the shaker.

"Yep. Dad was in charge of cooking tonight," I reply, adding a scoop of ice in the mixture and shaking.

Walker, knowing my parents' order, pours the dark lager into a frosted mug and sets it in front of me. "I'll make sure to head over and say hi," he says before moving down the bar to help another customer.

I coat the rim of a margarita glass with salt, pour in the mixture, and grab the drinks. When I reach their table, Angie is already there, ready to take their order. "They both want to try the Bangin' Bacon Burger," I state.

Angie looks up, confused.

"I don't think he's officially added it to the menu yet, but I had it yesterday, and it's good. Just make sure Jasper gets the ticket."

Her eyes narrow slightly. "So he can yell at me for making him prepare food not on the menu?" she teases.

"Believe me, he'll be thrilled to make it. He's like a peacock, remember? Sometimes you have to pat him on the ass and tell him how great he is."

That makes everyone laugh. "Fine, but if he yells at me, I'm telling him it was all you," she quips, jotting down the order. "I'll have these out to you shortly," she adds with a pleasant smile before turning and heading toward the kitchen.

"What's on the Bangin' Bacon Burger, besides the obvious?" Dad asks, sipping his beer.

"Brisket, sauteed onions, barbecue sauce, and some aged cheese," I reply, taking a quick glance around the room to make sure everything is as it should be.

"Oh, that sounds good," Mom replies, passing her menu over to me.

Suddenly, a familiar laugh catches my attention. I turn toward the bar and find the owner of said laugh, a beautiful smile on her gorgeous face. Walker is leaning against his wife's stool, kissing her cheek and whispering something in her ear. I probably don't want to know what it is. Reagan, Madelyn, Lyndee, and her sister-in-law, Dana, are all seated at the table, with what looks like their first round of drinks already in front of them.

"Is that Reagan Turner?" Mom asks, catching my attention.

"It is."

"I heard she quit the bank last week. I wonder where she went?" she inquires casually.

Part of me wants to tell her I don't know, but I know that won't get me far. When she learns the fact she works here, I'll be in trouble, and she'll want to know why I hid it from her. She'll start digging, and that's the last thing I need. Lydia Taylor is like a bloodhound when it comes to sniffing out gossip, and I'm one-hundred-percent certain she'd stop at nothing until she's figured out everything involving Reagan and me.

Trying to maintain a casual facade, I reply, "She's working here. She started last week as a hostess to help while Shantel is on maternity leave."

"Really?" she asks, a hopeful little gleam reflecting in her eyes.

"Stop it."

"What? What did I do?" she asks, innocently. Except I know her game. She's already matchmaking in her head, trying to figure out how to set me up with my newest employee.

"All right, I'll leave you two to gossip," I say, tapping the edge of their table. "Enjoy your meals."

"Thanks, son," Dad says, turning his attention to his wife.

I slowly make my way to the bar, where Reagan and her friends are sitting. "Ladies," I greet the moment I approach.

"Hey, Garreth," Madelyn replies.

"Hi," Reagan says, her voice a tad higher than normal.

"I see you all have drinks already. Have you placed your orders?" I inquire, stopping directly behind the woman I can't stop thinking about and gripping the metal back of her seat.

"Walker just took our order. He told me I had to try some Bangin' Bacon Burger," Mallory announces, reaching for her margarita.

"It's excellent. You won't be disappointed," I throw in as Reagan leans back in her stool and rubs against my knuckles. That slight touch, despite a layer of material between us, causes her to shiver.

"I ordered it too," Lyndee says, sipping what looks like lemonade. "Jasper talked about nothing else last night after work."

Needing to hear her voice, I bend down and ask, "And what did you order?"

Reagan looks back over her shoulder, meeting my gaze. Her eyes deepen to a beautiful golden color, and her pupils dilate. It's the same look she gets right before I kiss her. "I went with the majority," she replies.

Suddenly, she stiffens.

I look up, finding Madelyn's smiling wide eyes on me. I don't even realize what's happening until she looks down. So, I do too. That's when I see it. My hands are on Reagan's shoulders, lightly massaging.

Completely. On. Their. Own.

I pull my hands back and shove them in my pockets. Apparently, it's the only way I can keep from touching her. "Well, since you all are in good hands already, I'll go check on a few new customers."

As quickly, yet as casually, as my legs will carry me, I move away from the table—away from Reagan and the temptation she creates.

What the hell did I just do?

Worse, when I step into the restaurant, I look up and find my mom watching me, a knowing smile on her face.

Shit, did she just see that too?

I almost groan, outraged by my lack of control, especially when working. This is exactly what I didn't want to happen. Everyone saw me touch Reagan. Sure, I can try to play it off as innocent or flirty. Lord knows I've been flirting with her nonstop since we met, but something tells me that's not going to work in this case. Something tells me I was as transparent as a clear shower curtain where my attraction for her is concerned. For a man who has prided himself on silently watching from a distance, it took less than forty-eight hours of being with her to fuck it all up.

Figures.

I step inside my house and lock the door behind me. I leave the lights off, easily making my way through the small kitchen. I've lived here since I moved back home, thanks to Jameson. He was moving in with his girlfriend and offered me this place to rent until I figured out what I was doing.

I'm still deciding.

Fortunately, he hasn't been in a hurry to sell, and since my rent covers the payment and taxes, it works out well for both of us.

This place has been exactly what I need. A couple of bedrooms, a bathroom, and a large garage I can tinker with whatever strikes my fancy. I've loved this little place since the day I moved in, but tonight, it feels different.

Instantly, I feel the loneliness wrap around me like a wet blanket. It's suffocating.

Ignoring the nagging feeling in the back of my mind to call her and see what she's doing, I toss my keys on the old kitchen table and grab a Coke from the fridge. I don't usually drink caffeine this late at night, but something tells me I'm going to need a little sleep aid. Sure, some people try chamomile tea or Melatonin, but my go-to is Jack Daniels.

I have a feeling I'm going to need all the help I can get tonight.

I grab a glass and toss some ice in it before filling it halfway with whiskey. Then I add another splash just to make sure I'm good and numb come bedtime. Once the glass is topped with Coke, I take my drink into the living room and kick back in my recliner.

When was the last time I just sat here and relaxed? I took some time to rest on Sunday at Jasper and Lyndee's house, but even then, I was a little keyed up and focused on Reagan. My nights off are usually spent catching up on laundry, cleaning the house, and working in the yard. I usually stop by my parents and hang with them at some point, mostly around dinnertime. Nothing beats Mom's homecooked meals.

With a sigh, I grab the remote and find a movie on the premium movie channels I still pay for, but don't watch. Brad Pitt and George Clooney are plotting to rob a Las Vegas casino, and even though I've seen this one a dozen times over the years, I settle in to watch it again.

Except, I don't actually see the movie. I sit in my chair, sipping my Jack and Coke, and think about Reagan until I'm so hard, I can't think straight. It's just after midnight, and I know I shouldn't, but I do it anyway, because I apparently have no control where she's concerned.

Me: I hope you had a good time tonight with the wives.

I don't even get my phone set down when the little bubbles appear on the screen.

Reagan: I did, but I felt bad for sitting there when it was so busy.

Me: It was your night off. Plus, we had it handled.

The bubbles don't appear, but her name does on the screen when it starts to ring.

"Hey," I greet.

"Are you just getting home?"

"I've been home for about fifteen minutes. Just long enough to make myself a drink."

"A drink? Do tell. What are you having?"

"Jack and Coke."

She doesn't respond right away. "I wasn't expecting that. Bad night?"

"No," I insist, pushing myself back and reclining the chair as far as it will go. "Just knew I'd need a little help falling asleep tonight."

"You could try counting sheep," she suggests through a yawn.

I chuckle. "Sounds like you're ready to fall asleep yourself."

"Yeah, I just curled up in bed." There's a long pause, and I can't help but wonder if she's already falling asleep. "Can I tell you something?" she whispers.

"Always."

"I don't like my bed without you in it."

I close my eyes, absorbing the power of her words. "Can I tell you something?" I repeat.

"Always," she says with a smile in her voice.

"That's why I'm drinking. I can't stop thinking about you, and I can't get my mind to settle."

I listen to the steady sound of her breath, noticing how that simple noise calms me. "How can that be? It's only been a few days," she says softly.

"I wish I knew, love. All I know is I want to get to know you better."

"I want that too," she confesses through another yawn, bringing a smile to my face.

"Good. I think it's time to hang up so you can go to sleep."

"I don't want to," she murmurs, as if she's already starting to drift.

"I don't either, but we need to. I'll talk to you tomorrow."

"You don't work though, right?" she asks.

"No, I'm off tomorrow and Thursday, but I'll be there with you Friday and Saturday night."

"Okay. I can't wait," she replies. "Garreth?"

"Yeah?"

"Goodnight."

"Goodnight, Reagan. Sleep tight."

She mumbles something, but before I can ask her to repeat it, the line goes dead, leaving me alone with my thoughts once more.

I set my phone aside and take a big drink. The whiskey burns as it slides down my throat, making me hiss. "You just had to put extra in it," I mutter to myself.

I down the rest of my drink, noticing how heavy my limbs already feel. I should get up and go to bed, but I don't. Instead, I lie in my chair, watching as eleven men work together to rob a casino. And I think about Reagan.

About her smile.

The softness of her hair.

The sounds she makes when we're naked and about to come.

Most of all, I think about the way she makes me feel inside, even though it's way too soon to think about those feelings.

I haven't stopped to consider those feelings in a while, but I realize I'm not afraid of them. I've always been a relationship guy, even if it's been a long damn time since I've been in one.

As I drift off to sleep with my clothes on and a whiskey fog in my head, I can't help but wonder if this is my second chance to get it right. Maybe I won't fuck it all up this time. Maybe I'll actually be able to make a woman happy enough to want to stay.

Reagan

Madelyn: Sugar Rush. 10 a.m.

I sigh, slipping my phone into my purse and heading for the door. I don't know why I'm so nervous. I've gotten together with my cousin a million times since she moved to Stewart Grove almost four and a half years ago, but never have I worried about what she's going to say.

I already know the main topic of conversation will be Garreth. I could see the questions written all over her face. Well, on everyone's faces, especially when he reached out and started massaging my shoulders. I wasn't expecting that, and by the way he pulled back like he got burned, I'd say he wasn't expecting to do it either.

Everyone had questions the moment he walked away from the table. What happened when he took me home Sunday night? Why did he look at me like he wanted to strip me naked and get horizontal right there in the middle of the bar? Who finally made the first move? What's our official relationship status?

My answer was simple: We're taking it slow and trying to figure it out.

Of course, I left out the part about jumping him the moment he pulled into my apartment parking lot. Nothing was slow about what we did that night.

Even though my friends are awesome and wouldn't judge, I felt like what happened that night—and the ones since—is just for us, you know? I like keeping certain parts of *us* close to the vest, but I also know if I ever do need their advice, all I have to do is ask. Just like Sunday night, when I was confused about his flirting and then not flirting.

I jump in my car and head for Lyndee's bakery. With any luck, she'll be off this morning.

Ha!

I'm five minutes early when I pull into a spot in front of her business and slip out. I can't help but glance over to the bar and restaurant, which happens to be directly across the street. Even though I know Garreth is off today, I still find myself looking over, just in case...

The bell over the door rings, signaling my arrival. Madelyn and Jameson are at the counter, his arm thrown over her shoulder as she curls into his side. They're simply the cutest. As different as night and day, yet seem to complement each other perfectly.

"Hey, Reagan," Lyndee hollers from behind the counter, a warm smile on her face.

My cousin and her husband turn to offer a quick greeting as I wave to everyone. "Morning," I reply cheerfully.

Jameson takes two cups, while Madelyn grabs the white paper bag and points to a table along the wall. "I'll be over here," she says.

"What can I get ya?" Lyndee asks when I step up to the counter.

"I'll take a large mocha latte with skim milk and one of those raspberry Danish."

"Coming right up," she replies, turning to make my caffeinated drink first.

"How are you feeling?" I ask Lyndee.

"Pretty good so far today. I thought I was going to have an issue this morning when I walked in and caught a whiff of something in the trash I must have forgotten to take out yesterday, but I was saved by Dustin who quickly whisked it away before the yogurt I had for breakfast could make a reappearance."

"Aww, I'm sorry. That must be tough."

She finishes my drink and sets it on the counter in front of me, before turning to retrieve my Danish. "It's definitely not fun. Mostly because you never know what's going to set you off. When I was pregnant with Elliott, I remember the scent of certain meats made me queasy. It wasn't bad when I was here, but when you have a chef for a husband, who's constantly experimenting with new ingredients, it makes it tough to be in the kitchen."

"Thanks," I say as I take the sweet treat I'm enjoying for breakfast. "How much?"

She rings up my items, giving me what she calls the friends and family discount. Apparently, she used to give away free stuff all the time to her friends, and when they finally convinced her to stop, she agreed, but only if they allowed her to give them discount.

"Four thirty-five."

I hand her a ten and tell her to keep the change. "Hopefully this pregnancy is a little smoother than the last."

"Thanks." She beams at me, her hand automatically going to her still-flat stomach. "Head on over, and I'll stop by when Dustin gets back. He took a pie across the street to Jasper. It's Patrick's birthday, and he's a huge fan of rhubarb, so I baked him a pie."

"Yum," I reply, glancing in the display case for something rhubarb. There are several slices of pie, so I quickly add, "Will you box up one of those slices of rhubarb pie? It's my grandma's favorite."

"Will do."

Finally, I make my way over to where my cousin and her husband are waiting. Madelyn's sitting in a chair, while Jameson stands beside her. "I'll leave you two to gossip," he announces, bending down and kissing his wife firmly on the lips.

"We don't gossip," I counter, taking the seat across from her.

"Right," he replies, drawing out the word.

"You don't have to leave just because I'm here," I tease, sipping my latte.

"I was just getting my second breakfast in for the morning and spending a few extra minutes with my wife," he notes. "I have to head over to work. We have a big shipment heading out to a new customer. I want to make sure it goes right." To his wife, he gives a small smile and places a second kiss on her lips. "Love you, Mads."

"Love you too," she replies.

Then he does something I don't think I'll ever get used to seeing. He reaches down and places his big hand on her belly. "Be good to your mom, munchkin."

With his coffee cup in one hand and the white bag in the other, he throws Lyndee a wave before heading out the door and walking across the street to the brewery.

"It's so weird to see Jameson all soft and squishy," I note, taking a welcomed sip of my latte.

"He talks to the baby all the time. He's convinced it's a girl," she replies, unable to hide her smile behind her cup.

"What is that?"

"Some soy chai thing Lyndee said I should try. It's not bad. I was getting tired of drinking the same old tea over and over again. Plus, I had to switch it to decaf, so it wasn't the same. I figured a change was welcome, you know?"

I nod, pulling my Danish from my own bag and taking a bite.

Before I even swallow my first bite, she leans over and asks, "So what's the deal with you and Garreth? Obviously, something's going on. Jameson said his truck was still at your apartment Monday morning."

I look up and meet her gaze, instantly noticing her eyes are curious, but lacking the teasing humor I'd expect. "And Jameson said *we* gossip," I quip.

She grins widely. "Well, he was concerned, but not because it's Garreth. He trusts him with his life, and with yours too. He just wanted to make sure you're both on the same page. He thinks Garreth's had a crush on you for quite a while."

"What'd I miss, what'd I miss?" Lyndee hollers, practically running over to where we sit and dropping down in a chair beside me. "Did she confess to doing the dirty with him?"

"We're getting to that," Madelyn replies.

I sigh, lightly shaking my head. "Since I know you guys won't let this go, I will confirm we are seeing each other."

"Good," Lyndee states. "He's such a great guy."

"He is. I don't think he's dated much since he's been back home," Madelyn says, referring to the four years Garreth has been back in Stewart Grove and working for the guys.

"So, you've confirmed you're seeing each other, which is great, but what about the other thing... What happened Sunday night?" Lyndee asks, practically bursting at the seams for details.

Chuckling, I close my eyes for a brief moment, knowing they're not going to let it go. "We, uh, did...stuff."

They both lean in at the exact moment, almost comically. "Like, the good stuff?" Madelyn whispers, her cheeks already blushing a dark shade of pink.

"Oh yeah. Very good stuff," I confirm, taking another sip of my latte.

"I knew it! I told Jasper when he started massaging your shoulders last night, you two were hiding something. Spill it."

I contemplate how much I want to share with them. A big part of our time together is personal, and I don't want to share it. Even if his bedroom abilities are extremely boast-able, deserving of all the ego-boosting accolades. Glancing around, I see we're still alone in the bakery, with the exception of Dustin, who's behind the counter across the room. "Have you ever had sex so amazing you wonder if you even enjoyed, really enjoyed, it before?"

Immediately, they both nod. "Yes."

"Jasper is," she starts, clearing her throat, "...very talented in the bedroom, and if either of you ever repeat that, I'll kill you. That man's ego is already insufferable. The last thing he needs to know is I told my friends his cock is magical. I'll never hear the end of it." She takes a sip of her tea, as if she didn't just share dirty details about her husband's dick.

I can't help but laugh. Hard.

"I think some sex is better than other sex because of the chemistry," Madelyn states, her face as bright as the fuchsia coloring painted on the window.

"Totally," Lyndee agrees.

Madelyn smiles. "By the far-off look on your face, I'm assuming there's a lot of chemistry with you and Garreth."

"Tons," I confirm, that familiar rush of heat racing through my veins when I think about him. "He's pretty...wow." I glance around once more. "You know, Justin and I slept together plenty while we were dating, but it wasn't anything like being with Garreth."

Madelyn nods. "Chemistry."

"I love that for you, Reagan. Life's too short not to be having great sex," Lyndee proclaims.

"I'm going to pretend my sister didn't just say that aloud, because she's not having sex," Dustin hollers, making us all look his way. He's wearing a disgusted face, which causes us all to laugh.

"Keep telling yourself that, little brother. How do you think I keep getting pregnant?"

Dustin pretends to gag. "Stop talking, Lyndee."

"I love pushing his buttons," she whispers to us, as we all turn our attention back in front of us.

"I've always looked at Garreth as a friend. I mean, a really hot friend with a great ass, but a friend, nonetheless. Then, all of a sudden, Justin dumps me by text and Garreth is there, and it's like I see him in a whole new light. Is that weird?"

They're both shaking their heads. "Heck no," Lyndee says. "I couldn't stand Jasper. I mean, I secretly wanted him, but I wanted to punch him at the same time. It was a crazy feeling."

"And I thought Jameson was attractive, but I was drawn to the side of him he hid from the world. We were great friends for quite a while before we took it to the next level," Madelyn confirms, even though I know all about their relationship. I was along for the ride the entire time, and I'm so glad they both took the chance together.

I nod in understanding, and we sit together, enjoying our pastries and beverages, and chatting about anything and everything. When a few customers come in, Lyndee excuses herself to get back to work, leaving just Madelyn and me at the table.

"So, what's next? I know working together seemed to be a hang-up with him."

"Well, we agreed to date outside of work, but keep it professional while there." A memory of him pulling me into his office and kissing me until I was breathless pops into my head.

"Uh huh," she replies with a giggle. "And that face tells me it's a struggle for both of you."

I shrug my shoulders, picking up my trash from the table and sliding it into my bag. "Let's just say we both failed our first shift working together."

Madelyn shrugs. "I understand his concern because of his position over you."

Again, the dirty images...

She laughs hard this time. "And I take it by that face, you were thinking something dirty." She stands up and helps carry our garbage to the bin across the room. "When are you guys going out on a date?"

I stop in my tracks. "I'm not sure. He hasn't really said anything about that."

"I imagine trying to schedule you both off a night is difficult. Especially because I know he always works the nights the hostess is off."

"Yeah. He's off tonight and tomorrow, but I work both, so we'll have to see."

"You guys might have to schedule in some day-dates. There's plenty you can do before work," she suggests.

"That's a good idea," I agree, wondering if we can make something work.

We wave at Lyndee and Dustin and step outside. The summer air is hot, the sun unforgiving as it peeks over the building across the street. I can already tell it's going to be a scorcher.

"Let's do lunch with grandma and your parents soon."

"Deal. I'm off Sunday. I'll call Mom and see if we can get it worked out."

"Perfect," my cousin replies, stepping in and pulling me into a hug. It always cracks me up how different we are. She's much shorter than my five-nine body and grew up in New York. Our moms are sisters and as different as night and day. I grew up here, with family and friends in a small town, while she lived a penthouse, privileged life.

"I'll text you."

I head for my car but keep going. It's such a gorgeous day, despite the hot temperature, and I end up walking to the end of the block and checking out some of the storefront windows. When I worked at the bank, I rarely had time to just browse and shop, but now that I'm working evenings, my schedule is a little more flexible.

I stop by the clothing boutique down the block and am instantly greeted by Jane Honeywell, the woman who's owned the business since 2000. "Hello, dear. Lovely to see you today. Are you looking for anything in particular?" she asks.

"Not today, Jane. I'm just browsing."

"Well, holler if you need help. There's a summer section in the back that's all fifty percent off, and my special this week is in my lingerie section at forty percent discount."

"Thank you," I reply, slowly making my way through the racks of clothing.

There's a great variety of styles and sizes, everything from little girls to adult women. When I reach the sale section, I'm instantly drawn to a yellow sundress with pink and green flowers. Before I even know what I'm doing, I go to the dressing room and enclose myself in the small fitting area.

I slip the cool, smooth material over my body and turn to check out my reflection in the mirror. The spaghetti straps tie together at the shoulders, and the hem hits just above the knees. It's flowy and fun and the cooler color really complements my tanned skin. Admittedly, it's a bit more revealing in the front than I normally wear. I always wore more modest clothing to the bank, usually slacks and short-sleeved tops, and while this isn't the dress code I'd need to follow for the restaurant, I still can't seem to stop wanting to buy it.

It would make a great date dress…

If there ever is an official date.

This size fits perfectly, noting I can pair it with a cute pair of tan wedge sandals I have in my closet. Heck, I might not ever actually wear it, but at this price, I'm not out much if it just hangs in the back of my closet forever.

I change back into my shorts and tank top and step out. Before I can talk myself out of it, I head for the lingerie section, wondering if I can find something to wear beneath my new dress.

There's a small section of strapless bras, and one in particular jumps out at me. It's a soft pink, much like the pink in the flowers, but it's the design I'm loving. It has a darker pink lace that crisscrosses over the cups of the bra and runs around to the clasp at the back. Plus, it's forty percent off. I mean, why not?

Then I head over to a small table display of panties right next to the bras, pleased to find the matching panties to the bra. It's a thong, with that same dark lace crossing over the front and running around the hips and down the slim scrap of material in the back.

"Yes," I whisper, a bubble of excitement sweeping through me at the prospect of Garreth undressing me and discovering my new purchases.

With my new dress and undergarments, I head for Jane at the front counter. "Oh, I'm glad you found something, dear."

"Too pretty to pass up, Jane," I confirm, setting my stuff on the counter and praying she doesn't ask me about the panties. I'm sure it's common knowledge Justin and I broke up. I can only imagine what she's thinking, ringing up my sexy new things.

She scans the barcodes and places everything in a bag, one piece at a time. When she reaches the panties, she says, "You know, there's nothing more important than a pretty piece of lingerie. I've always said that. Buy the pretty things. It does wonders for a woman's confidence," she states.

After I've passed my credit card and she's handed me the bag, I consider her words. I think she's right. The thought of wearing that bra and panty set has me lifting my head up a little higher in anticipation. Sure, I can't wait for Garreth to see them, but it's more than that. I can't wait to wear them.

What the hell, maybe I'll just throw them on this weekend with my jeans and restaurant polo. After all, there's no wrong time to wear sexy panties, is there?

Garreth

I've never been bored sitting at home, but here I am, bored out of my fucking mind. Why? Because I know Reagan's at work tonight, and I'm not there. I'm stuck here, and I don't like it.

Usually I keep myself busy on my days off, but today has been a struggle. I've wanted nothing more than to go to her, but knowing she had to work tonight, I refrained. Instead, I resorted to texting her off and on, soaking up any ounce of contact from her I can get.

I'm so screwed.

Now, it's almost six, and the walls are starting to close in on me. I've cleaned my kitchen and bathroom from top to bottom and took care of all yard work for the week. I've even washed my bedding—maybe with the hopes of Reagan joining me in my bed sometime in the near future.

My phone chimes with a text, and I practically trip over myself to get to it. I'm a little disappointed it's not her name I see on the screen, but still pleasantly surprised to see my buddy Leo's name displayed.

Leo and I were good friends in school, and while I went to college after graduation, he went into the military. He spent eighteen years in the Army, serving our country, and did more tours overseas than anyone else I know. He had always planned to make a career out of it, but on his last trip to Afghanistan, something went wrong, and several members of his team were killed. He ended up discharging and has been working as a mechanic ever since.

> **Leo**: What the hell. I finally come up for dinner and you're off?
>
> **Me:** Sorry, man. Should have texted me earlier.
>
> **Leo:** No worries. There are some hotties working tonight, so sitting alone boasts my single and available status.

The hairs on my arms stand up. I know exactly who's working tonight, since I make the schedule. Kallie is behind the bar, as well as Max, and Angie and Lilli are working the restaurant side. But something tells me he's caught sight of Reagan, since she's the most beautiful woman in the world. Why would she not turn his head too?

> **Me:** Want me to come up and join you? I could use a drink.

Or five...

> **Leo:** If you don't mind having a beer at the place you work. If you'd rather go somewhere else, I can meet you.

I'm already up and shoving my feet into my shoes.

Me: I don't mind. Be there in ten.

Or sooner, if I keep thinking about Leo hitting on Reagan.

Women always seem to flock to him. It's like they can sniff the military man out at a thousand paces. When we were younger and would meet up for a beer, it was like I was invisible when the opposite sex discovered what he did for a living. I didn't mind, though. I was dating and eventually married, so it wasn't like I was taking any of those women home.

But I would damn mind now.

Reagan's mine.

I jump in my truck, not even sure I locked the back door when I walked out, yet refusing to take the two extra seconds to go check it. I head for the bar, grateful the downtown area isn't too packed with people.

Pulling into the back lot, I find a spot next to Jameson's Harley and make my way to the back door. As soon as I key my code in and step inside, I hear, "Aren't you off tonight?" Jameson is standing at the kitchen door, his eyes narrowed.

"Yeah, but Leo's here and invited me to have a beer with him," I counter.

"You sure it has nothing to do with the woman working up front you're still pretending doesn't affect you?"

"Fuck off," I mumble, refusing to acknowledge his statement and the truth behind it. I head down the short hall that leads to the bar and instantly spot Leo sitting at one of the pub tables in the middle of the room, his gaze locked on the restaurant side. "Hey, man," I say, as soon as I reach his table.

"Hey," he replies, bringing his attention back to the table. "Thanks for meeting me."

"No problem," I respond, taking a seat across from him and automatically glancing at the restaurant.

Reagan is standing at a table, talking to a couple, and wearing a big smile on her face. She looks stunning, her hair pulled up in a tight ponytail high on her head. I can't help but want to wrap my hand around that hair, lightly tugging it as I bury myself balls deep in her sweet pussy.

"You okay, man?"

I turn back to Leo and find a big grin on his face. "What? Yeah. Sorry. Just making sure everything is going well." It sounds like a lame excuse, even to my own ears.

"Mmhmm," he mumbles, clearly finding the humor.

I grab the menu from the center of the table, even though I have it memorized. I'm just using it as a buffer between myself and the desire to seek her out and watch her work. If my eyes are locked on the menu, maybe I'll be able to calm myself down and actually have a decent conversation with my friend, despite Reagan's presence.

"So…you and the hottie in the other room, huh?" Startled, I look up in shock and make him laugh. "Dude, you're not fooling anyone, especially me. It's practically written all over your face. Now the question is, does she know you love her or not?"

My mouth drops open. "I don't," I say, stopping to lower my voice to a whisper. "I don't love her, Leo. Jesus, we've been seeing each other for like three days."

"Ahh, so you're still in the lust and sex phase." He takes a drink from his beer. "I miss that phase."

I glance around the room, finding several sets of female eyes all trained on my friend. "In case you haven't noticed, there's about ten single ladies in this room who would help you with that problem. Hell, even a guy at the bar who keeps looking your way, if you've decided to switch teams."

He snorts a laugh. "No, sorry. Women only." He glances around the room, but his gaze doesn't linger on anyone specific for more than a couple of seconds. "So, what's her name? The future Mrs. Garreth Taylor."

I chuckle to try to cover up the reaction my heart has at the sound of his question. Keeping my voice lower, I reply, "Reagan. Reagan Turner."

He narrows his eyes a little, the wheels in his head spinning. "Did we go to school with her?"

"No, she was about six years behind us."

He nods, glancing into the restaurant to scope her out once more. When he meets my gaze, he asks, "And she's into you too? I mean, she has another option now that I'm here."

I bark out a laugh and shake my head at his antics. "I hope," I find myself saying, looking her way once more. This time she's standing at the hostess stand and wearing a surprised look when she sees me. Her face instantly transforms into a smile.

It so fucking hard to breathe when she does that.

She starts heading our way, my heartbeat kicking up a bit with every step she takes.

"I better be invited to the wedding," he mutters softly.

I pin him with a look. "I believe you were invited to the first one. Stood up at the altar with me and everything."

"Oh, I remember. What was that bridesmaid's name?"

"Eloise, and she was Shelby's sister."

"Ha! Now I remember. I hope she's not still waiting around for me to call," he replies just as Reagan reaches our table.

"Well, this is a surprise," she says in way of greeting. "Checking up on us on your night off?"

"Absolutely not. My friend Leo stopped by for a drink and invited me to join him."

I barely get the words out when my friend stands up dramatically and reaches for her hand. "Leo Martinez, and it is a pleasure to meet you, Miss," he croons, bringing her hand up to his mouth and kissing her knuckles. "And might I say, my friend Garreth has the most stunning employees."

Fucker.

"Reagan, ignore this asshole." I almost start grinding down my molars.

Reagan offers him a polite smile. "Very nice to meet you, Leo. I remember you from school, even though you were older than me."

"Older, yes, and might I add, wiser and more mature?" He leans over just slightly and adds, "You know what they say about older men, don't you?" He waggles his eyebrows at her, and I swear, I almost punch my oldest friend in the face.

She barks out a laugh, covering her mouth with the hand my friend's not holding. "Oh my God, does that line actually work?"

He gives her a smile, but it's not one he usually offers women he's trying to actually hit on. I know he's doing it to rile me up, but I refuse to show him it's working.

"No, not usually. I was hoping you'd be the first," he concedes, sending her a wink and releasing her hand. He takes his seat once more and flashes me a wide, cocky grin.

Asshole.

"Can I get you something to drink?" Reagan asks, and I realize when she just arches an eyebrow at me, she's talking to me.

"Oh, I can get it."

"No can do, boss. You're off tonight, so please allow me to be of service," she replies. I'm sure she meant the comment innocently, but my brain—and my cock—do not take it that way.

"Uhh, beer. Anything on tap."

"Coming right up. You still good?" she asks Leo, who nods in response.

She heads for the bar, and yes, my eyes follow her every move.

"You have it bad," Leo sings and chuckles, clearly enjoying my misery. Not that liking Reagan is miserable, but the fact I can't touch her, and I'd *really* like to is pretty sad.

Sighing, I don't reply, because anything I'd say would be a lie. The fact remains I do have it bad.

"What's going on with you? How's work?"

"Not bad. Crazy busy. OT's nice though, so I'm not complaining," he replies, taking another look around the bar. "Ran into ol' Archer yesterday. Brought his Mercedes in for an oil change and proceeded to tell me all about how amazing he is."

"The guy's a tool," I say as Reagan returns with my drink.

"Who is?" she asks, standing close to my side.

"Archer Stewart."

She groans. "Massive douchebag," she agrees. "Not only was he a crappy boss, but he'd always throw the whole Stewart Grove feud in my face, like I had anything to do with something that happened in the eighteen hundreds."

"Oh, that's right. I almost forgot about that piece of town history," Leo says. The legend goes Gerald Stewart and John Grove claimed the land as theirs, so when it was time to name the developing town, it was named Stewart Grove. Reagan's family is a direct descendent of John Grove.

"And I worked for the man. Well, when I started, I worked for his father, who was a decent guy, but when Archer took over the bank, everything went to hell, fast."

"I thought you looked familiar. I was having a hard time placing you, but that's where I remember you from. The bank," Leo responds, taking a drink from his beer.

"Well, I better get back up front before my boss fires me," she states, giving us both a grin. "Holler if you need anything."

"We'll be fine, but thanks," I tell her, returning the grin.

"Okay. Leo, it was nice to officially meet you."

"You too, Reagan. If you ever want a date, just ask Garreth here for my number. He's got it," Leo quips, a big smirk on his face.

She snickers and shakes her head. "I'll keep that in mind," she teases before turning and heading back over to the restaurant.

"Lock that one down, man," Leo mumbles.

My eyes trail her every move until she's out of sight. Only then do I glance back at my friend. "What was with all the knuckle kisses and the flirting? You want to get your ass kicked tonight?"

A loud roar of a laugh flies from his mouth. "Shit, you and what army, man? No, you know I was just kidding. I wasn't hittin' on her. It was all in good fun. Besides, if I was trying? You'd be licking your wounds all alone right about now," my cocky friend says.

"Hey, how're your parents? It's been a while since I've seen them," I say, settling in for the story I know is coming.

"Mom's doing okay. That last round of radiation really took a lot out of her, but the scans are showing shrinkage of the tumor in her stomach. Once they get it down to where they want it, they can go in an remove that part of her stomach."

My heart breaks for Leo. He had barely been home from the military, dealing with a whole mess of private shit in his head, when his mom was diagnosed with stomach cancer. She's been on a pretty aggressive regimen of chemo and radiation, and if they can get it all when they remove the tumor, she has a twenty to thirty percent chance of beating it. Not exactly great odds, but Valerie Martinez is a fighter. Always has been.

I listen to him tell me the latest, and guilt starts to nag at me. "Hey, I'm sorry I haven't been over to see her in the last few months. Work just always seems to be hectic, but no excuse. I'll get over there soon and catch up with them." Leo's parents were always in my life, considering I was good friends with their son growing up.

"Don't feel bad, Garreth. Life has everyone by the balls. If you want to stop in, I know they'd welcome the company, but don't feel obligated to do it. Dad's still trying to work as much as possible and still take care of Mom. I know it's hard on him, but he refuses to hire any more help. He says she's his wife, and he'll do everything he can to take care of her."

A lump forms in my throat. "That's gotta be tough. For all of you."

He nods solemnly. "I help when I can, but when they've got me working six days a week, ten hours a day, it's hard."

"If I can help, let me know. My evenings are pretty jammed here, but I don't usually come in until mid-afternoon. I'll help where I can."

He offers me a grateful grin. "Thanks, man. Appreciate it. Enough of the sad shit. Let's talk more about that hot girl you keep drooling over."

We spend the next three hours hanging out and catching up. We both switched from beer to water after our second drink and adding a plate of fries to munch on while we visited. My eyes continually moved, watching how the business flowed, and at one point, I almost got up to help behind the bar when it got busy, but Jameson was there, as if sensing my intent, and stepped in. Almost all the staff stopped by the table at some point to give me hell about coming in on my day off, but I took it in stride.

"Well, I think I'm going to head out," Leo says, standing up and stretching his arms over his head. "Oh, hey, does Jameson's sister still do tattoos? I've been thinking of adding a piece to my arm."

"Yep, she and Jax Forrester at Xpress Urself. Call Amanda and get on the schedule. There will probably be a little wait. Numbers says she's been busy."

He nods. "Will do." Something dark passes through his eyes, but it disappears just as quickly, so I don't ask. I know he's still dealing with some demons about whatever happened overseas with his team.

He reaches out his hand and pulls me into your classic bro-hug, even though he's never really been a hugger. Hell, I'm not either, but something tells me he has a lot on his mind and if knowing I'm here for him is what he needs, I'll gladly oblige.

"Let's not wait so long next time between drinks," I tell him, earning a nod in return.

"Deal. Talk to you soon," he replies before heading for the front door. Before he exits, I don't miss the way he casually turns and looks behind the bar, as if he's taking another glance at Kallie.

Interesting...

I glance around before looking down at my watch. It's nine thirty, which means the restaurant has been closed for almost thirty minutes. However, I haven't seen Reagan for a bit, and I can't help but wonder if she left without saying goodbye.

Shoving my hands in my pockets, I start to wander to the restaurant side, stepping over the rope we extend across the entryway when it shuts down. I find the two servers and Reagan standing at the servers' station, watching the screen.

"Hey, what's up?" I ask, leaning against the counter.

"We're short," Angie says, a nervous look on her face.

"How much?"

"One hundred, exactly."

"Okay. Why don't you guys go ahead and clock out, and I'll run through it," I reply, stepping around the short wall where the register is hidden.

"You shouldn't have to do that, Garreth. It's your night off," Angie argues, printing out all the final receipts and slipping them with the cash drawer.

"Numbers will be here in the morning. I'm sure he'll find it," Reagan adds.

I nod, taking the paperwork anyway. "I'll run it to Jameson. Have a good night, ladies," I reply, giving Angie and Cameron a smile.

I notice Cameron is a little...off. Her face is a little pale, and she appears to be a bit more fidgety than usual. She's been working for us for about three months now, picking up the server duties pretty quickly. She trained under Gigi during the day before moving to the evening shift.

Angie and Cameron both head for the break room.

"Cameron seemed nervous when Angie was counting the drawer."

I sigh and glance at Reagan. "I caught it. Did you see anything?"

She instantly shakes her head. "No."

At first glance, most of the receipts were charges, so it shouldn't have been too hard to balance at the end of the night. "Okay, well, I'll leave it for Numbers to look at. Maybe the day shift was over, which would explain why you were short tonight." It doesn't happen too often, but it does happen. It would be an easy explanation.

"Okay, well, I'm going to clock out too." She stops and turns to face me. "You heading home?"

I nod. "Leo just left, so I'll be taking off in a few minutes."

Her eyes seem to darken as she holds my gaze. She takes a small step forward, making sure we're not too close to draw attention. "Want some company?" she whispers, nibbling on that delectable bottom lip.

"Back door will be unlocked."

She flashes a quick grin and walks away, her hips swaying seductively and her ass looking amazing in her jeans. My cock is already getting hard.

Well, my night suddenly got a thousand times better.

Reagan

I don't even have to knock. The moment I step up on the back deck, the door opens and Garreth is standing there, leaning against the doorframe. "I was afraid you changed your mind."

"Oh, no. I ran home and changed my clothes." And grabbed a fresh set for tomorrow, but I don't mention that part, since I left the bag in my car.

A girl doesn't want to appear too eager.

"Come on in," he offers, stepping back to allow me room to pass. I notice the way his eyes slowly peruse my outfit, which consists of a pair of comfy cotton shorts, loose tee, and a pair of flip-flops.

The kitchen is familiar, yet so different. "I haven't been here since Jameson moved," I comment, even though he's probably well aware, considering he's the one who lives here.

Jameson was a minimalist. He had the basic necessities needed to live, while Garreth's got the place looking a little homier. There's a large wooden sign on the wall by the table that says 'Today's menu: Take it or leave it' and an artificial plant on a shelf beneath it. It's cute, homey, and not what I expected.

"My mom. She decorated when I moved in," he blurts out, clearly noticing my interest in his wall.

"Ahh." I turn around and lean against the counter.

"Can I get you something to drink?" He runs his hands through his hair, as if he's a touch nervous.

"No, thank you." Placing my hands on the counter, I lift myself up and take a seat.

His eyes glance down, specifically at the apex of my legs. I'm sure my loose-fitting cotton shorts are gaped open at the thigh. "Are you wearing panties?" he asks, his voice tight.

I slowly shake my head. "They seemed like such a waste of time, you know? Put them on, take them off again."

His gaze never wavers. He just stares at the bare skin exposed between my legs. "That does seem like a waste."

Moving my legs farther apart, a dry gargle bubbles from his throat. "So, I've been thinking," I start, leaning back, my head against the upper cabinet.

"I'm all ears," he replies, taking a step forward.

"I've always wanted to do it in the kitchen," I state boldly.

Garreth glances up as he moves the rest of the way to where I'm sitting. "Never had kitchen sex?"

I shake my head in confirmation.

"Well, good thing for you, sweetness," he starts, placing big, hot hands on my upper thighs and sliding them to where my shorts part open, "I'm a master."

"At kitchen sex?" I quip, slightly jealous of the fact he's done this before, even though I shouldn't be. Everyone has a past, right, and it's not like he was a virgin when we got together.

His gaze blazes fire, which seeps through my skin and ignites the desire in my blood. "No, at giving you what you want."

He takes my lips with his own, hot and demanding, as his fingers tease my pussy. I'm already wet, have been pretty much all night since I saw him sitting at the table with his friend and saw the lust brewing in those dark brown eyes.

He pushes two fingers inside me, making me gasp. "Fuck, Reagan. You're so wet."

"I've been picturing you naked pretty much all day," I confess, rocking my hips to take more of his fingers.

"Yeah? Why didn't you call me? I would have come running." He nips at my bottom lip before trailing his tongue down my neck.

"I didn't want to bother you on your day off." I'm practically panting now.

"You'll never be a bother to me, love. Not when you have a need I can take care of." He twists his fingers, burying them to the knuckle and curls them up.

I cry out and close my eyes, already feeling my orgasm build.

"Do you want to come, Reagan?"

"Yes." It's a plea.

He works his fingers out and then thrusts them back in steady rhythm. His unoccupied hand slips under my shirt, quickly discovering I also left off a bra. "Fuck," he groans, cupping my breast before pinching the nipple. "That's so hot."

"Again, it felt like a waste of time."

"Definitely," he agrees before slamming his mouth against mine. This kiss is fierce, dominating, consuming as he manipulates my body, driving me toward release. "You ready to come?"

I cry out as he cups my pussy, his palm pressing against my clit as his fingers curl against that magical spot inside me. He rolls my nipple between his thumb and first finger, his tongue delving deep in my mouth.

It's too much and not enough at the exact same time.

"Now, Reagan. Come on my hand."

My body immediately responds as my release washes through me. I feel the tightness as my internal muscles clench down on his fingers, glorious sensations sweeping from my nipples through my limbs. I rock my hips, taking everything I need, and then some. It's when my release has finally started to wane, I feel him move. His fingers slip from my body as he breaks the kiss. I'm just about to protest when I open my eyes.

Garreth is getting naked.

Fast.

His jeans are gone, followed by his boxer briefs. He tosses his T-shirt over his head and lets it drop to the floor. He fishes a condom out of his wallet and makes quick work of covering his erection. Then, he turns his attention back to me and does the same. My shirt is gone and my shorts tossed on the floor before I can even offer to help.

He steps between my open thighs and slides his cock between my folds. I cry out when he presses against my swollen clit and slips two fingers back inside. "Ready, love?"

I barely have time to nod in agreement before he's replacing his fingers with his dick, slowly filling and stretching me. My fingers itch to touch his hair, his shoulders, his incredible chest, but all I can do right now is grab the cabinet handle beside my head and hang on.

My body is already responding to the pleasure he provides, and all I can think about is...chemistry. There's so much here, it's practically a tangible force between us. I can feel it's power pulsating through the air. It's a heady, potent feeling.

"You going to come for me again, doll?"

"Yes, please," I reply, trying to meet his thrust but unable to from my position leaning back. All I can do is hang on and enjoy the ride.

"Your wish is my command."

He alternates between powerful thrusts and rocking his hips in the teasing manner he knows I like, and before I know, a second orgasm is starting to build. He grabs ahold of my ass and gently lifts me off the countertop. The movement changes the angle of his penetration and sends lightning bolts of euphoria through my veins.

I cry out as he pistons forward and drives me onto his cock at the same time. My nipples tingle and pucker as I do everything I can to hold on to the cabinet behind my head so I don't crash down to the counter. Even as the muscles in my arms burn, I feel the familiar start of another release.

"Garreth," I moan as my body tightens around his.

He thrusts twice before he stills, releasing himself inside me. I can feel his cock thicken as I squeeze, his body shuddering as he lets go. When the biggest part of his orgasm has passed, he moves with smaller, controlled thrusts, as if drawing out the pleasure.

Finally, he relaxes, leaning forward and placing his forehead against mine. "Jesus, Reagan."

"Yeah," I whisper, wrapping my arms around his shoulders and running my fingers through his hair.

Suddenly, I'm moving. He lifts me off the counter and carries me out of the kitchen, and yes, he's still buried inside me. Even though he's getting soft, I can feel every movement he makes. Carefully, he places me in the middle of his bed. "I'll be right back. I'm going to take care of this condom," he says, placing a kiss on my forehead before disappearing out of the bedroom.

I lie here, listening to the sound of another person moving about the house. I'm used to silence, with the exception of the occasional noise coming through the wall from a neighbor, but I can't help but note how much I like hearing someone else. It's relaxing.

Garreth returns a few minutes later with a warm washcloth. He helps me wipe off my most sensitive area and throws it in the hamper outside his closet. Then, he climbs into his bed beside me. "Do you want something to sleep in?"

"No," I reply, snuggling into his side. "I have a bag in the car if I need it."

"I'll get it in the morning before you wake," he says, holding me tightly against him.

"I didn't want to just assume I could stay."

"No assumptions. You can stay here any night you want."

Taking a deep breath, I feel myself relax as I close my eyes. His heartbeat thunders steadily beneath my cheek, and it's the perfect lullaby to lure me to sleep. It doesn't take long and I'm there, drifting away with Garreth at my side.

"Good morning," Grandma says, pulling me into a big hug. "It's been ages since I've seen you."

"It's been like a week, Grandma," I mumble, letting the familiar scent of her perfume wrap around me.

"Ages. Your parents are already here," she says, pulling back and looking me over from head to toe. "You feeling okay? You look a bit flushed."

My eyebrows arch upward. "It's a hundred degrees outside, Grandma," I quip. My makeup has already melted off.

"Hmm," she replies, watching me with a critical eye. "Anyway, come on in. We're just waiting on Madelyn. She's probably canoodling with that handsome husband of hers."

"Grandma," I groan. I follow her through the formal dining room and to the massive kitchen. I glance at the large spread of food on the counter, and instantly say, "We could have gone out somewhere."

She waves off my comment. "I had it catered in, honey. I didn't cook a thing," she boasts proudly.

The doorbell rings, so Grandma turns to let Madelyn in. I head over to where my parents sit and give hugs. "Hey, guys," I say, giving my mom a hug and then my dad. When I spy the amount of food waiting, I add, "Are we expecting more people? Like half the town?"

Mom smiles. "You know your grandma. She'll donate what's left to the church for families in need."

I do know Grandma. She's the kindest, most generous woman I've ever known. It doesn't surprise me she'd buy plenty of food for us and some to help others in the area.

"Hello, everyone," Madelyn says with a big smile on her face.

My mom instantly goes over to her and wraps her arms around her. "You're glowing, sweetheart. Look at you!"

"Thanks, Aunt Corrine," she replies, beaming happily at my mom.

Ever since Madelyn moved to Stewart Grove, she has gotten really close to the family. She moved in with me for several months before finding her own home, making us instant best friends, but she's also built relationships with our grandma and my parents. Family she didn't know she had until the untimely death of our grandpa several years ago. Ever since, she's an extended part of our immediate family.

Sort of like the sister I never had.

"Madelyn," my dad says, pulling her into a hug. "How are you feeling?"

"Good, Uncle Jerry," she responds, placing her hands on her swelling belly. "I can't believe I'm already four months."

"Are you going to find out?"

"We're still talking about that," Madelyn confirms, taking a seat the table.

"Where's Jameson?" Mom asks.

"Oh, he's working today. Numbers was on the schedule, but he wasn't feeling well, so Jameson volunteered to go in."

"Let's eat before the food gets cold," Grandma announces.

We enjoy a great lunch of lasagna, chicken alfredo, garlic bread, and salad, but it's the conversation that makes the meal so enjoyable. I've always valued time with my parents and Grandma, and now that Madelyn is a part of that, it makes it that much sweeter.

When we're finished and the desserts are brought out—tiramisu and a strawberry truffle cake—we decide to take it out to the sunroom. It's heated in the winter and cooled in the summer and overlooks Grove Park, a large piece of public land named after my family when my ancestors donated the space to the town for the sole purpose of a place for families to gather, hike, and fish.

Madelyn and I are the last ones to fill our plates, leaving us alone in the kitchen. "How are things going with Garreth?"

I instantly smile at the mention of his name. "Good."

"Have you told anyone about him?" she asks, glancing toward the back of the house where Grandma and my parents are.

"Not yet. It's still pretty new. I mean, we've only been seeing each other a week."

She nods slowly in understanding. "I get that, but you guys have been friends a long time, even if you didn't exactly hang out."

"True," I reply, slipping a little extra cake on my plate. "We're taking it pretty slow. We hang out after work"—code for sex—"and talk quite a bit throughout the day."

"Any dates planned yet?"

With my plate filled with too many sweets, I turn my attention to her. "Not yet. It's fairly difficult to organize something with our work schedules."

She considers my statement. "I'm sure something can be worked out. You deserve a nice evening out."

I shrug my shoulders. "I'm sure we'll get there, eventually."

It's the first time I've really thought about the fact we haven't had a date. Most relationships begin with one. Ours started with a confessed crush and hot sex. Not your typical "getting to know you" date, but I don't really care. In fact, I actually prefer our story this way. I've done the fancy dinners. Justin took me to some big steakhouse an hour away with a waitlist three months out. He made a big production of mentioning how he knew the owner and was able to get us a table without having to wait months like everyone else. Our dates after that were always public, where everyone could see him and watch him drop his cash, and while I concede they were great dates with delicious food, I'm much more a fan of low-key, private dinners.

Take me to the park for a picnic, and I'm a happy girl.

"I'm sure you will," she replies, plate in hand. "Maybe say something to him about scheduling you both off one night."

I shrug as we slowly make our way out of the kitchen and toward the sunroom. "I think it's a little more difficult than that. Since there's only one hostess right now, he makes sure he's working the nights I'm off so he can help the servers."

"He's such a great addition to the business. Jameson has mentioned on several occasions over the years how much they appreciate him. His hiring really took a load off all four of their shoulders, and now they're able to spend a little more time in the evenings at home with their families."

I nod. "And he's really good at his job. I've seen him in action. All the employees like him, and he treats them fairly." I stop outside the sunroom before adding, "I know that's why he's very careful about us. He doesn't want any of them to look down on him for dating an employee or thinking I'm getting preferential treatment."

"I don't think they would, but I get it. I'm sure it's not an easy position to be in," Madelyn confirms before I open the door and we enter the sunroom to enjoy our desserts.

We all stay for another hour and visit before Madelyn decides it's time to go home. Jameson will be getting off soon, which means Garreth will be replacing him. I can't help but feel sad I won't get to see him today, but that's life sometimes.

Perhaps he'll stop by after the bar closes tonight.

A girl can only hope, right?

"Can I help with the food?" I offer, noting the foiled containers filling the refrigerator.

"No thank you, dear. I'll take them to the church in a bit. There's a family of six, a husband, wife, and four children under the age of seven, who can use this. He was laid off from his job last week, and I know his wife is working extra hours at the grocery store to help until he finds something."

I pull my grandma into a hug. "You're a true angel on earth."

She waves off the compliment. "I just do what I can to help."

I give her a smile, hoping I'm half the woman she is when I'm her age. "Well, let me at least help you take this out to the car."

She grins widely. "I won't say no to that. Thank you, Reagan."

"You're welcome, Grandma."

As I head for home, I can't help but reflect on this past week. It's been a whirlwind, for sure, but I've loved every second of it. I enjoy my new job, which makes me wonder what will happen when Shantel returns from her maternity leave. I knew this position was temporary, yet the thought of having to step away upon her return leaves me filled with dread.

Of course, if I'm not working there, that gives Garreth and I more opportunities to take our relationship public, so that's not so bad either.

I don't know what the future holds with us or my job at Burgers and Brew, but I do know I'll just sit back and enjoy it while I can. I'll cross the job bridge when I get to it. As for now, I'll take the time working with him, even if we have to keep it completely professional, and live for the nights we're able to steal away in private.

Someday we'll be able to go public with our relationship.

Until then, I'll take what I can get.

Garreth

A few weeks later, it's packed on a Friday night. I've been jumping back and forth between the restaurant and the bar all evening, helping wherever needed. Right now, the dinner crowd is starting to thin out, as we approach closing down that side of the business.

"Hey," Jameson says as he meets me in the hallway by my office.

"Great crowd tonight," I reply, noting a small group of women headed our way and veering off into the restroom.

"Packed," he confirms, holding his guitar.

He's fidgety, but he always seems to get like that before he plays. I think a big part of it is the change in his routine. Jameson quit smoking a little over a year ago, when he and Madelyn were trying to have a baby. Since then, he's had to make adjustments that didn't involve him taking a few minutes to go outside and smoke before his shows. Now, he either hangs back with his wife, or if he does go outside, he goes behind the brewery, far away from any other smokers. He says he likes to just breathe in the fresh air.

"Need anything before you go on stage?" I offer.

"Nope."

I nod and pull my door closed, ready to head back over to the restaurant and help them close that side down.

"Hey, Garreth?" When I turn around, he catches me off guard by saying, "We're switching days off this week. I'll work for you Sunday night, and you're covering for me Thursday."

"What?" I ask, wondering what the hell I missed.

He steps toward me and lowers his chin. "Take your girl out on a date and quit scheduling yourself off on opposite nights as her." I open my mouth to argue, but he holds up a beefy hand and stops me. "I know why you do it, but it doesn't hurt one of us to cover for you a night here and there. I'm not saying change up your nights off every week, but every once in a while, it's fine. In fact, we insist."

My throat is dry. "We?"

The corner of his mouth curls up in a partial smile. "We. All of us. Just let us know when you want to switch, and we'll see who's available to cover. Hell, we're all here anyway, it might not even take much of a schedule change."

Dumbfounded, all I can do is stare at him. "I don't know what to say."

Jameson shrugs. "Just say thanks and be sure you show up for my shift Thursday. I'd hate to have to kick your ass because I had to cancel my own night with my wife to cover for you."

I instantly smile. "Thank you, Jameson. And don't worry about Thursday. I'll be here."

He holds my gaze. "I know you will." Then he turns and walks toward the bar, ready to play music.

The amount of trust these guys have in me is humbling. Professionally and personally.

I make my way to the bar, spotting Reagan and Madelyn right away. They're sitting at their usual table, facing the stage as Jameson plays. She's still in her restaurant polo, but she let her hair down. It's cascading in wild whiskey-colored waves, and my fingers itch to touch.

"Hey," Numbers says, coming up beside me at the edge of the bar.

"Busy night."

He nods, taking in the crowd, but I can instantly tell something's on his mind.

"You okay?"

"Yeah," he says, running his hand through his hair. "We were short again tonight."

That catches my attention. "How much?"

"Ten bucks."

I slowly nod in acknowledgement, absorbing the information. "Did you ever find what we were off last week?" I pray it was in the dayshift register.

"No." Before I can say anything else, he adds, "Let me do some more checking. It's not a lot, and we all know how easy it is for two bills to stick together."

"True," I agree.

"Give me until Monday and we'll discuss it in our meeting."

"Sounds good," I reply, hating I have to wait three days to have the conversation. Of course, by then, he could find the issue, and everything be right as rain again.

He slaps me on the back and gives my shoulder a squeeze. "Don't stress over it. We'll figure it out."

"You'll figure it out," I correct him. Lord knows if there's a problem with numbers, it's going to be this man who figures it out. They don't call him Numbers for nothing.

He gives me a cocky grin, because he knows I'm right.

With the restaurant closed and the patrons all congregated on one side, all eyes are at the front of the room. For nearly two hours, everyone listens to our resident musician play, singing along with him from time to time. The bar stays busy, but it's nothing Walker and Kellen can't handle.

Of course, throughout the night, I can't help but steal glances at Reagan as she listens. Her smile is small as she mouths the words to a song, and that one small gesture lights up the entire room. I'm not the only one who notices either. I spot three guys—including her ex, Justin—all watching her. Even from over here, she captivates an audience.

I'm completely smitten.

I know it.

My friends know it.

They've been teasing me about my lack of concentration at work all week, but I can't help it. Look at her.

Just as Jameson wraps up his set and we prepare for the onslaught of drinks and singing at the stroke of eleven, I head in her direction. She laughs at something Madelyn says, her head thrown back as she barks out a joyful sound. I place one hand on the back of her stool and the other on the tabletop and lean in, catching a huge whiff of her shampoo. My fingers itch to touch those wavy tendrils.

"What's it gonna take for you to go out with me? Like a real date," I murmur so only she can hear.

She startles, but only for a second, recognizing my voice. Reagan moves, pressing her back against my fingers. She turns her head, her kissable lips grazing across my ear. "Hmm, us both having the same night off would help," she whispers, her warm breath sending jolts of lust through my veins.

The corner of my mouth curls upward. "Done. What else?"

Her eyes widen, as if she wasn't expecting that answer. "Well, I guess you just need to ask me then."

I know we're in the bar, and I'm still technically on the clock. Right now, I don't care if anyone sees. All I care about is securing a date with the most gorgeous woman in the room. "Reagan, will you go out with me Sunday night?"

She smiles. And my heart? It fucking explodes. "I'd love to."

Now I'm the one grinning like a lunatic, and even though I want nothing more than to kiss her right now, I don't. The fact remains, I'm still at work, surrounded by a room full of people. No way do I want an audience when I finally get to kiss her tonight.

Chances are it won't be just one little kiss.

I tap on the table and back away, glancing over to Madelyn, who's wearing a grin from ear to ear. "You ladies need anything?" I ask.

"We're good, thanks," Reagan replies, while Madelyn winks.

Something tells me she was the driving force behind her husband offering to switch shifts with me, and if so, I'll thank her later. Because as much as I love my job, the prospect of going on a date with Reagan is the icing on the cake.

I can't fucking wait until Sunday.

Am I nervous? Hell yes, I am.

I'm thirty-seven, and I'm not even sure when my last real date was. Two years ago? Even then, I wasn't nearly as excited as I am tonight to pick up Reagan.

Planning this date took all morning Saturday, and a lot of time in the early afternoon to execute. I made phone calls, went shopping, and even bought a new shirt for the occasion, all before I was due at the restaurant.

Now, I'm pulling into her parking lot to pick her up, praying I made the right choice where tonight is concerned. I've second-guessed myself a million times, but it all came down to one thing: To give her an unforgettable evening.

I hope I succeed.

I wipe my hands on my jeans, grab the bouquet of daisies and lilies, and head for the front door of her building. I opt to take the elevator, hoping it'll give me a few moments to calm my racing heart, but it really doesn't. I'm still like a teenager, picking up his prom date, when I knock on her door.

She opens it right away and takes my breath away.

"Hi," she greets, opening to door wide. "Would you like to come in?"

Reagan's wearing a yellow sundress with small pink and green flowers on it. The straps tie at her shoulders, and all I can think about is what would happen if I gave those tiny strings a tug. I slowly glance down, taking in the stunning image she creates in this dress, and my mouth waters. It hits just above the knee and has a flowy skirt. Her feet are covered in wedge sandals that make her even taller than she already is. In fact, I'm pretty certain, if I were to step forward, my mouth would line up perfectly with hers.

"Want to? Yes. But I shouldn't. If I come in, we'll never leave," I reply, finally looking up and meeting her eyes. "These are for you," I add, holding out the flowers I grabbed from the florist.

Her smile is everything. "Thank you so much. I've never received flowers before," she says, bringing the bouquet to her nose and inhaling.

"Then you've dated the wrong guys."

She chuckles and glances at me over the lilies. "You're probably right. Let me put these in water, then we can go."

I follow behind as she slips around the corner into the kitchen. She moves easily around the small space, grabbing a vase from beneath the sink and filling it with water. As she arranges the bouquet, she asks, "Do you always give flowers on a first date?"

I nod. "Always. My mom would tan my hide if she found out I didn't. Lydia Taylor may look sweet and innocent, but she has a mean slap with a flip-flop."

Her wide eyes meet my smiling ones. "Really?"

A smile spreads across my lips. "Well, not in a while, but when I was younger, I used to test her regularly. One day at the park, it was time to go, and I refused to get off the swings. Let's just say, I listened to her the next time it was time to leave. It was either that or have a size six flip-flop imprint on my ass again."

Her giggle is like honey. Smooth, thick, and rich, and I can't get enough. "I can't believe she spanked you with a shoe."

I shrug. "I deserved it. And that was the day I learned not to push Mom." Our gaze remains locked, and it feels more intimate than ever before. "Ready to go?" I ask, clearing my throat. If we don't go now, we'll never leave.

"Yes," she replies, that one word dripping with eagerness and anticipation.

Once we step into the hallway and her door is secure, I take her hand and lead her to the elevator. The car is still on her floor, so we step in immediately and start our short descent down to the ground. "You look beautiful, by the way. Sorry I didn't tell you as soon as you opened the door, but I was a little awestruck."

"Thank you." There's a hint of a blush that creeps up her neck. "I hope this is okay for where we're going. You said casual."

I push open the front door of her building and escort her to my truck. "I did, and it's perfect."

She hops into the cab and fastens her seat belt. The moment I climb onto the driver's seat, she asks, "Where are we going?"

I flash her a quick smile. "That's a surprise," I reply, my palms getting sweaty once again. I pray I made the right choice for tonight.

We head to the private land I secured; the cab filled with comfortable silence. "So...how many girls have received flowers over the years?" she asks with a smile.

Chuckling, I think back over the last decade and a half. "You'd probably be surprised by the low number. You're only the second one to receive them since I've been home, and that date only led to two or three afterward."

She nods, and if she wants to ask more questions, she doesn't. I'd answer them if she asked. I'm not going to hide anything or lie to her, which is why I keep going.

"In high school, there were two. Emmie Lou Granger, my sophomore year, and then my senior prom date, who sadly only gave me a slight peck on the cheek at the end of the dance before leaving with a group of her friends. Then college, I thought it would be nothing but parties and girls, and while there was a lot of both available, I realized I was more of a relationship guy than into casual hookups, so the only woman to receive flowers during and after college was my ex-wife."

I can feel her shock all the way over here. "You were married?"

Nodding, I glance her way for a few moments before returning my eyes to the road. "I was. For seven years."

She's silent for a minute, probably absorbing this new piece of info. "We don't have to talk about this. It's probably horrible first date etiquette."

"I don't mind. I mean, we're getting to know each other, and our pasts are part of that. It wasn't a horrible marriage, but it wasn't the best either. Our problems started before we got married, right after I graduated college. I have an engineering degree but discovered my love for the restaurant business. She felt betrayed I wasn't using my education. Looking back now, we should have ended the relationship, but didn't. That's okay. Mistakes are made as learning tools, right? Shelby's remarried now and has two kids."

When she doesn't reply, I risk a look her way and find a soft smile on her lips. "You're an amazing man, Garreth Taylor."

I shrug, a little uncomfortable with the compliment, because I'm anything but. I try to be good and do good, but still stumble a lot. It's how you respond to the challenges and mistakes that show what kind of person you truly are.

Approaching the property I'm using for tonight's date, I slow my truck and turn onto the dirt lane. I notice Reagan looking around, trying to figure out where we are and what we're doing. "Is this the back side of the park?" she asks, referring to the massive piece of land known as Grove Park.

"It is not. This property belongs to Leo's family. I decided I wanted to do something different for our first official date."

"Like murder and bury me in the woods?" she quips.

A laugh rumbles from deep in my chest. "No, you're safe here. I bury my bodies in a field out by the river."

She giggles as I slowly wind my way down the long lane. We round the last big bend, and I can already see the lights. It's not nearly dark enough to enjoy them, but I'm hoping it will be the perfect ambiance as the night wears on.

When she gasps, I know she's finally seeing what I spent all day setting up. I take a quick moment to look her way and am so grateful I did. I can see the excitement, the wonder, the appreciation on her face, and suddenly, all the stress and worry about this being the right first-date set-up melts away.

"Wow," she whispers, the word barely audible.

I stop the truck and put it in park. "You like?"

She looks my way with tears in her eyes. "I love it," she croaks out, her voice hoarse and crackly. "It's so pretty out here. Peaceful." She reaches down and releases her seat belt without taking her eyes off the scene.

When I contemplated what to do tonight, my first thought was a picnic. Intimate, serene, and private. Not that I didn't want to take her to a restaurant and show the world the beautiful woman at my side, but I just wanted to do something a little different. Special.

Like her.

As soon as I called Leo and told him what I was thinking, he readily offered up his family's campground. They own a little over twenty acres, just outside of town. Most of it is timber, and Grove Creek runs through the northern park. That's where we are. I'm not sure when the last time their campground has been used, but Leo's dad maintains it well. The grass is mowed and there's electricity for campers. There's even a small beach area along the creekbank where you can fish and swim.

Of course, tonight, we won't be doing any of that. I have a picnic planned, along with sightseeing the trails on their side-by-side. I even have the large blanket for stargazing beneath the lights.

I was worried this wasn't enough, but when I see the awe in her eyes, I know I knocked this one out of the park.

"Come on, Miss Turner," I say, releasing my own seat belt and opening my door. "Your last first date awaits."

Reagan

Your last first date awaits.

If there was ever any doubt in my mind the type of man Garreth Taylor is, there isn't any now. He's...everything.

The moment I open my door, he's there, taking my hand and helping me step from the truck. There's a very light breeze, which flutters my dress around my thighs and cools my heated skin.

He leads me over to a large blanket under a shade tree. There are a thousand twinkle lights hanging from the branches, and even though it's still light enough to see their beauty, I know they're there and appreciate his effort.

On the blanket, he has a picnic basket and small cooler set off to the side and a radio playing country music. There are more flowers, this time in tin buckets sitting at all four corners of the blanket.

"I hope you're hungry," he says, toeing off his slide-on shoes and stepping onto the blanket.

"I'm starving," I confirm, reaching down and slipping off my wedges. The blanket is warm and soft beneath me as I sit in the spot he guides me to. "This is amazing," I add, taking it all in.

"I was hoping you'd be okay with something like this over a fancy restaurant. Don't get me wrong, that's a great first date too, but I just wanted something unique, if that makes sense."

"Perfect sense, and this is...perfect," I say, completely smitten with this man.

"Well, let's eat," he says, pulling plates and utensils from the basket. "I took another chance on the menu, so I hope you like it."

He opens the cooler and pulls sandwiches out of a container. "I have chicken salad and tuna salad, not knowing which one you'd prefer," he informs, opening the lid.

"Chicken salad sounds amazing."

Garreth sets a sandwich on each plate and places small containers of different things between us. Grapes, strawberries, and cheese cubes, as well as a bag of Cool Ranch Doritos. "These are my favorite," he replies sheepishly. "What's yours so I can bring those next time?"

I award him with a big grin. "Cool Ranch Doritos."

He shakes his head and laughs. "No shit? Well, I got lucky there, didn't I?"

I take the bag and dump a small pile on my plate. Then, I lift my top slice of fresh bread and carefully place four chips on the chicken salad, making sure to cover every corner with a Dorito. Finally, I replace the bread and take a bite. It's sweet, bold, and crunchy, just the way I like it.

"I think I just fell in love," he mutters, catching me off guard. His mouth is hanging open as he watches me eat my sandwich, and I try to ignore the way my heart rate spikes when I think about him talk about love.

"Sorry, I've always been a fan of chips on my sandwich. My favorite is ham and cheese with mayo and chips."

Again, he just stares before seeming to snap himself out of it. He reaches down, takes his own handful of chips, and shoves them beneath his top bread. "Only way to eat a sandwich," he proclaims before shoving a quarter of it into his mouth.

"Favorite color?" I ask before popping a cube of Colby jack cheese in my mouth.

"Black."

I can't help but sigh. "Black isn't a color."

"Is too," he counters between bites. "Fine, if it's not a color, then I choose hazel."

"Hazel? That's an odd color choice."

He holds my gaze as he replies, "It's the color of your eyes, and they're my favorite eyes in the world. Therefore, hazel is my favorite color."

I know I'm blushing. I can feel the tingling heat spread up my neck and stain my cheeks. "You're full of charm tonight."

"I'm always charming, sweetness. Only with you."

And cue the swoon…

We spend the next thirty minutes enjoying our food and chatting, sharing little details about ourselves so we can get to know each other better. When our plates are clean, he throws them in the unlit firepit and tosses the empty containers in the basket. "Ready?" he asks, extending his hands to help me up.

There's no hesitation. I place mine inside of his. I realize instantly I would follow him anywhere. We both slip our shoes back on before we walk. "What's next?" I ask, glancing down at the firepit. There are logs stacked inside with kindling, as if it's ready to be lit.

But that's not where we head.

Garreth leads me over to a shed at the far end of the campground and opens the double door. Inside, I find a mower, a variety of yard tools, and a large utility terrain vehicle. My eyes move to the shovels. "Are you going to make me help dig my own grave?" I tease.

"Keep getting sassy, and you'll get a spanking." There's a fire dancing in those eyes. It shoots through my veins, heat licks at my skin.

"Promise?" The word is husky and laced with desire.

"Oh, most definitely, love. Now, let's get to the next phase of the best first date ever."

That's when I realize we're getting on that UTV. It's much larger than a regular ATV, with two seats and a bed on the back like a truck. I've ridden on ATVs before, but nothing of this size. I'm actually a little excited.

I climb onto the passenger seat and fasten the seat belt, while he grabs two helmets and slides behind the wheel. "How fast will this go?"

"Sixty, but we won't go that fast. Leo's family uses it mostly to help clear debris off the trails and haul logs and tools and stuff," he says, starting the machine and slowing pulling it out of the shed. "I almost forgot. Here." He reaches into his pocket and pulls out a...scrunchie.

My eyes are wide as I take the blue and white hair tie.

"I got to thinking about the ride and figured it could be bothersome with long hair. The windshield and helmet will help with a majority of the wind, but it may still blow and tangle, so I stopped and grabbed this before I picked you up."

This is it.

This is the moment I realize I'm truly falling for this guy. After only a couple of weeks, I notice I'm feeling more for him than I ever expected, and fast.

I reach for the scrunchie, but don't stop there. I pull against the safety restraint until I'm able to press my lips against his. "Thank you," I whisper, hoping to convey just how much this simple little hair tie means to me.

Because it's not just the fact he grabbed one. He could have easily mentioned at my apartment that I should bring one with me. It's the fact that he thought about and planned every little detail, including the fact the wind might blow my hair and annoy me.

He cups my cheek, the tips of his fingers sliding against my hairline, as he returns the kiss. "You're welcome."

I pull back much sooner than I'd like, but I know how much time he's put into tonight's events, so the last thing I want to do is completely distract him by crawling on his lap and mauling him. Though, I don't really think he'd complain too much.

Once I have my hair secured behind my head and our helmets are on, he takes off. The sun is starting to drop so the heavily shaded parts of the land is much cooler than out in the open. We ride for what feels like forever, yet not nearly long enough.

Garreth points out an old, dilapidated treehouse he and Leo built back in fifth grade, which really only consists of a platform and half-walls. "We were so excited to sleep out in it, we used an old tarp from my dad's garage and ran it over the top of the wood. Of course, we could barely sit up in it, and the plastic top made it hotter than hell inside. Plus, it started to rain about an hour into our campout, so we ended up forgetting about it and running to the camper with his parents."

I look up at the structure and smile, picturing a blond-haired, brown-eyed little boy climbing the rickety ladder and running down the path. I'm sure he was an adorable little guy, if the gorgeous man he turned into is any indication.

When we finally return to the campground, I've never felt this relaxed and content in my life. In fact, I've never been camping before, but I may want to try. No, I don't think I'd like the bugs, but I'm sure the fire would help keep them away. Plus, sleeping beneath the stars, tucked securely against Garreth, definitely has merit.

"So you've been camping out here a lot?" I ask when we return the UTV to the shed and lock it up.

He takes my hand and leads me to a log positioned beside the firepit. "When we were little, we'd come all the time in the summer. Then, in high school, Leo and I used to camp as much as we could on the weekends, but sports and, later, work got in the way sometimes. Of course, his dad would either come out with us or stop by and check up on the situation a lot," he replies.

"To see if you were bringing girls out here?" I ask, smiling, as he crouches down to light the fire.

He meets my gaze and gives me a wolfish grin. "Felt my first boob over by that tree," he says, pointing to a large oak opposite of where we sit.

I can't help but laugh. "I bet all the girls wanted to come out here with you. I've seen your flirting game. It's pretty strong."

He chuckles as he lights the paper towel he's using to ignite the kindling. "Back then, I was just an awkward teenager, just like the rest of them. That's why I only had one girlfriend. I didn't perfect my game until I moved back here and could practice on you," he says, throwing me a wink and a smirk.

I want to roll my eyes, but I'm too distracted by how sexy he looks right now to bother.

When the fire is lit, Garreth comes over and sits beside me on the log. He links his fingers with mine and draws me into his side, wrapping his right arm around my shoulder. The hard wood isn't the most comfortable, but the entire ambiance makes it perfect. The sky is starting to darken, so the twinkle lights are starting to shine brightly overhead. Even though it's a warm summer night, the fire crackling and filling the air with the fresh scent only seems to add to the experience.

It's a truly remarkable date.

One I'll never forget.

"I've never been camping," I confess, looking out at the large grassy area.

"No? We'll go."

I glance over my shoulder and meet his gaze. "Yeah? I'd like that."

"Of course, I don't have a camper, so we'd have to rough it in a tent, but I'd bring an air mattress."

Snuggling into his embrace, I watch the fire glow as the night falls. I have no idea how long we sit here, talking and stealing a few kisses, but my legs are numb and I have to use the restroom.

"What's wrong?" he asks, instantly picking up my discomfort.

"Oh, uh…I have to use the restroom." I glance around, grateful there's at least the dark of night in the timber to provide cover.

"Shit, I'm sorry. I should have told you way before now," he says, standing up and practically pulling me behind him toward the shed.

Apparently, there's a spot behind it I can use…

But Garreth doesn't lead me to the back. Instead, he stops at a single door toward the rear of the shed and turns the knob. "Bathroom," he says, flipping on the light.

"Oh."

"I'll wait out here."

Then, I'm left alone in the small bathroom.

First thing I notice is the clean scent. Pine and ammonia, as if it has been cleaned somewhat recently. There's a single shower unit in one corner and a toilet and sink on the opposite wall. I can understand exactly why they'd want to build this space in the back of the shed. It's incredibly convenient.

After I go to the bathroom and wash my hands, I head back out and flip off the lights. I don't see Garreth on the log, but find him lying on the blanket, gazing up at the sky. "I have to admit, even though I've never been camping, a bathroom is a necessity for me."

He turns toward the sound of my voice and smiles. "Agreed. They didn't build that until we were in high school. You don't want to know what we did before then," he quips.

When I reach the blanket, I take off my wedges and crawl onto the soft material, stretching out beside him. "Did they recently come out and clean it?"

"I did," he confesses, reaching for my hand and linking our fingers. "When I came out to set up, I cleaned the bathroom and turned on the water and electricity."

"Thank you," I say right away, referring to him thinking of making sure the bathroom was in working order and clean, but my appreciation is for more than just that.

It's for the perfect night with a great guy.

"Of course," he replies, turning on his side.

I do the same, pressing my chest to his and placing a leg over his as I slip my fingers into his hair. He reaches behind me and grabs my ass, pulling me even closer. When he does, I feel his erection, hard and ready, between us. His lips are soft as he slowly coaxes my mouth open with his tongue.

He shifts his hand down to my outer thigh and slowly starts to slide it up, beneath my skirt. "Have I told you how much I love this dress?" he asks, slipping farther up my leg.

"I do recall hearing something about that," I tease, practically bursting with excitement for him to discover what I'm wearing under the dress.

I know the moment he does. His warm palm grazes across my bare ass cheek before stilling. His fingers shift, sliding along the thin strip of material between the globes of my ass. "What are you wearing?" he asks, the smile evident in his voice.

"I might have bought a little something else the other day when I was shopping for this dress."

Fire reflects in his eyes, and not just from the bonfire nearby. These flames are fueled by lust. "You might have? I think you're holding out on me, love. Stand up and let me see."

I carefully get to my feet and reach for the ties at my shoulders. Garreth rolls to his back and places his hands behind his head, clearly getting comfortable as he prepares to watch me undress. With one little tug, the first bow releases, spilling the ties against my body. Then, I grab the second bow and pull.

With my eyes locked on his, I grasp the zipper at my side and slowly pull it down. The dress starts to part before falling to my waist and eventually down around my ankles. He holds my gaze before his slowly drops. I can feel the power of his eyes like a caress. Warm. Intimate. Consuming.

"Jesus, Reagan."

"Do you like it?" I ask, slowly spinning around so he can get a complete view.

He makes a gurgling, pained noise when my back is to him, and I can't help but smile. When I'm facing him once more, I let my desire for him take over and straddle his body before slowly lowering myself down. His thick erection presses into the apex of my legs, and I can already feel wetness coating my panties.

"I really don't want to see you lose this," he starts, running a finger across the cup of my bra, "but I'd really like to see you naked right now."

Reaching behind my back, I release the clasp of my strapless bra and let it fall to his chest. "Like this?"

"Getting better," he mutters, his eyes locked on my breasts.

"I think you're wearing way too much clothing," I say, placing my hands on his chest and arching my back.

"Agreed. What do you say we do something about that?"

I slide off his waist so he can undress and just sit there and enjoy the show. He strips off his shoes, socks, pants, boxer briefs, and T-shirt, and grabs a condom from his wallet. Garreth lies back down and sheathes his cock. I actually feel my internal muscles clench with anticipation.

Standing up, I slip the thong down my legs, kicking it off to the side, before returning to my original position straddling his waist.

"Ready?" I ask, reaching down and gripping his erection.

"For you to ride me? Fuck, yes."

I adjust myself and place the tip of his cock where I crave him, and then slowly sit down, feeling the stretch as he fills me completely.

This.

This right here.

It's passion and rightness.

It's two people, coming together as one.
It's magic.
It's us.

Garreth

I've never been to heaven, but I imagine this is exactly what it looks like.

This.

Her.

Hair cascading around her bare shoulders, nipples hard, as she rocks and takes every inch of me.

Her skin glows beneath the star-filled sky and twinkle lights, and I'm pretty sure I'll never forget this night or the way she looks. I grab her hips but let her set the pace. She rocks with slow, determined motions, her sweet pussy tight and wet.

She moves a little faster, her glorious tits bouncing. "Take what you need, love," I instruct, reaching over and taking both her hands in mine.

Using them for leverage, she lifts up and slams down, her hazel eyes wild and unfocused. "I need you," she whispers so softly, I almost don't hear it.

Squeezing one hand, I lift my other to cup her neck, running my thumb over her jaw and bottom lip. "You have me. Always."

She has no idea how true that statement is.

Reagan cries out, her pussy starting to squeeze around my dick, and I know she's close. I thrust up, meeting her rocking motion and hitting that spot deep inside her. The one that makes her come hard. Just a few more thrusts and…

"Garreth," she moans, her muscles gripping me so tight, it makes it hard to breathe.

Her release triggers my own, and all I can do is ride the waves of pleasure.

When the tremors start to subside, she slides off me, curling into my side. "Well," she starts, taking a deep breath. "I've never done *that* outside before."

"That was a first for me as well."

"I think I really like this camping thing," she mutters, snuggled into my arms.

"Me too, love. Me too." I place a kiss at her temple and breathe her in. I'll never tire of the way she smells. Like sweet vanilla and sex.

My favorite combination.

I don't know how long we lie here together, but long enough for us both to get chilled. Plus, I have this damn condom to deal with. "We should probably get dressed. You have goosebumps."

"I don't really want to move," she mutters, holding my arms as I hold her.

"Me either, love, but I have to get rid of the condom and put the fire out. I didn't bring enough supplies to have an actual campout."

She rolls enough to be able to look up at me. "What if we camp out at your place?"

I give her a smile. "I don't have a sleeping bag," I quip.

"No, but you do have that big bed."

"Ahh, yes. That big bed."

"I really like your bed," she says, trying to stifle a yawn.

"Let's go, Cinderella. Midnight is approaching," I say, sitting up and reaching for her hands.

"Are you saying I'm going to turn into a pumpkin?"

"No, I'm saying it's time to get you home and to bed."

My heart skips a little beat at the thought of taking her *home.* Together.

She leans forward and presses her soft lips against mine. "Thank you for the best date ever."

"You're most welcome. I'm glad you had a good time."

"The best time," she confirms.

"Let's get dressed and this mess cleaned up so I can get you naked again and in my bed."

"I like the way you think, Mr. Taylor," she teases, reaching for her dress. "I really like the way you think."

"We need to talk."

I look up from the report left on my desk and find Numbers standing in the doorway. "I was just reviewing everything," I start, but essentially stop talking when he enters my office and shuts the door.

"I've found something."

He has my full attention. "What?"

"You know the two times we were short at the front register a couple weeks ago?"

"Of course. Did you find it?"

His face says I'm not going to like what he has to say. "It wasn't two incidences of being short. There were actually four."

"Seriously? At the restaurant register, right? Not the bar," I confirm, even though I already know the answer.

"Not the bar. That's the one we expect to come up a few bucks over or short, because lots of cash runs through that one. The restaurant is seventy-five percent charges, which leaves a much smaller margin for error."

I nod, already knowing this.

"The first time was one hundred dollars. We've never had that kind of shortage before, so I started digging. A few nights after that, we were ten off. There was a time we were ten off again, way back in late July and I never thought anything of it until now. Plus, Saturday night we were twenty short."

"What?" I ask, instantly pissed. "Why didn't someone say something?"

He holds up his hands. "Settle down. They didn't say anything because I asked her not to."

"Who?" I bite out.

"Cece. She got called in to work for Angie, remember? Well, Cece is a dayshift girl, so if something was going on, I knew it wouldn't be her. I asked her to help close out the register and bring me everything. We were twenty dollars short."

"Son of a bitch," I mumble, running both hands through my hair. "Who?" I ask, even though I have an idea.

"There were two employees working all four instances."

I wait, since I can already confirm one wasn't Angie, considering she wasn't working Saturday night.

"Cameron and Reagan."

I blink once, twice, as I try to process. "No way. No fucking way, Numbers. It wasn't Reagan," I insist with a little extra heat.

"Hold up, man, I'm not saying it was," he starts, but I'm already on my feet.

"It wasn't Reagan," I state once more, carefully punctuating each word with anger. "I know this woman, Isaac. Better than I know myself. She'd never do something like this. She'd never steal from her cousin's husband's business. Never. Plus, she used to work at a fucking bank, man. If she was ever going to steal money, don't you think it would have happened by now? You're wrong about her. Fucking. Wrong."

When I finally stop to take a breath, I find him sitting there, smiling.

"What?" I snap, ready to rip someone's head off.

"Does she know you love her?"

I just stare at him for several long seconds. "No, but that's not the point."

"No, it's not, but we can circle back to that one, because I definitely think we should talk about it."

I plop down in my chair. "We're not talking about that."

He smiles again. Asshole.

"I never thought for a second it was Reagan, Garreth. I was just pointing out there were two employees working up front on the nights the money was missing. We both know Reagan doesn't handle the register."

He has a valid point. I was so worked up at hearing her name mentioned, I didn't even stop to think about the fact she doesn't touch the money.

Numbers relaxes in the chair and meets my gaze. "So we have a problem with Cameron. What do you know about her?"

I let out a deep sigh and rub my temple. "Nice girl. Young. Twenty-two, I believe. Interviewed well. Worked at the diner in high school. References checked out. The only time she's been late was when her car wouldn't start, and she phoned right away. Jameson went over to give her a jumpstart. Has never called in sick. No customer complaints. The other staff enjoy working with her. She's basically an exemplary employee. I'd hire a dozen Camerons in a heartbeat."

Or so I thought.

He nods. "How do you want to handle this?"

I glance at the printed schedule hanging on my wall. "We gotta let her go. She's on tomorrow night. I'll bring her in before she can start her shift."

Numbers stands up. "Sorry, G. This was never my favorite part of the job either," he replies, referring to when he did the hiring and firing before they brought me on.

"It's the worst part, but it's the job."

He nods. "If you want a witness, let me know. I'll be here."

"I'm sure I'll be fine, but I'll buzz you if I need anything."

"Perfect. Thanks, Garreth."

"No, thank you for finding it. I hate that it's happening, but at least we know who. I'll take care of it tomorrow."

He heads to the door and pulls it open. "I'm not going to say anything at the meeting today. We'll wait until you talk to her, and then I'll fill the other three in."

I give him a small smile. "Sounds good."

He walks out, leaving the door open the way he found it before he stepped in and ruined my entire day. In the back of my mind, I've known something was off with Cameron. I just didn't know what. I take it personally when someone—*anyone*—steals from the business I'm overseeing. I feel it looks bad upon them, but also me. I take a lot of pride in my work, so when something like this happens, I can't help but wonder why I didn't see it or what I could have done differently to stop it.

I know I couldn't have known this would happen, but still.

This fucking sucks.

"Cameron, do you have a minute?" I ask before she can clock in on Tuesday afternoon.

"Of course," she replies, following me from the employee break room to my office.

"Have a seat," I state politely, closing the door behind us. The moment I sit across from her, I know. I can see her guilt written across her face.

She knows what's about to happen.

"There's something that's been brought to my attention," I start. I barely have the words out when I see tears gather in her eyes. "You know what this is about, don't you." It's not so much a question, but a statement.

She nods, dropping her gaze down to her chest as the tears start to fall. I'm not one who normally gets worked up over tears. I've fired people before—women and men—who have cried. I'm prepared for it, really, but what I'm not prepared for is the agony I see mixed with the guilt.

Cameron reaches into her purse, her hands shaking, as she retrieves a bar napkin. "I took it," she confirms, handing over the wrinkled paper. On it, I see four dates with a dollar amount. The same dollar amounts that equal what we figured was stolen. "One hundred and forty dollars," she whispers, looking completely forlorn and dejected.

She takes a deep breath, meets my eyes, and continues. "After the first time, I swore I was going to put it back the next day with my tips, but I wasn't able to. I know it was a small amount. I mean ten bucks. Who can't repay ten bucks?" she asks with a sniffle.

I give her my full attention, because something tells me this is bigger than someone with sticky fingers.

She sniffles again and wipes tears from her cheeks. "You have to know, it was never my intention to take what didn't belong to me, and I have every intention of paying it back. I still will. I am honored to be an employee here, or former employee," she whispers, crying a little harder as she covers her face with her hands.

I lean back and watch, surprised she just confessed so easily. In my experience, when an employee is cornered like this, they tend to turn defensive or try to lie to get out of it. It was someone else.

You can't prove it. You just don't like me and are trying to get me fired. I've heard them all.

This? This is different.

"Cameron? What's going on?" I ask softly, needing to know why she did it.

She gives me a small smile, but it's a sad one. "I'm a walking cliché for 'my mom told me not to date him.'"

"Who?"

"Cage Bronson."

I know the name. Local thug who has been busted a few times for selling drugs.

"We started dating a year or so ago. I had heard all the stories about him, but he just seemed so...nice. I knew for sure they were rumors. You know, kid from the wrong side of the tracks," she says with a small shrug. "We moved in together after a few months. It wasn't anything fancy, but I was happy."

"What happened?"

"I found a stash of drugs hidden under our bed. It was...a lot. A suitcase full. All different kinds. Baggies of pills, powder substances, and cash. A lot of cash. I remember just staring at it, trying to figure out why it was there. He came home and I confronted him about it." She pauses and closes her eyes for a few moments. I can see the pain she's feeling play out across her face. "He yelled at me, accused me of snooping, and told me to forget I ever saw the suitcase. It wasn't his, but he was going to return it to the owner."

"And you believed him," I deduce.

She flashes a small grin. "Actually, no. I knew it was his. It was like all the pieces just sort of clicked into place.

"Later that night, I was going to tell him I was leaving, but he didn't come home. When I went to look for the suitcase the next morning, it was gone. Along with a bunch of his clothes. I thought for sure that was it, that I was home free. I applied for the job here, because I knew I'd need a bigger income in order to cover the rent and utilities.

"About a week after I started, there was a knock on the door. Turns out, Cage didn't just run out on me, but his supplier too. A man known as Johnny Cats. He's from Cleveland, I believe, and it turns out, he owned that suitcase. Drugs, money, everything. And he wanted it back."

Dread fills my entire body. "What happened?"

"He wasn't very happy to hear Cage was gone with his stuff. He told me it was owed to him, and if Cage couldn't pay, I'd have to."

"Jesus, Cameron," I mutter, trying to wrap my head around what I'm hearing. I'm a pretty good judge of character, and my gut is telling me she's speaking the truth. Not some crazy made-up story to get herself out of trouble. If anything, she's owned her mistakes from the very beginning.

"He's come to the house every Thursday morning to collect his weekly payment and made it very clear what would happen if I didn't have the money."

"So you took the money to pay off your boyfriend's drug dealer."

She shakes her head. "No, I use my own money to pay him off. I took the money to cover rent and food. The utilities are mostly cut off at this point."

Now it's my turn to close my eyes and take a deep breath.

"I'm very sorry, Garreth," she whispers, crying once more. "I never meant to hurt you or the guys. I never meant for any of this to happen."

When I open my eyes, I can see the pain. It's downright excruciating, and my heart breaks for this young girl who is trying to get herself out of a horrible situation that's not even hers to begin with.

"How much?" When she just looks at me, I elaborate. "How much do you still owe him?"

She visibly swallows hard. "Just over seven thousand," she whispers, as if saying the words aloud makes it that much more real.

"But I'll do it. I'll figure it out," she adds miserably. "And I'll pay them back the money I took from here. I promise."

"I believe you," I find myself saying, because I do.

"What will you do now?"

She shrugs. "Hopefully I'll find another job. I know you have every right to give me a bad reference, and I'd understand completely if you do. Hell, if I walk out of here and there's a cop waiting to arrest me, I'd go quietly and willingly. The guilt I've been living with, the disgust at myself is almost too much to bear, and it seems redundant for me to keep saying it, but I am truly sorry. For everything." She stands up and turns around, most likely expecting the police to be waiting.

"Cameron?" I say before she's able to make it to the door. "I want to help."

"No. This is my mess. I'll clean it up," she insists, lifting her chin as she makes the vow.

"I'm sure you will, but the truth is, it's not your mess to clean up, so I'm going to help you. You don't have to do this alone. You have friends."

Her chin wobbles as she fights the tears once more. "I can't ask," she starts, but I cut her off.

"You didn't ask. I'm offering." With a deep breath, I add, "I'll loan you the money to pay the jerk off who's harassing you. You'll make smaller, more manageable payments to me until the debt is paid. You'll also pay the guys back right away. And…you can keep your job, as long as you promise to never do this again and promise to come to me if you get in a bind."

Cameron cries so hard, her petite body shakes. "I can't…"

Standing up, I move to the opposite side of my desk and place a careful hand on her shoulder. "You can. I remember what it was like to be your age. I truly believe you got yourself into a situation and have been doing what you can to get out of it. Have a little more grace for yourself, Cam. Everyone makes mistakes and falls down. It's how you get up and take that first step that matters."

I meet her shocked gaze and add, "You'll get through this. I believe in you."

And I do.

I feel a lot of bosses would have washed their hands of her, trashed her name at every turn, and never looked back, but I can't do that. Not when her entire future is laid before her. She needs someone to take the chance on her, to believe in her and help guide her through the rocky roads ahead.

I'll be that person.

I'll be her friend.

Reagan

I pull into the lot and park in the back near Garreth's truck. Like a schoolgirl, I give myself a quick once-over in the rearview mirror, making sure my makeup is flawless and my lips are stained a light pink. I rarely wear lipstick but couldn't stop myself from adding a little color, in hopes of drawing someone's eyes to my mouth.

With a pleased look, I slip from my car and head for the back entrance of the bar. Before I reach the door, a noise to my left catches my attention. I turn and find Cameron there, sitting at the picnic table. Her head is down, and she appears to be crying. My feet carry me toward her immediately.

"Hey," I say softly as I approach as to not startle her.

She looks up, her pretty eyes puffy from crying. "Hi," she replies with a sniffle. "Ignore me."

I slip onto the wooden seat across from her. "Sorry, can't do that. Are you okay?"

She looks up and just stares at me for several long seconds. I start to think she's going to brush me off, to insist she's fine, even though she clearly isn't, so I'm surprised when she replies, "I've had a rough few months."

"Do you want to talk about it?" I find myself asking.

I've always liked Cameron. She's young, about twenty-two, with a bubbly, friendly personality. My only hang-up with her has been the fact I can't let go of the feeling something is up with her and the money we've been short recently.

She sighs and meets my gaze. "You're into Garreth, right?"

Okay. I wasn't expecting that.

"You don't have to answer, but I've caught the way he looks at you. I think he really likes you, if that matters at all. He seems like a great guy, so I thought I'd just... I don't know, mention it?" she states with an awkward chuckle. "I'm not trying to be nosy, really. Actually, now that I think about it, you two would make an awesome couple."

"Oh." That's all I got.

"Anyway, I guess I was just saying, if you're into him, you should totally ask him out."

I try to clear the lump in my throat, but it just won't go away.

"I did something I'm ashamed of. Something I can't take back," she whispers, breaking through the silence.

"Okay," I reply, afraid this conversation is going where I think it is.

Cameron proceeds to tell me about the money and why she took it. I can't help but feel sympathy for the young woman who found herself in an impossible situation, especially because she's so remorseful about it. I can tell the guilt is eating her alive.

I'm not at all surprised by the fact Garreth is helping her out. Since I've gotten to know him, I've discovered him to be so much more than the flirty guy I first thought him to be. Sure, he's still that way, but he's also sweet, romantic, and passionate. He proved that by our amazing first official date.

"What can I do to help?" I ask, reaching out and placing my hand on hers in support.

"I don't think there's anything you can do. Garreth promised he wouldn't tell anyone. Well, except the owners. He did say he had to tell them, not that I blame him. I guess they could still insist he fire me, and I'd understand that too."

"They won't," I insist. "They trust Garreth and if he believes in you, so will they."

She closes her eyes. "I just don't know if I can face them, you know? I'm so embarrassed by what I did," she murmurs.

"They'll understand, and broken trust can be repaired. If you pay them back right away and continue to make payments to Garreth, they'll see the real you. Just like he does."

She nods and sighs. "I still can't believe he didn't fire me. Or have the police come and take me away. Honestly, I think I've been expecting that all along."

Squeezing her hand once more, I reply, "He's a good man."

She gives me a knowing grin. "So, does that mean you'll think about dating him?"

I can't help but laugh. "I'll consider it," I say, feeling a little guilty myself about holding back, especially since she just shared something extremely personal, incredibly embarrassing with me.

"Thanks, Reagan." The smile she gives seems to hit her eyes for the first time in...awhile. Now that I think about it, this guilt she's been carrying has to have been eating her alive. I'm not sure when the last time was I saw a genuine grin on her face, but I'm happy to see it now.

"If you need anything, call."

She nods. "I will."

Standing up, I ask, "Are you coming inside?"

Cameron shakes her head. "No, I was taken off the schedule tonight. I'm pretty sure Garreth thought he was firing me, so he covered my shift for the night."

I nod in understanding. "Well, you're welcome to come inside and have dinner with me and my friends."

She shakes her head. "I can't. I look horrible, and honestly, I think I just need to go home and go to bed. I haven't been sleeping well lately."

I don't ask about the utilities she mentioned were shut off. I can't imagine trying to sleep without air-conditioning in the temperatures we've had this summer. And she did mention she was going to her mom's house to shower and wash her clothes when her mom was at work, telling her mom her washing machine was on the fritz.

"I'm serious, Cameron. Call if you need anything."

She gives me a grateful smile. "Honestly, I think I just need this. A friend. I lost the ones I had when I was dating Cage. They all knew he was bad for me," she says with a sigh. "I just wish I would have seen it sooner."

"Don't beat yourself up," I insist. "We've all made questionable choices where men are concerned," I add with a wink.

"Thank you." Then, she does something I wasn't expecting and pulls me into a hug.

"Anytime."

I watch her walk away, noticing her steps seem a little lighter. I'm sure she still has plenty of weight on those young shoulders, but I'm hoping today brought her a little relief. She climbs into an old car that looks like it's seen better days, and when she starts it up, I notice a ticking sound.

I make a mental note to ask Jameson to look at it for her.

Then, I turn back to the building and go in search of the man I've fallen in love with. Tonight only proves how deeply I care for him, and all I want to do is kiss his lips and tell him.

But I won't.

Not here, at least.

Inside, the music plays, and the ambiance is lively. I can hear laughter spilling from the bar, which makes me grin. There's something about this place that brings a smile to my face. Or perhaps it's the man sitting behind his desk, writing something on a sticky note. He doesn't see me standing in the doorway, so I quickly step inside and close the door.

That's when he looks up, and I can see the stress written all over his handsome face.

"Hey," he says, giving me a soft smile.

"Hello," I reply, walking around to where he sits behind his desk.

Garreth pushes back, so I climb on his lap, straddling his legs and wrapping my arms around his shoulders. Then, I place my mouth to his and just breathe him in.

"Well, this is a fine hello," he mumbles before deepening the kiss.

When I finally come up for air, I reply, "You just looked stressed. I thought I'd kiss away your worries."

His eyes dance with happiness. "Well, you succeeded. I feel much better."

However, I can still see the worry lines around his eyes. "Do you want to talk about it?"

He shifts in his chair, adjusting me against his body. "Yes, but I can't. It's an employee matter, and I promised I wouldn't say anything."

"I understand," I agree immediately. "I would never ask you to break employee/employer confidence, but just so you know, I ran into Cameron in the parking lot and she told me everything."

He seems surprised by this, but doesn't say anything outright.

"I think what you're doing is an amazing thing for her, and I respect you even more now than I did as a boss before. I always knew you were an incredible man, but this just proves how remarkable you truly are."

He blushes an adorable shade of pink and tries to hide his face. When he looks back up at me, he says, "I keep expecting to feel regret, like I'm doubting I'm doing the right thing."

"You are," I insist, kissing his forehead and sliding my fingers into his hair. "I'm proud of you. I made her promise she'd call me if she needed anything."

He gives me a small grin. "That's because you're a remarkable woman too."

I lean forward and press my chest against him. "It sounds like we make a remarkable team," I reply.

"I agree, love."

"Have you told the guys yet?" I ask, knowing this entire ordeal is weighing on his mind.

"Numbers just left my office. We'll tell the others tomorrow. It's too big of an issue to wait until next Monday's meeting."

I nod, agreeing. "He wasn't mad, was he?"

He shakes his head. "Not at all. I thought maybe he would be, considering I was supposed to fire her, but when I told him everything, he just seemed to understand."

I give him a chaste kiss. "That's because they're all equally amazing. I had no doubt they'd react that way."

"Really?" he asks curiously.

"They all have their own crosses to bear too."

He holds me close, hugging me tight. "You're amazing, you know that?"

"I'm not, but you can keep saying that if you want," I retort.

"Deal." Garreth kisses me soundly once more before pulling away. "You should probably get out there. I'm sure everyone is waiting on you."

"Probably."

"Plans after you leave here?" he asks with hopeful eyes.

"Where would you like me to be?" I can feel the moisture gathering between my legs.

He flashes me a wolfish grin. "In my bed, screaming my name."

With another chaste kiss to his lips, I reply, "Deal," as I climb off his lap.

Glancing down, there's no missing his erection. "We'll take care of *that* later," he replies as he reaches into his pocket and pulls out his keys. He removes one and hands it over.

This seems like a big deal kinda moment.

He presses his lips against mine. "It is a big deal," he whispers, as if he could read my thoughts. "I'll see you at my place when I get off."

"I'll be there," I confirm, slipping the key into my pocket. "And then we'll get off together."

With a little extra swing to my hips, I walk to his door and pull it open. Looking over my shoulder, I find his eyes glued to my ass the entire time. He glances up and gives me a smile. "Yes, we most definitely will be."

As soon as I step out into the hallway, I meet Lyndee, who's rounding the corner, as if coming from the kitchen. "Hey, we were wondering if you were coming."

I feel my face flush as I recall our plan for later this evening. "Yep, sorry. I had something I needed to run by Garreth."

She gives me a wicked smile. "Oh, I just bet you did."

I chuckle and roll my eyes. "And what were you doing back in the kitchen?"

"Stealing a kiss from my sexy husband," she confirms as we make our way to the table where the rest of the ladies are sitting.

"Where's Madelyn?" I ask when I take a seat beside BJ.

"She wasn't feeling well. She covered that festival thing at the preschool for the paper over the weekend, and says she thinks she caught a little cold from one of the kids. She opted to stay home," BJ replies, sipping a beer.

"Hey, Reagan," Max greets, setting a napkin down in front of me. "What can I get you?"

I open my mouth, ready to order a beer, but my stomach gets a little queasy for the second time today. "Uh, I think I'll just have a water with lemon right now."

All eyes are on me, but I just shrug off the question. "I haven't been drinking as much as I should lately. I think my body is telling me to hydrate," I respond.

"I get like that, especially in the summer," BJ says. "When I'm a work, I forget to drink. Amanda has to force me to take breaks between clients."

He sets down the glass in front of me, and I practically chug half the contents. "Sheesh, I guess you were thirsty," he says with a laugh. "I'll just bring a pitcher over for you," he adds with a wink.

Movement catches out of the corner of my eye as I see Garreth enter the bar. His dark brown gaze instantly finds me, those eyes penetrating every part of my being.

"You two are so cute," Lyndee says quietly.

I can't help but smile. We've been seeing each other for almost five weeks now, spending as much time together outside of work and trying to hide our attraction to each other inside of it, but I also can't help but remember what Cameron said earlier. How she's seen the way he looks at me. If she's seen this, does that mean everyone else has too?

I may have to ask Garreth what he thinks later when he gets home.

Until then, I'm not going to worry about it. I'll just sit here with some of my friends, enjoy a little food and their company, and steal glances of him while he's working. No one will know I plan to devour him later tonight like a Fudge Pop.

Easy peasy.

I just make it out of the bathroom when I hear the door open and close.

Dammit, he's home already.

Well, at least I was able to brush my teeth first.

Garreth appears in the living room, his eyes devouring me from head to toe. Suddenly, his fiery eyes transform to ones of concern. "What's wrong? You're pale and...are you sick?"

I wave off his concern. "I probably got what Madelyn has. I've been feeling a little off today, but I'm fine now."

"Did you get sick?" he asks, putting the back of his hand on my forehead.

I shrug, not really interested in talking about puking with the guy I've been seeing.

"Come on, love," he whispers, pulling me into his arms and leading me to his bedroom. "Get into bed."

I do as instructed, climbing under the covers and reveling in the cool sheets against my flushed skin.

"I'm going to get you a glass of water. Do you want anything else?"

"No, I'm good," I reply through a yawn.

Garreth snickers and places a kiss on my forehead. "You don't feel feverish, which is good. Maybe it's something you ate."

"Probably," I reply, my eyes already drawing closed. Why am I so exhausted all of a sudden? Oh yeah, probably because you just threw up everything you had in your stomach in a violent fashion.

"Rest, love. I'll leave some Tylenol and water on the nightstand before I jump in the shower." He runs his fingers across my cheek, sliding them into my hair.

I sigh and turn my head into his touch. "I was really looking forward to licking you tonight," I grumble.

"Well, as fun as that sounds, we'll wait a bit until you're feeling better."

"'Kay."

He bends down again and brushes his lips across my cheek. "Rest. I'll be back in just a bit."

I don't reply. I can't. Sleep is already claiming me.

I'm just sliding from bed when I hear the front door shut. I tiptoe down the short hall and find Garreth standing in his living room, dressed for the day. "Hey," he says with a smile as soon as he sees me. "How are you feeling?"

"Much better," I announce, stretching my arms over my head. "How long did I sleep?"

"A while. It's almost ten o'clock," he states, coming over to place a kiss on my forehead.

"Ten? Seriously? I haven't slept this late since I was younger."

"Well, your body was needing the rest," he replies, heading into the kitchen with the bag in his hand.

"What's that?" I ask, the sudden aroma hitting my nose. "It smells like heaven."

"You must be feeling better then," he says, pulling the container out of the bag. "It's my mom's chicken noodle soup."

"Your mom brought you soup?"

He meets my gaze. "No, my mom brought you soup."

"Me?" I croak out over a sudden Sahara dry throat.

"Yes, Reagan. She called this morning and was going to stop by for a visit on her way to the market. I told her today wasn't a good time, since you weren't feeling well. She showed up an hour later with this." He holds up the container.

"So, wow. Your mom…she knows about…us?"

"She does now," he says, pulling a spoon out of the drawer and pointing to the table.

When I sit down, he places the still-steaming bowl of soup in front of me, my stomach growling angrily the moment I catch another whiff. "Oh my God, that smells like heaven."

"That's a good sign. Your appetite has returned," he says, retrieving a bottle of water from the fridge and placing it in front of me. "It must have been a quick bug."

"Thank God. I hate being sick," I reply, tasting the soup for the first time. "Jesus, this is good." I slurp up another spoonful. "What are we going to do about your mom?"

He gives me a big smile. "She used to make that soup for me all the time when I was little and not feeling well. She always said it had magical powers. And to answer your other question, we're not going to do anything until we're ready. She knows you're here. She knows we're seeing each other. She's anxious to officially meet you, but says she'll wait until we're ready. In reality, we've probably got about two, three days tops." He flashes me a knowing smile.

"Okay, well I'm happy to meet your parents," I state easily, inhaling the delicious chicken broth like it's prime rib. "But today probably isn't the best day. What are your plans?" I ask after chewing a piece of carrot.

"I have nothing planned for today. How about you hang out here with me? We can relax."

I nod in agreement. "I have to work at four."

"Are you sure you should be going in?" he asks, taking the empty seat across from me.

"I'm sure. I feel great today."

"If you're sure, but you have to promise me you'll tell me if you're not well again. I can go in and hostess for you tonight and let you rest."

I give him a warm smile, one filled with the love I feel but am too scared to actually say yet. "I'm fine. Promise."

"Good. Now, eat up. There's a chick flick marathon on TV calling our names."

Garreth

It's my day off, but I have to go in. Numbers just called and said the owners are all there, and now is a good time to have a quick meeting to discuss the Cameron issue.

"I'm going to run home and get ready for work anyway," Reagan replies. "You need to go in."

"I know, but I wanted this last hour with you," I grumble, pulling her into my chest and kissing her cheek.

She chuckles, throwing her arms around my neck. "I was going to have to leave soon anyway to get ready."

"You know, you could just leave some clothes here. This way, you don't have to run home to get ready for work or remember to bring a bag over at night," I suggest, waiting for her response. I've been thinking about it for a while now, how much I'd love to have her stuff mixed in with mine. I also knew we hadn't been dating very long, and even though we were both on the same page, I didn't want to rush it and freak her out.

"Hmm," she purrs, meeting my gaze. "I might be able to do that."

A smile spreads across my lips. "No rush, but if you want me to go over to your place while you're at work and get some of your stuff, just say the word."

She giggles the sweetest sound. "I was thinking maybe this weekend."

I can't but feel a little disappointed, but I push it away. The fact she's agreeing to bring some stuff over here this weekend is still a pretty big declaration, and I can live with that. "I'll say goodbye before I leave the restaurant," I tell her, giving her one last kiss before I go.

"Oh, I have your key," she says, turning to grab her bag.

"Keep it. It's yours."

I place a too-short kiss on her stunned lips and swat her on the ass to pull her out of her stunned state. "See you soon."

"Bye," she squeaks out as I shut the door.

I smile the entire way to work.

I slip in the back entrance, dressed casually in a pair of jeans and an old tee. I know the guys won't care, considering I'm not on the clock. I take the steps two at a time until I reach Numbers' office on the second floor. Jasper and Walker are already there, sitting in the two seats across from the desk, so I move to stand beside Isaac.

"Jameson should be here any minute," Isaac confirms, handing me a bottle of water from the small fridge he keeps beside his desk.

"We can start without him," Jasper grumbles, crossing his arms over his chest. Clearly, he's running low on patience today.

"Whatever it is has to be big, to call us in here on a Wednesday afternoon, so don't get your panties in a bunch," Walker counters, kicking his boot-covered foot up on his opposite knee.

Jasper responds by flipping him off.

I hear heavy boots on the stairs, letting us know the fourth owner has arrived. "Sorry I'm late. The last shipment of the day was late," he announces, stepping inside and closing the door behind him. He leans against the back of it and crosses his arms over his chest.

"Garreth and I thought it was best to have this meeting today instead of waiting until Monday," Numbers starts. "I think you're all aware we were short a couple of nights in the restaurant."

I watch as Walker and Jasper both sit up a little straighter in their chair, while Jameson pushes off the door and stands directly between them.

"We recall," Walker says.

Numbers looks over at me and nods, letting me take the reins and tell them the rest of the details. No one says a word as I outline what Isaac found out and how he narrowed it down to Cameron. I share every part of the conversation I had with her, including how I felt hearing her reasoning.

"Wrong or right, what's done is done," I conclude, waiting them out while they process.

It's Jasper who speaks first. "So, she steals from us and...we keep her on?" he asks, the annoyance evident in his question.

"Yes," I reply. "I really feel like she felt trapped. You should have seen the agony in her eyes, man. She was miserable."

"I don't understand why she wouldn't just come to us for help," he says.

It's Jameson who replies and has the biggest impact on the discussion. "You'll do just about anything to survive when you're alone."

We all turn our attention to him. His hands are shoved in his pockets and his eyes are cast down. I know he had a rough childhood. I'd heard all the rumors back in the day, especially when we were in high school. His mom was a shitty provider, leaving him to take care of his sister, BJ.

Suddenly, I respect the hell out of this man even more than before.

"I hear ya," Walker agrees, turning to Jasper. "It wasn't that long ago you made a pretty big mistake where Lyndee was concerned." I can feel the anger spreading through Jasper's body like an ocean wave, and apparently, Walker can too. He quickly continues, "But you righted that wrong, man. We all make mistakes. It sounds like Cameron realized hers and came clean immediately, and it's not like she was doing it for fun. If Garreth says she can be trusted to make this right, then I trust him."

"Is this guy going to keep fucking with her?" Jameson asks, staring straight at me.

"He shouldn't. I gave her the money. She's going to completely pay him off tomorrow and be done with it. I want that debt wiped clean now."

"I agree," Jameson says. "What time does he stop by? I'll be there, just to make sure it goes well, and he knows not to come back."

"I'll find out and let you know," I reply, earning a nod in return.

Jasper's gaze turns to me, pinning me hard with his intense stare. "Now she owes you."

"She does, and she's agreed to make smaller, manageable payments. That's after she repays the one-forty she owes to you guys."

Everyone is quiet for a few minutes, as if running through everything in their own minds.

Jasper looks up. "You're sure?"

I nod immediately. "Yeah. She's a good kid, just needs help getting back on track."

"I agree with him. I think cutting her lose and throwing her to the wolves, so to speak, would be bad. Who knows what this Johnny Cats guy would do," Numbers says, speaking up for the first time since I laid the situation out for them.

Jameson nods. "I agree."

"Me too," Walker chimes in.

All eyes look at Jasper. He takes a deep breath. "Well, I do agree everyone deserves a second chance, so I'm willing to give it to her. But if she fucks up again and takes money, she's gone."

"I agree with you, but I don't think she'll do it again," I answer as they all start to stand up.

It's Walker that turns first and asks, "What about her utilities? You said she took the money for part of the rent and food."

I shrug. "I assume they're already shut off," I reply.

He closes his eyes and swallows hard. When he opens them, there's a plethora of emotion running through them. "When I met Mal, she was barely hanging on. Sleeping on her couch because she didn't have a bed. Doing everything she could for Lou so she didn't know how hard she was really struggling," he says, swallowing hard. "If Cameron needs help, let's help her."

A ball of emotion gets lodged in my throat, making it hard to breathe, let alone speak, so I just nod.

"Tell us what she needs." This from Jameson.

Clearing my throat, I say, "I'll ask Reagan. Cameron confided in her yesterday."

They all nod before eventually walking out of the office, their descent all but silent.

"You're a good man, Garreth Taylor," Numbers states, slapping me on the shoulder and giving it a squeeze.

"Just doing what anyone would do," I reply, even though I know that's probably not true.

"No, you're wrong. You did what was right, not what should have been done. You're a hell of a manager and an even better man. We're lucky to have you."

I nod in appreciation and take my leave, desperately needing a little fresh air. Before I go, however, I head for the restaurant to see Reagan as promised. I find her standing at the hostess stand, cleaning menus and prepping for the dinner rush. She looks up, as if sensing my gaze, and gives me a small, private smile.

"Hello, Garreth," she whispers politely.

"Hi, Miss Turner. How was your day?"

"It was okay," she replies with a shrug, a playful gleam filling those gorgeous hazel eyes.

"Just okay, huh?" I ask, glancing around to make sure no one is nearby. Leaning in, I whisper, "You'll pay for that later."

She flashes me a wide, knowing grin. "I'm counting on it."

I reply with my own smile and take a step back. "Back door will be unlocked."

"Well, if not, I do have a key."

I have to shove my hands in my pockets to keep from reaching out for her. "You do, indeed. See you later."

"Bye," she sings, throwing me a wink before returning her attention on her task.

Spotting Cameron at the servers' station, I stop by and say hello. When I see she's alone, I let her know of the meeting and the fact everyone agreed to let her stay. She tears up, but blinks rapidly to keep them at bay. "Thank you, Garreth. From the bottom of my heart. I know turning me into the cops was probably the easiest and safest decision, but you didn't, and I won't ever forget that."

"Let me know what time he's supposed to pick up the money tomorrow. Jameson will stop by and just make sure it goes okay."

She visibly swallows and nods. "Thank you." The words are barely audible.

"We're a family here, Cameron. You're part of that. Just promise you'll let me or even Reagan know if something ever happens again, okay?"

She nods, looking over my shoulder. "You know, I think Reagan likes you. She keeps staring at your backside."

I snicker a laugh. "Yeah? She can't help it. It's such a nice ass."

Cameron laughs outright, and I have to admit, it's been a while since I've heard it. That makes me feel a fresh wave of guilt for not realizing she was in trouble. "You should ask her out."

I look back, confirming the woman I love is watching me. Then, I turn back to Cameron and reply, "You know, I just might do that."

"Mom? Dad?" I holler, stepping into the house I grew up in and finding it silent. I move through the living room and to the kitchen, spotting them sitting on their back patio. "You hiding from me?" I ask when I step outside, closing the door tightly behind me.

"Hey," Mom greets, standing up to accept a kiss on the cheek.

"Son," my dad says, holding up a beer. "There's more in the fridge."

"No, I'm okay. On my way home, and I can't stay long," I state, dropping down into one of the padded chairs. "How was dinner?"

"Well, your mom cooked, so it was edible," Dad quips with a wink.

"There're some leftovers in the fridge if you want some. I just put them in there a few minutes ago. I bet they're still warm," Mom offers, ready to jump up and run inside to fix me a plate.

"No, I'm good. I'm gonna grab a bite to eat when Reagan gets off work."

My mom smiles so wide, you could probably see it from the International Space Station. "How is she feeling?" she asks, practically chomping at the bit for details.

"She's better. Just a quick bug, it sounds like."

"Good," she replies with a nod.

"She loved your soup."

"I'm glad." She stares at me, expectantly, which is why I just sit there for a few long seconds. Finally, the silence gets to her. "So?

When did that happen? How long have you been seeing her? When can we officially meet her?"

Dad starts laughing and checks his watch. "Two minutes four seconds. Must be a record."

She narrows her eyes, but there's no heat behind her gaze. "Hush, you. I can't help it I'm excited for my son to date a lovely woman. And the first one since he moved home four years ago, I might add."

I was waiting for that.

"Anyway, tell me all the things," she insists, leaning forward as to not miss a single one.

"Well, we've been seeing each other for a few weeks now." I leave off the part about already sleeping with her when they were at the restaurant a few weeks back. "We're taking it slow because of work"—lies—"and you can officially meet her soon." I glance down at my hand, the one that used to wear a silver band around the ring finger, and realize for the first time since I took that ring off, I might be ready for another one.

Too soon?

Yep.

I know it, but that doesn't stop me from feeling at peace with the prospect of someday marrying her. She's that fucking amazing, and I'd be an idiot not to see it. Like Justin and the other douchebags before. They didn't value the gift they truly had.

"I can't wait to meet her. She seems great, and anyone who can put that smile back on your face is a winner in my book," Mom says, grinning from ear to ear.

"Well, I really like her." It feels good to say those words.

"Proud of you, son. I know it wasn't easy after you and Shelby divorced, and then to move back home after more than a decade away. You've made a great life for yourself here, and if you share that with Reagan, you'll be a rich man for sure."

"Don't get ahead of yourself there, old man. No one said anything about sharing my life with someone," I counter, wanting to argue with myself immediately, considering I just asked her to bring some clothes and personal items over.

Dad gives me a knowing look. "Didn't you?" He's always had a way of seeing past the bullshit and to my heart. Dad and I have always been close, even when I was living in Cleveland.

"All right, if I promise to set up lunch or something soon, will you get off my ass?"

"Yes," they both reply at the same time.

"I won't even start on you about grandbabies yet," she sasses, sipping something fruity from her glass.

I roll my eyes dramatically as my phone rings. Fishing it from my pocket, I see Numbers' name on the screen. "Hello?" I answer, stepping away from my parents.

"Garreth, I want you to listen to me and not freak out. You hear me?"

My heart starts to pound. "Yeah."

"Good. Reagan started to not feel well tonight. She excused herself to go to the restroom, and when she didn't come back, Cameron found her passed out on the floor. We called an ambulance, and they should be here in a few minutes, even though she begged us not to."

"She's..." I can't even get words out.

"She's awake and insisting she's fine, but clearly not well. Cameron said she was pale before she went to the bathroom and seemed short of breath. She's got a little color in her cheeks again, but we're making her sit in a chair in the break room. We're not sure if she hit her head or not."

"I'm on my way," I state, already heading for the side of the house. "If the ambulance leaves before I get there, call me and I'll meet it at the hospital."

"Okay. Drive safely. I really think she's okay, but it's best to get checked out," he says.

"Thanks, man," I reply as I disconnect the phone. I quickly turn to my parents and say, "Reagan just passed out at work, so they called an ambulance. I've got to go."

"Keep us posted," my mom hollers as I wave goodbye and take off at a jog to my truck.

I jump into the cab, forget about fastening my seat belt, and throw it in reverse. I have to literally tell myself to keep it together and not to speed more than just a few miles over the twenty-five miles per hour in town, but fuck, it's hard. I just want to get there, to see with my own eyes that she's all right.

To hold her and tell her the things I should have told her before.

Fuck it if it's too soon. I don't give a shit.

I love her.

Period.

And dammit, I'm going to tell her before it's too late.

Reagan

I don't remember much of what happened. One minute, I was trying to get to the bathroom, the contents of my stomach about to make an appearance, and the next, I was on the floor.

"I really don't need an ambulance," I maintain for the third time—or is it the fourth? Either way, my insistence falls on deaf ears.

Numbers ignores me, so I turn pleading eyes to Jameson. If anyone can be reasoned with, it's him.

He walks over and crouches down in front of me. "How ya feeling?"

"Fine." Lies. My stomach is still churning, and I think I have a bump on the back of my head from the fall.

He gives me a small, knowing grin. "I'm sure you are, but it would make a lot of us feel better if you went and got checked out."

"Fine, I'll get checked out. Just let me drive over there."

He pins me with a look.

"Okay, so you can drive me."

Jameson sighs and takes my hand in a rare show of affection, giving it a squeeze. "Your cousin would have me by the balls if I didn't just have you ride in the ambulance, and I'm particularly fond of them."

I sigh, because I know this is a losing battle. "I just," I start, glancing around at the people hovering nearby in the break room, "I hate everyone being in here, watching. It makes me feel like I did something wrong."

"Well, not wrong, but you did pass out, and there has to be a reason for it. That's why we want you to go in the ambulance. If something happens to you en route, you'll be with people who can help, and there's a lot of people who care a great deal for you, so best not to argue with us anymore and just go along with it. If you do, I'll buy you an ice cream."

A bubble of laughter spills from my lips. Of course, it makes my head hurt a little, but it still feels good to smile. "Ice cream?"

He shrugs. "Works on Rorik, so I thought I'd take a chance," he answers, referring to his nephew.

I hear the sound of the ambulance approaching, and all I can think about is the attention it's going to bring.

"Don't worry, Reagan. Jasper went out front to direct them to the back. No one will see you," Jameson states, very calm and collected, as usual.

I nod and look around once more, wishing Garreth were here. Not that he could really do anything, but just having him nearby would be comforting.

"Hi, Reagan," Ellen greets. She's the first EMT to walk in, her partner right behind her.

"Hey, Ellen."

"What's going on?" she asks, squatting in front of me and starting her assessment.

I run through what happened, about not feeling well and excusing myself to use the restroom. Numbers jumps in and adds the part about Cameron finding me on the floor unconscious.

"How have you been feeling leading up to this episode?" she asks, slipping a blood pressure cuff on my arm.

"Last night I didn't feel so hot and threw up, but this morning I woke and felt fine."

"Okay, we'll take a few stats and get you checked out. When you fell, did you hit your head?" she asks, writing something down on a clipboard.

"I think so. There's a sore spot on the back of my head," I confirm.

She stands and checks. "You didn't break the skin, which is good, but there's a goose egg. I definitely think you should get checked out. The possibility of a head injury is worthy of concern. Do you have someone you want to ride with you?"

I look around, again, wishing Garreth were here. "I'll go," Jameson says, stepping forward. "I'm her cousin." He flashes me an easy smile and a wink. No one refutes the fact he's actually married to my cousin, not mine by blood. I'm just grateful I'll have someone along for the ride.

Ellen asks me a few more questions, and then they load me onto a stretcher. I hate this. I hate having people stand around, watching me, their concerned eyes filled with worry.

As we start to move, I turn to Numbers and say, "I'll be back as soon as I can."

He gives me an incredulous look, as if he can't believe what I just said. "You'll be back when you're good and rested. Don't worry about this place. We've got it covered."

They wheel me down the hall, where Jasper waits to open the door. Then, I'm outside and taken toward the waiting ambulance. As soon as I'm loaded, Ellen starts to hook me up to monitors and runs an IV. Jameson slips inside, his large body filling the small space for a passenger. If this whole ordeal wasn't so unbelievable, I'd laugh at him, but my head feels a little foggy, so I think I'll just close my eyes for a bit.

"Reagan? Stay awake, okay?"

I open my eyes as the driver shuts the ambulance doors.

"We'll be there in a few minutes, and once the doctor checks you over, you'll get to rest, okay?" Ellen says with a polite smile.

I nod, resolved to sit back and do as I'm told. I still wish I would have been able to drive myself—or have someone drive me— to the clinic, but there's no point in arguing. If the shoe were on the other foot, I'd probably do the same thing. If it were Madelyn who was passed out on the floor, you're damn certain I'd make her go get checked out.

"I'm ready, Greg," Ellen announces to the other EMT, who gets behind the wheel.

Just as we get ready to pull away, there's a loud bang on the door.

"Hold up!" Ellen hollers, stepping to the back door and turning the latch.

A man jumps in. The most amazingly beautiful man I've ever seen, and suddenly, the wave of emotions is too much to bear. I feel the first tears slide down my cheeks as I watch Jameson try to slide past him at the door.

"I'll grab your truck and meet you there."

"Keys are inside," Garreth says, but he's not looking at his boss.

His dark eyes are on me.

Relief washes over me like spring rain, and the tears come down as softly.

He takes the small seat Jameson occupied and reaches for my hand, careful not to jar the IV they just inserted. He brings it to his mouth and presses his lips to my knuckles, leaving them there for several seconds as he closes his eyes. I can feel the same relief I felt moments ago ebbing from his body as he continues to touch me.

"Reagan, we're almost there. As soon as we arrive, Garreth, I'm going to ask you to get out first and step back so we can remove Reagan from the bus. You can follow behind as we proceed into the hospital, but stay back while we move her into a room and give the report," Ellen says, looking over to Garreth.

Ellen has lived in Stewart Grove her whole life, so it doesn't surprise me she calls us both by first names. I remember her coming to the grade school when I was little, showing us all how to take care of minor wounds and discussed when to call 9-1-1 through a partnership program between the school and hospital. There probably aren't many people she doesn't know or cared for at one time or another.

The moment the ambulance stops, Garreth leans over and kisses my forehead before jumping out when the doors open. Everything after that happens so fast, I barely have time to process it. I'm taken into a room and transferred to a bed in the emergency department.

"Good evening, Reagan. I'm Dr. Andrews. Can you tell me what happened?" he asks, taking a seat on a stool and sliding over to my bedside. When I finish recounting the evening, he nods and stands. "Okay. We're gonna do a blood draw and run labs, as well as send you down for a CT scan to make sure that bump on your head isn't causing any problems. I don't necessarily think there's an issue, but we'd always like to be on the proactive side of head injuries. Do you have any questions?"

I shake my head, slightly overwhelmed with the turn of events for the evening. One minute I'm seating patrons at the restaurant, and the next I'm being taken to X-ray for a CT scan.

"Hang tight," he says, standing up and patting my leg. "The lab and X-ray will be here shortly."

"Thank you, doctor," Garreth says, waiting until the physician leaves the room before taking his stool and wheeling himself to where I sit. "Worst phone call ever, love," he whispers, lacing his fingers with mine and resting our joined hands on my lap.

"I'm sorry. I really thought I was fine. Like now, I don't feel bad, other than the bump on the back of my head throbbing."

He stands up and leans over my head, carefully examining the lump with a gentle hand. When he sits back down, I can see the tightness in his mouth and the worry in his eyes. "There's no need to apologize. I'm just glad you're getting checked out."

Before I can reply, there's a knock at the door and a younger man walks in. "Good evening, Miss Turner. I'm Brodie, and I'll be taking some blood."

My stomach clenches, but not like before. "I'm not a fan of this," I confess as he sets down his kit of supplies beside my leg.

"Not a problem. I'll make it quick, and if you start to feel woozy, let me know."

"Look at me, love," Garreth instructs, taking my arm without the IV and drawing my attention away from what's about to transpire. It's not that blood draws are painful or anything, but I've always preferred to keep my blood inside my body. I don't like seeing it on the outside.

"Let's talk about this weekend," he says, bringing my hand to his mouth. "My parents want to meet you officially. What do you say we plan lunch sometime in the coming weeks. We can even invite your parents if you want."

My eyes widen, and suddenly, I'm not paying any attention to what Brodie is doing to my arm. "Really? That's…huge."

"Thank you," he boasts, smiling widely and making me laugh.

"You're incorrigible."

"I am, but only for you. And to answer your question, yes, really. I want to spend all my free time with you. We discussed you bringing a few personal things over to my house, so I think it's only logical we meet the parents."

I don't even realize I'm grinning until he returns the gesture. "Okay." It just seems so simple. When has any relationship I've ever been in ever felt this way?

Never.

"All done, Miss Turner. I'll get this to the lab, and we'll get your results back soon," Brodie says, drawing my attention.

I glance down, not even realizing he was drawing blood at all. "Thank you," I reply to the younger man before he walks out the door.

It's only a few seconds later when there's another knock. "I'm Aleah, and I'm going to take you down for your CT scan," she says politely, walking over to disconnect any machines I'm attached to. "You can stay here in this room. I'll have her back once the scan is complete," she adds, this time speaking to Garreth.

He comes over and kisses my lips, resting his forehead against mine. "I'll be right here."

I nod, my throat suddenly too thick to speak.

The next thirty minutes go by fairly quickly, as I'm taken to X-ray for the scan of my head. When I'm brought back to my room, I find Garreth standing off to the side with Jameson. The moment Garreth sees me, he smiles and walks over to greet me with a kiss.

"The doctor should be in shortly with the results," Aleah announces, locking my wheels on the bed and exiting the room.

"Hey," he says, taking my hand.

"Madelyn sends her love," Jameson states, setting my purse down on a chair. "I brought this."

"Thanks," I reply, not even realizing I didn't have it until now.

"I'm not going to stay. Walker is in the parking lot, gonna run me back to my car," he says, coming over and kissing me on the forehead. "Message us and let us know what's going on, please?" He turns to Garreth and adds, "Oh, and don't worry about working for me tomorrow. Take care of Reagan."

I nod, moved by the kindness and emotion in his eyes. "I will. Tell Madelyn not to worry. I'm sure everything is fine," I insist.

He snorts. "Right. She won't rest until she hears from you," he replies, and I know he's probably right. I'd be the same if the roles were reversed.

When we're left alone, Garreth brings a chair over and takes my hands again. "How are you feeling?"

"Okay, really. I feel a little silly for being here, for worrying everyone, for making a scene at the restaurant. I'm sure that's not the PR you guys want for the business," I reply, unable to swipe the hair off my forehead because he's holding my hand.

He lifts our joined hands and does it for me, as if knowing exactly what I was thinking. "Stop. You can't help if you're sick, Reagan, and the business is fine. No one cares how this could possibly make Burgers and Brew look. Everyone—and I do mean everyone—is only concerned about you," he says, bringing our joined hands to his lips and kissing my knuckles.

We sit together, waiting for the doctor, which fortunately, only takes about another fifteen minutes. "Okay, Reagan, we have some test results I wanted to discuss with you. Can we talk in front of your friend, or would you like to do this privately?" he asks, taking the stool beside my bed once more.

Nervousness seems to sweep through my entire body, and I think Garreth can feel it. He holds my hand a little tighter.

"Well, the results of your CT scan came back normal. You'll have a bump for a few days, and it'll probably be tender, but there are no signs of bleeding or swelling. There were two red flags in your lab work, however. The first one is your iron levels are extremely low. It would definitely account for some of your symptoms. The fatigue, shortness of breath, pale skin your friend noted. I think it's safe to say you're anemic, which is treatable and manageable."

He looks up from the paper in his hand and continues, "The other test result will also contribute to your symptoms, including nausea and vomiting. It appears you're pregnant."

What?

My brain tries to process the information, but it keeps focusing on one word.

Pregnant.

"I'm guessing by the look on your face, you were not aware. I'd say you're pretty early, between six and seven weeks. When was the first day of your last period?"

I clear my throat and rack my brain for an answer. When I look back at the last couple of months, the date I come up with is a little shocking. "July, around the 30th, I think."

He nods. "That would be about right. I'm going to prescribe you some prenatal vitamins, and I'd like you to start an iron-rich diet. Leafy greens, fresh vegetables and fruits, especially ones high in Vitamin C. Call your OB-GYN and make an appointment. I can send over the lab work so they're prepared to monitor it. I'm hoping between the vitamins and the diet additions, you won't have to take additional iron supplements, but that'll be up to your provider. Do you have any questions?"

I shake my head, still trying to wrap it around tonight's development.

"You, sir?"

Garreth clears his throat. "Uh, no. Thank you, Doctor."

The older man gives me a small smile and stands. "Okay, I'll get your discharge papers ready. A nurse will be in shortly to remove the IV and go over everything. If at any time the symptoms get worse, please come back to the ER."

"We will," Garreth answers for me.

The physician exits the room, but I have a hard time seeing him through the tears welling in my eyes. I turn to look at Garreth, prepared to see panic or maybe even anger, but all I see is understanding and maybe a touch of excitement.

"Garreth, I..." I start but can't seem to find the right words.

"Shh, shh, shh," he replies, sitting on the edge of my bed and pulling me into his side. "We'll talk when we get home, okay?"

I nod, sniffling, because those pesky tears decided to fall despite me trying to keep them at bay.

The nurse comes in a few minutes later. "Let's get this IV out of you, so you can be on your way, shall we?" she asks politely, flashing me a quick smile. I'm not sure I return the gesture, though. I think I'm still in a state of shock.

"These are your discharge papers, and we had the hospital pharmacy fill a thirty-day prescription for a prenatal vitamin," she states, handing over the bottle. "This is a list of things to watch for over the next few days in regards to the iron deficiency, as well as the head injury, and if you have two or more of these symptoms, please return to the ER. Make sure you schedule an appointment with your OB-GYN, and tell them about your ER visit. You should be seen within the next five days. They can find the lab results on the hospital portal. Any questions?"

"No," I reply numbly, ready to get out of here.

She hands over the clipboard for me to sign and gives me a stack of papers. "Have a good evening," she says, and then she's gone, leaving just Garreth and me in my room.

Our gazes meet once more as he reaches for my hand to help me stand. "Come on, love. Let's go home."

Twenty-Two

Garreth

Pregnant.

I'm in a state of complete...elation.

Reagan's pregnant. With my baby.

Our baby.

We exit the ER on our own two feet—much better than how we arrived, I might add—and head for my truck. I pull open the door and spin around, grabbing her hips and gently lifting. She squeals in shock, placing her hands on my shoulders for stability, as I turn and deposit her on the passenger seat.

"I can get into a truck by myself," she sasses, that hint of defiance I love about her starting to show.

I paste on a bright, cocky smile. "I'm sure you can, but why do it alone when I can help you?"

She rolls her eyes and reaches for her seat belt. I almost comment about keeping precious cargo safe but think better of it. Reagan's definitely a little—okay, a lot—shocked by the news. I'm going to have to approach this slowly and carefully until the full weight of the information is absorbed.

When I climb into the cab, I start the truck to get the air going and reach for her purse. She doesn't say a word as she watches me pull her phone out. There are dozens of notifications on the screen, most likely from the wives of the owners and maybe her family, but it's not my place to check them. I hand over the phone and say, "You should probably call or text Madelyn. I'm sure she's going crazy with worry."

Her eyes go wide with panic.

"You don't have to tell her everything. Maybe just the part about being anemic. You can fill her in on the rest when you're ready," I suggest.

That seems to calm her a bit, as the wildness in those beautiful hazel orbs starts to subside. "You're right," she says, tapping away on her phone before bringing it to her ear.

I back out of the parking spot and drive toward the exit. Madelyn must be waiting by the phone, because she seems to pick up immediately.

"I'm okay," Reagan says softly, a smile evident in her voice. "We're leaving now." Pause. "I was diagnosed with anemia, which explains why I was pale, tired, and light-headed. I'll have to take a supplement for a while," she says, intentionally leaving out the other cause of her symptoms. She listens for a few seconds before answering, "I'm not sure." She looks my way. "Yes, he's right here." Another pause. "What? No, Madelyn," she argues before sighing deeply. "Uh, fine. You're such a pain in the ass. Hold on."

She looks down at her phone, hits the screen, and looks my way. "Madelyn is insisting she talk to you."

"Hey, Madelyn," I say, knowing the phone is already on speaker.

"Hi, Garreth. I'm so glad you're with Reagan. Are you staying with her tonight?"

"I am," I reply, turning onto my street. "I'm going to stop at my house and grab some clothes, and then take her back to her apartment so she can rest."

"And you won't leave her side?" she asks, her question laced with worry.

I turn and meet Reagan's gaze. "Not for one second."

She has no idea I'm talking about more than just for tonight. I'm in this for the long haul, even if a future with her isn't in the cards. I'm a father, which means I'm connected to her for the rest of my life.

But I'm not giving up on the idea of building a life with this woman. I'd want it even if we didn't just learn of her pregnancy.

"Thank you, Garreth. Reag, I'll stop by tomorrow around noon. How about I bring lunch? Maybe something from the deli," she offers, making Reagan smile.

"That sounds good."

"Okay, I'll let you go so you can get some rest. Call if you need anything."

"I will. I'm sorry I worried you," Reagan says.

"I'm just glad you're okay. See you tomorrow," she replies before signing off. Reagan sets the phone down on her lap and exhales deeply.

"She cares a lot about you," I say, even though it's not necessary.

"As I do her."

I park the truck. "Do you want to come in while I grab a change of clothes?"

She looks over at me before she shakes her head. "I think I'm just going to wait here."

I can tell she needs a few minutes of quiet to think. "Okay. I'll be quick," I tell her, releasing my seat belt, leaning over the console, and kissing her lips.

Somehow, I casually walk to my back door and pull out the spare key from under the mat. I still have to get another one made after I gave Reagan my key. I don't even flip on a light as I make my way through the kitchen, to the living room, and down the short hall to my bedroom. After retrieving an old duffle bag from my closet, I start tossing in clothes. At least two of everything, in case I stay two nights. Anything after that, I can make a quick trip home to get more.

I stop in the bathroom and grab my comb, toothbrush, and shower kit, even though I don't know I'll need it. With one quick look around the room, I flip off the lights and head back to where I left Reagan, locking the door and returning the key beneath the mat as I go.

Slipping inside the cab, I toss my bag in the back seat and give her a small grin. "Ready?"

She nods but doesn't say anything.

After fastening my belt, I throw the truck in reverse and reach for her hand. She gives it to me willingly, her slender fingers holding on to me tightly. We drive the rest of the way to her apartment in silence, but it doesn't feel uncomfortable. In fact, it feels…right. I know she's lost in her own thoughts right now, but the fact she's sitting here, hanging on to me like I'm her lifeline, goes a long way at soothing my nerves.

I park outside her apartment, grab my bag, and then escort her inside. We ride the elevator to her floor, her arms wrapped around my torso. The door opens, so I slip my arm around her shoulders, kiss her forehead, and lead her toward her apartment.

"Do you want anything?" she asks the moment we're inside and alone.

"Yes," I reply, setting my bag down on the couch and reaching for her.

She comes willingly, locking her hands behind my neck and rests her cheek against my shoulder.

"This. This is what I needed," I tell her, running my fingers into her hair. "Just you."

I feel her body start to shake, letting me know she's crying once more. "I'm so sorry," she mutters, gripping the back of my shirt as she holds on for dear life.

"Come on," I whisper, taking her hand and leading her to the bedroom. I kick off my shoes and help remove hers before pulling her onto the bed. We both lie on our sides, facing each other.

Reaching out, I swipe away the tears from her cheeks, hating to see them fall. "Now, let's talk. You said you're sorry, and I'm going to assume, since you've already apologized unnecessarily for the hospital visit, you're referring to the other news. Am I right?"

She nods and worries her bottom lip.

"So, here's the way I see it," I start, cupping her cheek with my hand. "You have absolutely nothing to be sorry about where that's concerned because I'm nothing but elated to find out you're pregnant. In fact, they might have to come up with a whole new word for the level of happiness I feel, Reagan."

I take a deep breath and slowly let it out. "I guess, I sort of became numb to the idea of ever becoming a dad. I always thought Shelby and I would have a kid, but the longer we were married, the less likely it seemed. We fought a lot, and it was never the right time. As the years went on, it just seemed like that dream of parenthood slipped away."

There's a sadness in her eyes as she listens, but the fact remains, I'm thirty-seven. If it was going to happen, I just assumed it would have happened by now.

"When that doctor said you were pregnant, my first thought wasn't that I was going to be a dad. It wasn't that I was *finally* living my dream. My first thought was this baby is going to have the best mom she could ever have, because despite protective measures, I get to watch you bring this baby into the world. *Our* baby, and *that* is the dream. Having this baby with you, watching your belly grow as she does, that's what I want. *You're* what I want, Reagan, so don't have any doubt in that pretty little head of yours that I'm not excited to take this next step in life with you. There's no one I want to walk beside but you."

More tears fall, and it guts me. I hate these fucking tears, but the moment she smiles, the worry just seems to fade away. "You keep saying she."

I shrug and use the pad of my thumb to brush wetness away. "It's a girl. I can feel it."

She chuckles and brings our hands to her mouth, kissing the back of my hand. "You're a romantic."

"Only with you, love. Only you."

"I'm really excited, even if this is a little soon."

I nod, my hand moving down to cover her flat stomach. "It is. But I think I've always been drawn to you, Reagan. From the first moment I saw you, I knew you were special. Who cares if we've only been seeing each other for a month or so? This is our story. We get to tell it."

She smiles widely. "Your mom is going to hate me," she states with an awkward laugh.

"False. My mom is going to love you, with or without a baby. Speaking of my mom, I need to send her a message and let her know you're okay." When she looks at me curiously, I add, "I was at their house when Numbers called."

"Oh. I'm sorry to cut your night with them short."

I pin her with a look. "Stop apologizing for something you didn't have control over," I insist, reaching into my pocket and pulling out my phone.

Then, something hits me...

"Shit."

"What?" she asks, concern filling my favorite pair of eyes.

"That first time. The night after Jasper and Lyndee's cookout. The condom, it was different. I remember it looked off. I was going to tell you, but then I walked out of the bathroom and—"

"And I was running my hands over myself," she says, finishing my thought and bringing that delectable image to the front of my mind.

"Yeah," I say, meeting her gaze. "You were touching your pussy and it was all I could do not to come right there like a teenager."

She giggles the sweetest sound. "That was a good night."

I pull her into my arms. "It was the best night, and if that's the one that gave us this little one, then it will forever be the best night of my life. It gave me you *and* her."

She presses her lips to mine for a quick kiss and snuggles into my arm. I tap out a message to my mom, letting her know Reagan is okay and I'll call her tomorrow. She responds right away with an okay.

Reaching over, I place my phone on the nightstand. "Do you have to call your family?"

Reagan yawns. "Yeah, I should. I don't think they've heard yet, but I'm sure they will soon. You know how gossip spreads in this town."

"Very true. Are you going to tell them about the baby?"

She looks up and holds my eye. "Yes. I thought about keeping it to ourselves for a little while, maybe until I'm out of the first trimester, but then I remembered this town has a way of finding things out, even when you try to bury them."

"If you don't want to tell, we don't have to. We can keep it just between you and me."

Her grin starts small, but spreads to cover her entire face. "I don't think I can. I'm really excited."

"Good." I place a chaste kiss on her lips. "Then, we'll tell your parents and mine soon."

"When will you tell the guys at work?" she asks through another yawn.

"Maybe Monday? Chances are they'll hear it before then, but Monday's meeting seems like the perfect time."

"Madelyn will probably tell Jameson," Reagan says.

"Probably," I confirm. "That man's like a vault though. If he knows, he won't blab it around the restaurant until we're ready."

She goes still in my arms. "What are we going to do about that?"

I turn her on her side and snuggle against her back. "Let's tackle that one another day. Deal?"

She yawns loudly, as she tries to cover her mouth with her hand. "Deal. We can talk about that tomorrow."

"Tomorrow, love," I confirm, holding her tight as she starts to drift off to sleep.

"Hello!" Mom hollers as she comes in the back door, Dad hot on her heels.

"Hey, guys," I state, heading over to take the pan from her hands. "I thought I told you not to bring anything."

She grins innocently. "Did you say that? I don't remember you saying that," she argues, practically pushing me aside and heading straight for Reagan. "Reagan, it's so lovely to see you again."

"Hello, Mrs. Taylor," Reagan replies, reaching out a hand.

"Oh, none of that," Mom states, waving off the hand and pulling my girl into a big hug. "And please, call me Lydia."

Reagan blushes. "Okay," she agrees easily. "Can I get you something to drink?"

"I'll just have water, but I can get it, dear. Do you like strawberries? I made a strawberry shortcake, hoping you'd like it," Mom says, pulling a bottle of water from the fridge.

"Did you make me cookies?" I ask, checking the pan and finding her strawberry cake concoction.

"Why would I make you cookies? You weren't the one not feeling well," Mom says, placing her hands on her hips and narrowing her eyes at me.

"Well… I had to take care of her while she was recouping," I argue. Even I can tell it's a weak defense.

Mom rolls her eyes. "Oh, please. You did nothing but probably hover over her and get in her way. It's the same thing you used to do to me when you were five."

I point my barbecue brush at her. "You're mean in your old age."

Mom gasps. "I'm not old! Darren, am I old?"

"Of course not, my love. If you're old that means I'm old, and I'm not old. I haven't even bought my midlife crisis convertible yet," Dad chimes in.

All I can do is shake my head at their antics. "I was adopted," I tell Reagan lightheartedly, making her giggle.

"You were not. I labored for three days to birth you. Four hours, I pushed and pushed."

"Okay, that's enough. You two can leave now," I tease, brushing the sweet sauce over the chicken breasts.

"Too late now. I'm talking to Reagan," Mom says, pulling her over to the table and sitting across from her. "You see the size of that head? It's hereditary, you know," she adds before sipping her water.

I go completely still.

Does she know?

We've been careful not to tell anyone since we found out Wednesday, but it's a small town and sometimes it just slips out. I mean, four whole days is a lifetime to keep a secret in a small town. I'm surprised it's not already posted on a billboard somewhere.

I meet Reagan's gaze, and I think we both realize it's time. The door doesn't open any wider than this. "You know, Mom, if you're going to talk about hereditary traits, maybe you could stick to the pleasant ones, like how good-looking I am or how smart? Those are the ones I'd like to focus on for the next nine months."

"That wasn't a complaint. Just stating a fact. Besides, I don't—" As if realization sets in, Mom's mouth falls open and no words are spoken.

"Huh, I think you rendered her speechless for the first time in her life," Dad quips with a chuckle.

I walk over and take Reagan's hand, bringing it to my lips. "Mom, Dad, not only did we discover Reagan's anemia this week, but we also found out about another thing we've got cookin'."

"Oh my God!" she proclaims, standing up and throwing her arms around Reagan. "A baby? You're having a baby?"

She nods eagerly as she's pulled into another fierce Lydia Taylor hug.

"I'm going to be a grandma," she says, her voice full of awe as her eyes fill with tears.

"I know it seems soon," Reagan starts, but is cut off by my mom once again.

"That doesn't matter. When you know, you know, am I right, Garreth?"

Smiling, I can't help but agree. "Right."

"Now, sit back down here and tell me everything. Don't leave a single detail out," Mom insists, hanging on Reagan's every word.

I stand back and watch, taking in the sight of the two most important women in my life, talking and carrying on like they've been friends forever.

Life doesn't get much better than this.

Reagan

"Grandma?" I ask, stepping through the front door of her gorgeous home.

"In the kitchen," she hollers from deep in the house.

I head in that direction and find her and Madelyn sitting at the kitchen island. "Good morning," I say, dropping my purse on the chair and moving to give them both a hug.

"Where's that strapping young man of yours?" Grandma asks.

"He had to go to work early," I reply, taking the seat beside them.

"I heard you two met your parents for breakfast this morning," she says, watching me closely over her coffee cup.

"We did."

"So, it's official? You two are dating, meeting the parents, and all that jazz?" Madelyn asks, her eyes dancing with excitement.

"It's all official," I confirm, unable to contain my smile.

"Excellent! Now, what about the other thing?" Grandma asks innocently.

The hairs on the back of my neck stand up as I gauge her question and the expected response. "You mean from last

Wednesday?" I ask, referring to passing out and going to the hospital.

She shrugs casually as she says, "Well, that, yes. But the *other* thing."

"What other thing?" Madelyn asks, her eyes volleying between mine and our grandma's.

My mouth falls open, because there's only one thing she can be referring to. The question is, how in the hell did she find out?

"Oh, don't look at me like that. A grandma knows these kinds of things," she replies, with a casual flip of her hand.

"What kind of things?" Madelyn asks, trying hard to stay caught up in the conversation.

I narrow my eyes at the older woman and shake my head. "I don't know how you know, but Garreth and I found out we're pregnant," I confirm.

Grandma, of course, gives me a big, knowing smile, while Madelyn whoops and throws her arms around my neck. "You're pregnant? Really?" she asks, practically vibrating off her seat.

"I am. We go to the doctor for the first time in a little bit."

"I'm so excited! I can't believe we're pregnant together. Our kids are going to be best friends," my cousin boasts eagerly. "You told your parents at breakfast? What did they say?"

I can't help but grin. "Mom cried, she was so happy. Dad seemed a little...surprised, but by the time our plates were clean, Garreth and he were discussing cars, so he was completely fine."

Madelyn looks over at Grandma and asks, "How did you know? Who did you hear it from?"

The older lady just gives us a smile. One that says she has a secret and she'll never tell. "Lucky guess."

"Come on, Grandma. How did you know?" I ask, extremely curious.

Finally, she reaches out and takes my hand, holding it tightly in hers. With her other hand, she cups my cheek, her eyes filled with unshed tears. "My sweet girl, you are glowing. My mother used to tell me there was this magical glow surrounding a woman when she was first pregnant. It's hard to see, but my mom used to say, if you look close enough, you'll witness the magic of motherhood right before your very eyes."

I don't know why my own eyes fill with moisture, but they do. "Thanks, Grandma. You're the best."

She sighs dramatically and replies, "I know."

We giggle, and suddenly Madelyn is being pulled into the hug. "I'm so blessed to have two amazing granddaughters, and now, two great-grandbabies on the way. I'm the luckiest Queenie alive."

"Queenie? I thought you were Grandma," Madelyn says.

Grandma shrugs. "Well, to you two, I am. But to these two angels, I need a name hipper than Great-Grandma. So, Queenie it is," she declares.

Madelyn just shakes her head. "All right, Queenie, what do you have for snack? Your great-grandbaby needs something sweet."

"Reagan," the nurse announces from the doorway, signaling my turn to see the doctor.

Garreth takes my hand, gently squeezing it, as he leads me toward the open door where the nurse waits. My nerves kick up a little as we step around the corner into an alcove.

"We'll start here," she says, pointing to the chair inside the small space. "Sir, I'll have you head down the hall to room four. Miss Turner will be down in just a couple of minutes."

Garreth releases my hand, and surprises me when he steps forward and kisses my forehead. "I'll see you in a few," he says before doing as instructed and heading to room number four.

"At the beginning of each appointment, we'll take your vitals and weight. Then, you'll take one of the plastic cups to the bathroom right across the hall for a urine sample." She goes over the steps for taking a clean sweep sample, as well as what to do with it when I'm finished. Once that's out of the way, she asks me to step on the scale and takes my blood pressure, pulse ox, and temperature. Finally, she says, "If you'll follow me, we'll head to your room now."

Slipping inside the room, I find Garreth sitting at a chair against the far wall. Once he sees me step inside, he jumps up and takes two steps toward me. "Everything okay?"

I nod as the nurse says, "Go ahead and have a seat on the table."

We take a few minutes to go over my medical history, as well as adding notes to my chart regarding my recent hospital visit. When I had called the OB's office on Thursday and explained what happened, they scheduled me for an appointment the following Monday. Those few days were the perfect amount of time to tell our immediate family about the pregnancy before someone saw us going into the office and started the phone tree chain to work its rumor-spreading magic.

"Okay, Dr. Ross will be in shortly," she says, pulling a paper gown out of a cabinet. "Please remove everything from the waist down. Gown opening can be in the back, and here's a sheet to cover your legs with."

"Thank you." As soon as she's out of the room, I get to work.

I've always hated this part about getting undressed at the gynecologist's office. You never know how much time you really have before the doctor comes knocking. I've been in the middle of undressing when they arrive for your exam. Other times, you wait fifteen or more minutes before the knock comes, so today, I'm not taking any chances.

Plus, I have a pair of eyes watching me intently from across the room.

I kick off my slip-on shoes and start shimmying out of my cutoff shorts.

"I didn't realize I was gonna get a show," he says, taking a seat and kicking back in the chair. When I pause, he waves his hand and adds, "Please continue."

I roll my eyes and snicker. "You're too much."

"You're referring to my penis again, aren't you?"

I can't stop the laughter that belts out from my mouth. I cover it quickly, hoping everyone in the building didn't just hear me, but I'm sure they did. "Stop it or you'll have to go sit in the car."

He sobers quickly. "I'll be good, I promise."

Noticing the slight bounce of his foot on the tile floor, I walk to where he sits, take the sides of his face in my hands, and plant a kiss on his lips. "I was just teasing."

"I know. You're standing in your underwear right now, and I can't touch you. I'd say you're doing a fine job of teasing me."

Rolling my eyes dramatically, I stand up, hook my fingers in my panties, and slide them down my legs.

"That's mean."

Shrugging, I scoop up my shorts and place them on the second empty chair, stuffing my panties inside them. Why I always do that, I'm not sure. I mean, the doctor is about to check my vajayjay, so it's not like I should be embarrassed about leaving my underwear sitting out for him to see. "You'll live," I sass, reaching for the paper gown and slipping it on. Once it's in place, I climb on top of the table and unfold the thin paper sheet.

"So, now what?" he asks, glancing around at the diagrams of male and female reproductive organs on the walls.

"Now, we wait for the doc. He usually runs on time, so hopefully, we won't have too long to sit here."

"He? What doctor are you seeing?"

"Ross. He's been my lady doctor since I was sixteen."

Garreth nods as a knock sounds at the door. "Well, hello, Reagan. It's lovely to see you on this gorgeous Monday," Dr. Ross greets, that familiar, friendly smile on his face.

"Hi, Dr. Ross."

"I see you've recently been to visit the Emergency Room," he says, taking a seat at the small desk and placing my open chart on the counter. "Tell me what led up to your hospital trip."

I run through everything, and when I get to the part about finding out I was pregnant, he smiles warmly.

"I'm guessing that wasn't the diagnosis you were expecting," he replies with a grin.

"Not at all," I state, glancing over at Garreth. "We have always used protection, but one might have broken or ripped."

"Unfortunately, that does occasionally happen." He looks over at Garreth. "I take it you're the father?"

"I am, sir. Garreth Taylor," he replies, reaching out his hand for the doctor to shake.

"Nice to meet you. Do you have anything to add regarding the incident last Wednesday?"

"No, sir. I wasn't there when it happened but was able to arrive right before the ambulance left. I can confirm she was horribly pale, especially her lips and under her lower eyelids."

Dr. Ross nods. "Okay, this is what I'd like to do. Let's order another blood draw to check your iron levels. If they remain low, we'll start an iron supplement daily, in addition to the prenatal vitamin you're on. If it's leveled out, then we won't add it. Sound good?"

I nod.

"Great," he says, pushing the chart aside and turning to give me his full attention. "Now, do you want to see your baby?"

Again, I move my head up and down, suddenly unable to form words.

He pulls out the stirrups and asks me to lie back, placing my feet in the uncomfortable metal contraption. Garreth moves to my head and reaches for my hand. "I'm going to do an external ultrasound, as well as a vaginal ultrasound," he informs us, pulling the wand device from a drawer and placing in onto the cart he moves beside the table. "You're too early to detect a heartbeat with a doppler, so we'll use this to see if we can hear your baby's heartbeat. Are you ready?"

"Yes," we both reply at the same time.

Dr. Ross uses the ultrasound machine first, squeezing a small amount of cool gel on my abdomen before placing the handheld wand onto my skin. "Just very slight pressure," he states, moving it around until he apparently finds what he's looking for. He turns the cart so the screen faces us and points. "See this little spot that looks like a bean? That, Reagan, is your baby."

It's hard to see because of the tears suddenly filling my eyes, but I feel it in my heart. That indescribable, all-consuming love. This is the moment I fall helplessly in love with a child I wasn't expecting, but immediately can't picture my life without.

Garreth bends down and rests his head against mine, his cheek pressed to mine. I feel wetness but realize it's not mine. It's his. He kisses my temple and squeezes my hand before turning and meeting my gaze. I see the same love and adoration I feel reflecting in his eyes, and I know in my heart, whatever happens between the two of us, this child will have the very best father I could give him. He will do anything for this child.

"I'll take a few shots of baby's first photoshoot and print them out for you. Sound good?"

I nod numbly and wait as he turns the monitor around. First, he prints out photos, and then begins to take measurements. The whole process takes a few minutes, so I just close my eyes and soak it up. I think about the baby I'm carrying and the man standing beside me. The only thing I know without a shadow of a doubt is I've fallen completely in love with them both.

"Everything looks great here," the doctor says, turning off the ultrasound machine and grabbing the wand. "Let's see if we can detect baby's heartbeat, shall we?"

The next part is a little uncomfortable, but it's quickly forgotten when the sweetest sound fills the room. It's fast and a little fuzzy, but I know it's the first sound of life for our baby and I'll never forget this moment as long as I live.

I look at Garreth and see him holding his phone, recording the heartbeat, the softest smile on his kissable lips.

"Everything looks and sounds good, guys," he says, removing the wand and helping me remove my feet from the stirrups. "Once we get the lab results, I'll call you and discuss what they say. In the meantime, keep taking the vitamins and eating iron-rich foods. I'm hoping we can raise your levels without adding another supplement, but if we do need to, that's okay. They won't hurt the baby."

"What does an iron deficiency mean for her pregnancy and the baby?" Garreth asks.

"Babies tend to have a lower birth weight, but are still perfectly healthy," Dr. Ross replies, giving us his full attention. "Any other questions?" When we don't come up with any, he adds, "Then we'll schedule you for your next appointment in four weeks, unless I feel we need to meet sooner based on your labs. Go ahead and get dressed and see Jessa at the front counter to schedule your next visit."

"Thank you, Dr. Ross," I state as Garreth reaches out his hand to shake the doctor's.

"Thank you, doctor."

He excuses himself, leaving us alone in the room. I quickly jump up to get my clothes back on, knowing Garreth is close by. He's perfectly respectable while I slip back on my clothes and doesn't turn around until I'm covered. When he does, I feel the heat of his gaze as he heads toward me and pulls me into his strong arms.

"Thank you," he whispers, his voice hoarse.

"For what?"

"For allowing me to be a part of this."

My eyebrows draw together. "Of course you'd be a part of this. This baby is yours too, Garreth, and as long as you want to be here, you're welcome every step of the way."

He gives me that sexy grin, the one I can't help but fall for every time I see it. "Good. I'm going to be so far up your ass you'll feel me there even when I'm not nearby."

Something dirty and hot sweeps through my veins, rendering me completely speechless, because now I can't stop thinking about him...there, and even though I've never been a fan of ass play, I suddenly want to strip off my clothes and let him have his wicked way with me.

He gently grabs my head and kisses me hard. "You're picturing it, aren't you." It's not a question. "Ass play later, babe. I've got to go to work," he says, slapping me on the ass and winking before he grabs my purse and pulls open the door.

I walk through the doorway on wooden legs and somehow make it to the front counter to schedule my next appointment. They also give me my lab order, which I decide to go ahead and do this afternoon when Garreth goes back to work. As much as I hate bloodwork, I want to get it over with sooner rather than later. Plus, that gives me a little time to relax before I go in at four.

Once everything is taken care of at the doctor's office, we head outside to our vehicles. We drove separately, knowing Garreth would have to go to work right away for the owners' meeting at two.

Garreth opens my car door and steps back for me to take a seat. "I'll see you in a couple of hours?" he asks, as if seeking confirmation.

"Yes."

He leans in and kisses my lips softly, and I can't help but savor the feel of his mouth against mine. Kissing him never gets old. There's nothing better.

"Drive safely," he says, stepping back and shutting the door.

He doesn't get into his truck yet, just watches me drive away. Happiness is all I feel right now, knowing our baby is doing well and my iron deficiency is manageable. In fact, since I started the prenatal vitamins I feel a lot better. I'm still nauseous from time to time and the exhaustion can be a real bitch, but I don't look nearly as pale when I see my reflection in the mirror.

All in all, things are starting to look up.

Now, I just have to figure out what to do about my job.

Garreth

I take a seat at the table, anxious to share my news with four of my closest friends. Jasper enters the bar with a tray of food and starts distributing plates. My stomach growls as soon as I catch a whiff of the amazing aroma, reminding me I missed lunch to attend Reagan's doctor's appointment.

"Who are we missing?" Jasper asks, glancing around the table. "Numbers. Where the hell is he? He's usually the first one down here."

"Sorry, sorry," Isaac says, hurrying into the bar from his upstairs office. "BJ called and I lost track of time." He takes the remaining seat and glances around. "What did I miss?"

"Nothing. We haven't started," Walker replies, taking a big bite of his sandwich.

"How's everything with Cameron?" Isaac asks, squeezing a big glob of ketchup on his plate.

"Going well. We haven't had any more issues, if that's what you're referring to," I reply.

"No, I know that, since I've been watching the reports closely. I mean emotionally. Is she doing okay?"

See? This is why I love these guys. They care about their employees as much as I do, even when said employee made some poor decisions that hurt their business. "Okay, I believe. She's in much better spirits lately, and I think a big part of that is because of the huge weight lifted off her shoulders."

He nods, running a fry through his ketchup. "And Reagan? How's she feeling?"

I sit up straight and clear my throat, recognizing the opening I need. "Actually, she's doing well. She worked all weekend, despite my insistence she take a few more days off and didn't have any problems."

"Garreth was a total helicopter parent the entire time. You should have seen him," Jasper announces, a smug smile on his face.

"How would you know? You were in the kitchen," I counter, narrowing my eyes at the cocky chef.

He, of course, just gives me a smug grin and pops a fry in his mouth.

I clear my throat a second time and decide to just go for it. "Actually, Reagan went to the doctor today for a follow-up."

"Everything okay?" Walker asks, taking another big bite.

"Everything's...perfect. We learned on Wednesday we're having a baby."

I'm met with silence and a few pairs of wide eyes.

"No shit?" Walker finally asks, swallowing hard as he tries to get his food down.

I nod and smile. "Yeah. Baby's due next year, around the tenth of May."

"Wow, man, congratulations," Numbers says, standing up and walking over. He throws his arms around my shoulders and gives me a hard slapping hug. "You're gonna rock the dad thing."

"Agreed," Walker adds, doing the same and giving me a one-armed hug.

After Jasper shakes my hand, I turn and look at Jameson. He has yet to say anything, and the blank look on his face gives nothing away. In fact, if I had to guess, I'd say he looks completely blasé to the whole announcement.

Then, he gets up, the scraping of his chair legs on the floor echoing through the bar as he walks my way. I straighten my spine, unsure of what to say, but I know I'll hold my position, despite what he says or does.

I think a part of me was expecting him to be pissed, since he's somewhat protective of Reagan, so when he grabs my shoulder and squeezes before pulling me into a hug, I'm slightly caught off guard. "I'm happy for you, man," he says when he slaps me on the back.

Hard.

He pulls back and meets my eye. "You're gonna make a great dad, Garreth, and even if you haven't said it yet, I know you love Reagan. Make sure you tell her, man. Don't be a dumbass like me and not say what needs to be said." He swallows hard before adding, "Besides, I really like you, so don't fuck it up with her. I'd hate to have to kill you."

I bark out a laugh, but when I see no indication he's joking, I sober a little and stop laughing. "I won't. I promise."

He nods and returns to his seat. "Let's get this meeting started. We have important shit to talk about."

It's a typical Friday night with the restaurant filling to capacity almost immediately after the five o'clock crowd gets off work. I spot Reagan seating another table of four and can't help but steal a few lingering glances at her amazing ass as she works. Fuck, I love her ass, even if she hasn't let me get too handsy there yet. The thought of touching her there, sliding my finger into her tight hole has me fighting a chubby within a matter of seconds.

"Wipe your chin off. You're drooling," Cameron sasses as she passes on her way to the server station.

"Smart aleck," I reply, just loud enough for her to hear.

She laughs, and I admit it's a great sound. She's young, pretty, and so full of life. To see that light in her dimmed because of a mistake she made with an ex has been tough, but watching that smile slowly return has been energizing for everyone she's near.

I bounce back and forth between the two sides of the business, but I can't help but notice how well everything flows tonight. Max is going great, his speed as a bartender and occasional server improving tenfold. He's on with Kallie tonight, and their flow seems to be going well.

Right as I go to spin around, I spot a familiar face at the far end of the bar. Smiling, I head in his direction. "Wasn't expecting to see you here on a Friday," I say to Leo, patting his back as I take the empty seat beside him.

He gives me a small grin, but it reflects what I would consider a long, stressful day. "Just got off work and needed a beer," he replies, sipping from a mug.

I nod. "Well, you came to the right place for a cold drink," I reply.

Leo's gaze flickers down the bar to where Kallie serves a drink before dropping back down to his napkin. "I can't stay too long. I'm dying for a shower, but was even more desperate for a beer," he says with a smile that actually reaches his eyes this time.

"We have that in spades. By the way, since you're here, I wanted you to hear something from me before the streets," I start.

"That pretty woman you've been seeing finally kicked you to the curb, huh? Does she need my number?" he asks with a teasing smirk on his face.

"Actually, quite the opposite. It seems she's pregnant with my child, and I'm hoping, will be hanging around for a while."

This time, Leo smiles. A real smile, one that reaches his dark eyes, making them shine a little brighter than normal, hiding the ghosts that usually haunt him. "Seriously? Congratulations, man. I know fatherhood is something you've always wanted."

I nod, unable to contain my own grin. "Thanks. It has been, and I feel like I finally have everything I've ever wanted within my reach, ya know?"

"I do, and no one deserves the wife, kids, and dog thing more than you." He holds up his glass in salute and adds, "You need another best man, I'm your guy. Though, don't get mad at me when the bride realizes she picked the wrong friend and runs off with me," he jokes, elbowing me in the stomach.

The haunted shadows I saw in his eyes are gone, and my easygoing friend is back. "You know, one of these days, you're gonna get a dose of your own medicine, and I'll be standing off to the side, pointing and laughing at your ass."

He smirks. "Whatever. I'll never be in the same boat as you," he professes, making me shake my head. "But in all seriousness, I'm really happy for you, man. She seems like a great girl. Now you just gotta put a ring on it."

I smile. "One step at a time, my friend," I state, slapping him on the shoulder and lightly squeezing. "Enjoy your beer, and let's get together soon and have one together."

"Deal." When he turns his attention back to his drink, I can't help but notice his eyes casually sweeping over to where Kallie is. She turns and flashes him a bright smile before making her way over to where he sits at the far end of the bar. I watch as she places her arms on the top and leans forward, Leo leaning in to hear whatever she has to say. I don't know what's going on there—if anything—but I think Kallie could be good for my friend.

The rest of the evening progresses quickly, as it tends to do when we're busy. I keep moving from restaurant to bar, but rarely do I have to actually step in. I visit with patrons and make sure their meals are good before moving to the next table and doing it all over again. By the time the restaurant is ready to shut down and the bar to start live music, I can use a few minutes of quiet.

I head toward my office, remembering I need to review next week's schedule before I post it. The moment I step inside, I close the door to cut off the noise and take a few minutes to breathe. Instantly, I think about Reagan and the baby and pull out my phone. I find the audio file I created and press play, letting the sound of her heartbeat fill my office. It's fast—so fucking fast it's almost scary—and sounds a little fuzzy, like the equipment is underwater. I play it twice before slipping the device back into my pocket and making my way to my desk.

A piece of paper catches my eye, mostly because I can already see her name on it. My eyes scan it once, then twice, trying to process what she's saying.

Dear Garreth and management team,

I am respectfully submitting my two-week resignation from Burgers and Brew. I appreciate the opportunity to work with such an incredible team. I've learned a lot in the last month and a half, and truly value the faith and trust placed in me during my time here. My last day will be two weeks from today, unless you don't need me before then.

Thank you for everything. I will always look back fondly on my time here.

Reagan Turner

What. The. Fuck?

I still can't process what the letter says. She's quitting? Why? Because of me?

I toss the paper on my desk, determined to find her and get to the bottom of this. I'm not letting her go. No way, no how. I head for the door, pulling it open with a little too much force. I turn to the right, walking through the busy bar and past the small stage where

Jameson is preparing to play, and into the restaurant. When I look to the front where the hostess stand is positioned, I stop dead in my tracks when I see her standing there with a guy.

No, not a guy.

With Justin.

Her fucking ex.

I move to the side and away from the large doorway where the sound of Jameson strumming his guitar pours through. I stay back, trying to not impose on their conversation, but staying close enough to intervene if needed.

"I don't understand. Why are you here?" Reagan asks, hands on hips as she waits.

"I heard, Reagan. About the baby."

"Okay," she says, the question evident in that single word.

"When were you going to tell me?" he asks.

She gives him a look, clearly not understanding him. "Why would I tell you?"

"Because! You think that's something you can just keep to yourself? Not tell the father of your baby?" he argues.

His words register and my blood runs cold. I take a step forward, prepared to lose my job for beating the shit out of him, but before I can grab the giant douche by his preppy polo shirt and toss him on his ass, Reagan starts laughing, causing me to stop in my tracks.

"Oh my God. You think this baby's yours?"

"Well, yeah. We just broke up. Who else's can it be?" he counters, as if he's never even considered the fact it might not actually be his baby.

"We broke up over a month and a half ago, but more importantly, we hadn't slept together for like six weeks before that. Probably because you were too tired from boinking your secretary," Reagan argues, pinning him with a glare that makes me proud. "This baby isn't yours, Justin."

He seems completely dumbfounded. "You cheated on me?"

She sighs loudly and rolls her eyes. "Of course I didn't. I met someone after we broke up, you big idiot." As if he's trying to do the math in his head, she adds, "Stop trying to find holes. It's not your baby."

I watch as he steps forward and places his hand on her arm. She flinches, jerking it back, but he doesn't seem to notice. "Listen, I don't care about what mistakes you might have made after we broke up. I've been doing some thinking, and I broke up with Tia. I think we should give it another shot."

"Another what?" she asks incredulously, and all I can do is stand here and watch it go down.

"You and me. What do you say?"

Her mouth drops open for a brief moment. "I'm dating someone. I'm having his baby," she replies a little slower this time.

I can't help but smile at her sassy insistence.

"Come on, Reagan. We were good together," he insists, trying to reach out and touch her cheek.

She swats his hand away. "If we were so good together, we'd still be together. You wouldn't have sent a stupid breakup text so you could bang your assistant. No, what you did was actually a blessing in disguise, because I met someone who makes me smile every day, who is amazing, and treats me better than I deserve. I'm having *his* baby, and I couldn't be prouder or happier. I'm sorry, but our ship has sailed. I've moved on. So should you."

My heart. Jesus Christ, I didn't think it was possible to love the woman any more, and then she goes and proves me wrong.

She spins around, ready to walk away from her ex, and stops when she faces me. Her smile starts small, but eventually takes over her entire face. She really is the most amazing woman I've ever known.

I walk toward her, completely ignoring the man still standing beside her. "You're wrong, you know."

"About what?" she asks, her eyebrows drawing together in question.

"You deserve to be treated like the gem you are, and if I have to spend the rest of my life doing so, I'm going to prove it to you."

She steps forward, invading my personal space. I catch a whiff of her intoxicating scent, the vanilla in her lotion and the hint of jasmine in her shampoo. "You don't have anything to prove to me, Garreth."

The urge to kiss her is so powerful, I almost give in, even though we're standing in the middle of the almost-empty restaurant, but then something hits me. "Wait. You can't quit. I won't let you."

She seems a little confused by my statement. "Why?"

"Because you're amazing at this job, and I realize I don't care about professionalism as much as I thought I did. Yes, I want to remain professional while I'm here, but I refuse to hide my feelings for you any longer. You're not some dirty little secret I only indulge in when we're alone. I want to kiss you and hold you, and I don't care where we're at or who sees. If those who work here can't respect the fact we're in a relationship, then fuck them. I won't hide you anymore."

She smiles. "I don't want to hide you either, but that's not the reason I'm quitting."

Now it's my turn to be confused. "It's not?" I ask, reaching for her hand and linking our fingers together.

Reagan shakes her head. "No. I was visiting with Jane Honeywell yesterday at Style on Main. I was gushing about some of the new merchandise she recently got in, which includes a new maternity section. She mentioned she was hoping to retire within the next year and is looking for someone who can take over the shop, possibly purchasing it when she's ready. I don't know why, but something inside me told me this was an amazing opportunity, and I'd be stupid not to consider it. We talked for another hour, and she offered me the job. I took it."

I can feel the excitement radiating off her, see it in her eyes. I know instantly this is the right move for her. "That's amazing, Reagan. I'm so happy for you."

She removes her hands from mine and places them on my chest. "Shantel is set to come back from her maternity leave next week, and you and I both know this job is hers. I'd never want to get in the way of that."

"I'd find another place for you," I counter, ready to fight to keep her here.

"I know you would, but you don't have to. Plus, I'll have a little more flexibility with my evenings now. We won't have to worry about you having to work on my nights off, and vice versa. I know I'll be working days now," she says, but I cut her off.

"But we'll make it work. If this is what you want to do, then I'm one-hundred-percent behind you. I just didn't want you to quit because of my hang-up about keeping our relationship on the down low here."

She shakes her head and curls her fingers into my shirt. "I'm not. This is what I want to do."

"Then by all means, do it, because I know you'll be great. And if you decide you want to be the person who buys it, I'll support that too."

Her hands slide up, her arms wrapping around my neck as she presses herself against me. "I knew you would. I never had a doubt."

My own arms wrap around her, holding her close. "That's because I love you. I'm sorry I haven't said it yet, because I do. I'm madly in love with you."

Her smile takes my breath away. "I love you too," she whispers right before she kisses me.

She might initiate the kiss, but I take complete control, sliding my tongue into her mouth and trying to show her just how much she means to me with a single kiss.

"'Bout damn time!"

Our private moment is interrupted, a not-so-subtle reminder that we're really not alone at all. We both turn and find Cameron, Jasper, and Angie standing there, all wearing matching, knowing grins.

"You're all fired," I tease, making them laugh.

Then, something else hits me. I glance behind us, expecting to still find Justin standing there, watching. "He left before the make-out session started," Jasper confirms.

"Yeah, I think he had no clue what to do at first. He just stood there and watched you two. Then, when he realized he wasn't going to get her back, he slithered out like the snake he is," Cameron adds.

I turn back to the woman I love. "That's right. He's not getting her back. She's mine."

Reagan beams up at me, a smile so bright you could see it from space. "All yours," she confirms, sliding her hands into my hair.

"Damn right, love. You, me, and our baby girl."

She gives me a look. "You don't know it's a girl."

"I do. Just you wait."

Reagan

3 months later

"Do you think we need more twinkle lights?" I ask, holding the last box of Christmas lights in my hand and gazing up at the big tree. This thing is huge, spanning from floor to ceiling in front of Garreth's living room picture window.

"I think if you add any more, it'll be considered a fire hazard," he quips, leaning against the doorjamb between the kitchen and the living room.

I can't help but roll my eyes. "I want it to be perfect," I insist, gazing back up at the huge tree.

I hear his footfalls on the hardwood floor and know he's heading my way. "It's perfect because you're here. Speaking of that, I wanted to talk to you about something," he says, taking my hand and leading me over to the couch.

He crouches down in front of me, still holding my hands in his. "I've been thinking, you've been talking a lot these last few days about starting to prep a nursery. What if you move in here with me, and we do it together here? You already sleep in my bed. The best part of my day is waking up and falling asleep with you in my arms.

So, what's it gonna take to make it official and you live with me permanently?"

I can't help but smile. "Well, I don't think it would take much at all, actually. I rather enjoy waking up and falling asleep in your arms," I reply, repeating his words.

"Perfect. What do you say we move all your things here after Christmas? I have some vacation time built up, I can take a few days off, maybe enlist Leo or Jameson to help. I'd drop everything and do it right now, but this next week leading up to the twenty-fifth is swamped with parties and gatherings. I think Numbers would kill me if I requested a few days off right now."

I cup his scruffy jaw with my palm. "After Christmas is perfect. While you're at work, I can pack up what I'm bringing here and figure out what I'm donating."

"Okay. Just don't do any lifting. My baby mama doesn't need to lift a finger right now," he informs me, running his hands down the very slight swell of my stomach.

I officially hit four months last week, and it seems like my belly just sort of popped out overnight. Garreth has always been obsessed with touching me, but even more so now that he can see the baby growing.

"Your baby mama is perfectly capable of lifting a few things within reason."

He tsks. "But there is no reason. I will do it for you. That's my job. And your job is to keep growing our daughter."

"No one's said it's a girl," I remind him.

He's insisted the baby's a girl since the moment we found out I was pregnant, and even though I don't care either way, I secretly get a thrill out of him referring to the baby as a she. There's so much cute stuff at the boutique for a baby girl, there's no doubt I'd spend every last penny I have shopping for her.

"I know," he reminds me, kissing my nose. "We're gonna go to that ultrasound appointment on Thursday and just confirm it."

I shake my head, his lips sliding easily against mine. "You're unbelievable."

He flashes me that cocky smile. "Thank you."

I can't help but snicker. "That wasn't a compliment."

"Says you," he replies before kissing me soundly.

"Reagan," the nurse calls from the doorway.

Garreth and I both rise, his hand wrapped firmly around mine, as we follow behind. This time, we don't stop for a weight check or urine sample. We bypass all of the usual appointment stuff and walk to the end of the hall to the last room. The sign on the door reads Ultrasound.

"No need to get undressed this time," the nurse says, pointing to the table. "Have a seat." We go through a few questions before she rises. "Marta is our ultrasound tech. She'll be in shortly to get started."

I sigh anxiously and look around, trying to keep myself from going crazy. I barely slept last night in anticipation of today's appointment. It was all I could do to keep myself from checking the clock every thirty seconds throughout the day at work. When it was finally time to leave, my part-timer, Hope, was ready to kick me out for being so distracted.

"Ten bucks says it's a girl," Garreth challenges, breaking through my inner thoughts.

"I'm not taking that bet," I counter, crossing my arms over my chest and narrowing my gaze.

"Because you know I'm right."

"Because I don't care either way. I just want to see a healthy baby with ten fingers and ten toes on that screen. The sex doesn't matter," I reply.

He humphs and comes my way. He places both hands on the table where I sit and lowers his face to mine. "You know I don't care either way, right?" He places a gentle kiss on my lips. "I just happen to know it's a girl," he adds with a wink.

A bubble of laughter flies from my mouth as a knock sounds at the door.

"Good afternoon, Reagan. I'm Marta, the ultrasound technician. I'll be conducting your scan today. Is this the baby's father?"

"Yes, this is Garreth."

"Nice to meet you, Garreth," Marta greets, extending her hand to shake. "Are you ready to get started?"

"I am," I confirm, lying back on the table.

Marta pulls out the extension for my legs and prepares the ultrasound machine. She squirts a glob of warm goo onto my abdomen and places the handheld wand against my skin. "I'm going to take some measurements," she states as the image of our baby fills the screen. "Oh. Wow."

"What?" I ask, trying to figure out what she's looking at.

She clicks around on the keypad as she asks, "Do you want to know the sex of your baby or is this a secret?"

I glance at Garreth, who's standing right beside me, his eyes riveted to the monitor. He looks my way and smiles in confirmation. "We want to know," I tell her, my heart trying to pound out of my chest.

"Well, it was very easy to tell. She flashed me the moment I brought her up on the screen," Marta replies with a chuckle.

"She?" I whisper, my voice hoarse with the sudden onset of emotion.

"Oh, yes. Look," she says, pointing to the screen. "This is most definitely a little girl. She wasn't shy at all."

I turn to look at Garreth, my eyes filled with tears. "A girl."

He's smiling so beautifully, so proudly, it brings a fresh wave of emotion to the surface, and the tears fall in earnest now. "We have a daughter," he whispers, his words filled with awe. "I knew it. She's just like her mother. Flashing her stuff at me."

"I do not do that," I argue, feeling happier and lighter than I have all day.

"Maybe you should," he counters quietly, waggling his eyebrows suggestively.

A clip of laughter flies from my lips. "You're going to be impossible to live with now."

He gives me that cocky smirk I love. "You bet your sweet ass I will be. Now, shhh. Let's watch and enjoy the show."

And we do. For the next several minutes, we watch as the technician measures every part of our baby girl, printing off images along the way for keepsakes.

When she's wrapping up, she says, "Everything looks great. Your baby is measuring right on track, and I don't see anything of concern." She hands over a strip of four ultrasound photos.

"Thank you," I reply, wiping away the last of my tears and giving her a grateful grin.

"You're most welcome. I'll share my report with Dr. Ross. Have a wonderful rest of your Thursday," she says before exiting the small room.

I finish wiping off the gel from my abdomen and hop off the table. The moment my feet hit the floor, I'm wrapped in strong arms and pulled against my favorite chest in the world.

"A daughter," he mutters for a second time, as if seeing how those words sound on his lips. "If she's anything like you, I'm going to have my hands full."

"You're going to have your hands full regardless. Her dad is pretty ornery."

He kisses the side of my neck and hugs me tightly. "Damn right he is."

"He's also pretty incredible."

"Only because I have a pretty incredible woman at my side," he states, placing one last kiss on my neck before releasing me and taking my hand. "Ready to go show off our daughter?" he asks, holding up the ultrasound photos.

I think about our parents, my grandma, and my cousin, who's ready to have her own baby any day now. The guys at the restaurant and their wives. A few former co-workers, like Cameron, who I still talk to regularly. All the people in my life I can't wait to share this exciting news with. In one way or another, they've been with me every step of the way through this journey.

Then I look at Garreth. The shameless flirt who slipped past my protective wall and showed me how easy it is to fall deeply in love when you've found the right person. The man who convinced me to take a chance on him and has proven to me daily it was the best decision I've ever made.

He is, without a doubt, the best man I've ever known, and I'm honored to share this journey with him. Who knows, maybe there'll be more to us in the future, but all I know is I'm happy and content with how it's going so far.

Garreth once said this is our story. We get to tell it.

So that's my plan. To live our life and tell our story.

Together.

Garreth

3 months later

She's miserable. I can tell, even though she tries to hide it.

The last two weeks have been rough on her. Her ankles are swelling, which means she needs to sit for longer periods of time while she's working. She hates that. Reagan is a busy person, always moving, and being forced to sit and put her feet up, all while watching someone else do the work she's supposed to do, has been a challenge.

She's also more exhausted now than she was in the beginning. Her sleep is interrupted by frequent bathroom trips, and she has heartburn at least once a day. Not to mention, her anemia came back last month, and she had to be put on an iron supplement through the end of the pregnancy. She has seven weeks to go, and I think she's starting to doubt she's going to make it.

But she will.

My girl is strong. She's a fighter. She'll endure whatever she has to for the sake of our child.

Why?

Because she's simply the best person I've ever met, and I'm so fucking lucky to have her in my life.

It's that exact sentiment that's gotten my mind working overtime these last few weeks. There's something I want to do—specifically, something I want to ask—but there never seems to be a good time. My schedule. Her schedule. The nesting phase she went through, in which she cleaned and recleaned the entire house at least three times a week. If you interrupted, she'd start all over. Not to mention rearranging the furniture—with the help of Jameson—and reorganizing the kitchen cabinets because they just don't flow right.

And through all the crazy mood swings and cravings, she's still the most beautiful woman in the world.

We finally have a day off together. I've been planning it for two weeks now, enlisting the help of Leo and the guys at the restaurant to cover for me. We're driving out to Leo's family campsite, a place that will always remind me of her, even though we haven't been back since our first official date all those months ago.

"Are we going camping?" she asks when I turn down the private lane to go back to the site. She flashes me a smile, but I can tell she's a little concerned. It's not exactly camping weather for the third week of March.

"Not camping, my love," I reply, stopping the truck so the windshield is facing the wide, open space. "Date night."

"Is the water on in the bathroom? I have to pee," she grumbles, releasing her seat belt and getting out of the truck before I can answer.

I move quickly, jumping out and making my way toward her. "The water's on," I confirm, taking her hand in mine.

"Good, because if it wasn't, you'd have to hold me up while I pee in the woods. There's no way I'd be able to hover behind a log with my belly this big. I'd tip over and never get up," she says, pushing her way into the bathroom and closing the door in my face.

I can't help but laugh.

"Don't laugh at me!" she hollers from the opposite side of the door.

"Not at you, my love. I promise."

She mutters something I can't quite hear, which is probably for the best. Everything I do seems to irritate her more now than ever before, and don't get me started on the meltdown that ensued after I left my wet bath towel on the floor in front of the hamper. I thought for sure that was it for me. She was going to kill me and bury me in the backyard. My only solace was the fact she was in no condition to dig a hole, considering she can't even walk to the kitchen without getting winded.

The door flies open, and she pins me with an annoyed look. "I almost got stuck on the toilet."

"You're in the home stretch," I remind her.

"So you keep saying," she argues, taking my offered hand and walking with me toward the already-lit fire—thanks, Leo. "I'm pretty sure I'm going to be pregnant until the end of time."

"Just a handful of weeks more. You got this," I state, leading her to the padded chair already sitting near the warmth. I knew getting down and up from the log would be a challenge, so I figured I'd make her relaxation a little more comfortable.

She sighs deeply and slowly drops into the chair, kicking her feet up on the stump I placed in front of her. "You're too good to me," she says, meeting my gaze as I sit beside her. "I know I'm all crazy with these hormones right now, and you're probably wondering what in the hell you got yourself into."

This is my opening...

"Actually," I state, turning my body just enough so we're angled toward each other, "I think it's the exact opposite. I keep wondering what in the hell am I waiting for."

Her eyebrows pull together in confusion. "What do you mean?"

With her hand tucked inside of mine, I say the one question I've been dying to ask. "What's it gonna take for you to marry me?"

She holds my gaze and replies, "A ring."

I reach into my pocket and pull out the one piece of jewelry I've been hiding in my shaving kit, too afraid to leave it in my original hiding place of my sock drawer. The way this woman has been cleaning and organizing, I was certain she'd find it within two days.

Holding up the ring, I ask, "Like this one?"

She gives me a watery grin and nods. "That one would work just fine."

"Good," I say, glancing down at the single solitaire diamond in the middle of the band. "This one was my grandmother's on my mom's side. She made my mom promise it wouldn't just sit in a jewelry box forever, collecting dust. She always said this ring was made for love and deserved to be worn. I never forgot that, so when I knew I wanted to spend the rest of my life with you, I asked my mom if I could have it. She readily agreed."

I look over and find Reagan crying.

"Why are you crying, my love?" I ask, fighting a grin, as I wipe tears off her cheeks.

She inhales hard and sniffles. "Because that was the sweetest thing I've ever heard."

This time, I do smile as I get off my seat and drop to one knee in front of her. "Reagan, I think I've loved you since the first time I laid eyes on you, and every day I discover another reason why I fall even harder. You're my purpose for being put on this earth. To love and care for you for the rest of my life. I'll never love another the way I love you, because you're the other half of my soul. All I want is to love you and be with you forever. Will you marry me?"

She nods, her whimpers turning into wails. "Y-yes," she mutters.

I slip the ring onto her shaky finger and bring it to my lips. I kiss her knuckles, the ring, and finally move to her lips. When I've kissed her soundly, I pull back and say, "I don't want to wait. I want to marry you as soon as you'll let me."

She wipes away the tears on her cheeks with her coat sleeves and gives me a grin. "I want that too. I didn't even realize it until now, but I want us all to have the same last name on our daughter's birth certificate."

"A wedding in under seven weeks? Done."

Reagan

1 month later

"Ready?" Madelyn asks, grinning at me as she passes me a small bouquet of lavender and lilac flowers.

"Definitely. Let's hurry up, though, or I might have to pee again before I make it down the hall." If only I was joking. This baby has been using my bladder like a bongo drum all evening.

"Let's go. The groom is waiting."

I follow my cousin out of the break room and down the hall where my dad is waiting, ignoring the slight ache in my lower back. He smiles widely and fights to keep the tears I see in his eyes at bay. "Wow," he says, taking my hands and bringing me in for a hug. "You look stunning."

"Well, I don't know about that," I counter, referring to the fact I'm thirty-seven weeks pregnant and wearing a dress that barely contains my stomach.

"I do" he insists, kissing my cheek. "And I know another man who will think the same. He's anxiously waiting for his bride."

I can't help but grin. "So he didn't run off?" I quip.

"Are you kidding? He's been standing in his spot for the last fifteen minutes, waiting for you." His words bring more tears to my eyes. "What do you say we put him out of his misery and walk you down the aisle?"

I nod eagerly. "Yes, please."

Dad extends his arm, and the moment I place my hand in the crook of his, he slowly leads me toward the bar.

I never pictured myself getting married in a bar, but there's no place else I'd rather this moment take place. This is where we met, where our friendship turned to more, where our love grew and bloomed, even if we didn't know it at the time. Plus, it's sort of a tradition to get married here. All four of the owners said "I do" in this very location, and it just seems fitting for us to follow suit.

Jameson begins to play "The Wedding March" on his guitar, signifying it's time. Madelyn walks out first in a dusty blue dress. The skirt hits just below her knee and the neckline shows modest cleavage. Of course, since she gave birth to her daughter, Rose, Madelyn's having a hard time containing the girls. They seem to have their own zip code at this point.

When she's around the corner, I know it's my turn. "Ready?" Dad asks, giving me a look of both wonder and sadness.

"I'm ready," I confirm, and together, we take the first steps toward my forever.

The moment I see Garreth is one I'll never forget. He's standing on the small stage, rocking back and forth, but as soon as he sees me, he stops moving completely and just stares at me. His jaw drops and his eyes roam my off-white dress from head to toe, as he watches me walk toward him.

When I reach his side, my dad kisses me on the cheek and steps back, holding out my arm for my groom to take. He does eagerly, guiding me to our position on the stage.

"Dearly beloved," the minister starts.

My eyes dart to the man I'm marrying. He's watching me intently, the softest smile on his full lips. "You look beautiful," he whispers when I'm trying to pay attention to what the minister is saying.

Smiling, I murmur, "It's the belly. They're all the rage these days."

He leans in, his warm breath tickling my ear. "Don't I know it. I'm going to strip this dress off you later and make love to my wife."

My eyes are wide with shock, praying to God and anyone else who's listening that our minister did *not* just hear what he said.

"Repeat after me…"

I can't take my eyes off him as he says his vows before a small group of family and friends. When it's my turn, I do as instructed, stating each line slowly and confidently. We exchange rings and seal our union with a kiss to a resounding cheer of applause.

"I love you, Mrs. Taylor."

Smiling, I whisper, "And I love you, Mr. Taylor."

He grins from ear to ear as he replies, "I'll never get tired of hearing you say that."

Taking my hand, he leads me down the short aisle, past our friends and family who gathered with us tonight for the ceremony. Jasper excuses himself to add the finishing touches to the meal, and Lyndee goes over to make sure the cake is picture-perfect.

Leo walks over and pulls me into a hug. "Congratulations, guys. I mean, you did okay with this guy, even though you could have had better," he teases, trying to get a rise out of his friend.

Garreth doesn't take the bait though. Instead, he pulls me into his arms and kisses me once again. "I heard there's a hotel room with our name on it across town." He waggles his eyebrows suggestively.

"What do you say we cancel that reservation and make a stop by the hospital instead?"

It takes a few seconds before my words register. "What?" he asks, looking down in a panic.

"I'm pretty sure my water just broke," I confirm, glancing down and seeing wetness marking the front of my wedding dress.

"Holy shit!" Garreth bellows, turning around in a panic. "It's baby time."

Everything happens fast from that point. I'm ushered out of the bar and into a car. The slight ache I've felt off and on throughout the day starts to hit me harder and harder as the minutes wear on.

As we race to the hospital to deliver our baby, I can't help but look over at the man I love and appreciate everything life has given me. Even the bumps in the road because those blows led me to this moment.

They led me to him.

The one squeezing my hand as he drives way over the speed limit in a race to get me to the hospital as quickly as possible.

Life isn't always easy, but it's one beautiful ride.

This is our love story.

And I'll do whatever it takes to tell it.

Another Epilogue

Leo

The room is a buzz over the latest development. One minute we're celebrating a marriage, and the next the groom is rushing the bride out the door to deliver their baby.

Talk about a crazy story.

I make my way over to the far end of the bar, away from everyone, and take a few minutes to soak up the quiet. No, it's not exactly quiet over here, but at least I'm not in the direct line of fire in the barrage of questions being asked across the room.

How long before we hear anything?

What do you think they'll name her?

Leo, how's your mom doing?

Do they think they'll be able to shrink the tumor this time?

"What can I get you?"

Finally, a question I want to answer.

"Night Crüe draft, please," I reply.

The pretty bartender gives me a smile, one that seems to make my heart skip a beat or two. I watch as she heads over to pour my drink, bringing the full glass over and placing it in front of me. "How much?" I ask, reaching for my wallet in my back pocket.

"Bar bill is being taken care of tonight," she says.

I fish a ten out of my wallet anyway and slide it across the hardwood. "Consider this a tip then."

She grins and takes the ten-dollar bill, tapping it against the bar top and holding my gaze. "Thank you. My name's Kallie, by the way," she says, holding out her hand.

The moment my rough, larger hand wraps around hers, I feel a jolt of electricity sweeping through my veins. "Leo."

"Nice to officially meet you, Leo," she replies, holding my gaze much longer than normal. In fact, it suddenly feels like we're the only two left in the room.

"Likewise, Kallie."

After a few long seconds, I finally release her hand and grab my beer instead. It's not nearly as satisfying, but it'll have to do. "If you need anything else, just holler," she states before slowly turning and heading down to the opposite end of the bar. Halfway there, she pauses and glances over her shoulder, her blue eyes locked on mine and rendering me completely speechless.

I bring my beer to my lips and take a long drink, trying to flush the image of those blue eyes from my mind.

Kallie.

A temptation for sure.

One I don't need.

That doesn't stop me from spending the rest of the night watching her, wishing things in my life were different. Wishing I could ask for her number. Wishing I could flirt and see where the night leads.

Wishing I wasn't fucked up in the head, drowning in my own thoughts.

In the memories that haunt me.

For the first time in a long damn time, I'm picturing a happier me, wishing things could be different.

Wishing they were but knowing they can't.

Because that is my life.

All the ugly and the broken.

The End

Want more Burgers and Brew Crüe? Book 6 will feature Leo and Kallie and will release January 10, 2023! Preorder Home Sweet Home today!

Don't miss a single reveal, release, or sale! Sign up for my newsletter.
http://www.laceyblackbooks.com/newsletter

Books by Lacey Black

Rivers Edge series
Trust Me, Rivers Edge book 1 (Maddox and Avery) – FREE at all retailers
  ~ #1 Bestseller in Contemporary Romance
Fight Me, Rivers Edge book 2 (Jake and Erin)
Expect Me, Rivers Edge book 3 (Travis and Josselyn)
Promise Me: A Novella, Rivers Edge book 3.5 (Jase and Holly)
Protect Me, Rivers Edge book 4 (Nate and Lia)
Boss Me, Rivers Edge book 5 (Will and Carmen)
Trust Us: A Rivers Edge Christmas Novella (Maddox and Avery)
  ~ This novella was originally part of the Christmas Miracles Anthology
BOX SET – contains all 5 novels, 2 novellas, and a BONUS short story
With Me, A Rivers Edge Christmas Novella (Brooklyn and Becker)

Bound Together series
Submerged, Bound Together book 1 (Blake and Carly)
  ~ An International Bestseller
Profited, Bound Together book 2 (Reid and Dani)
  ~A Bestseller, reaching Top 100 on 2 e-retailers
Entwined, Bound Together book 3 (Luke and Sidney)

Summer Sisters series
My Kinda Kisses, Summer Sisters book 1 (Jaime and Ryan)
   ~A Bestseller, reaching Top 100 on 2 e-retailers
My Kinda Night, Summer Sisters book 2 (Payton and Dean)
My Kinda Song, Summer Sisters book 3 (Abby and Levi)
My Kinda Mess, Summer Sisters book 4 (Lexi and Linkin)
My Kinda Player, Summer Sisters book 5 (AJ and Sawyer)
My Kinda Player, Summer Sisters book 6 (Meghan and Nick)
My Kinda Wedding, A Summer Sisters Novella book 7 (Meghan and Nick)

Rockland Falls series
Love and Pancakes, Rockland Falls book 1
Love and Lingerie, Rockland Falls book 2
Love and Landscape, Rockland Falls book 3
Love and Neckties, Rockland Falls book 4

Standalone
Music Notes, a sexy contemporary romance standalone
A Place To Call Home, a Memorial Day novella
Exes and Ho Ho Ho's, a sexy contemporary romance standalone novella
Pants on Fire, a sexy contemporary romance standalone
Double Dog Dare You, a new standalone
Grip, A Driven World Novel
Bachelor Swap, A Bachelor Tower Series Novel
Perfect Kiss, Mason Creek Series book 9
Waiting For Love, The Love Vixen Series book 11

Burgers and Brew Crüe Series
Kickstart My Heart
Don't Go Away Mad

Same Ol' Situation
Wild Side
What's It Gonna Take

Co-Written with *NYT Bestselling* Author, Kaylee Ryan
It's Not Over, Fair Lakes book 1
Just Getting Started, Fair Lakes book 2
Can't Get Enough, Fair Lakes book 3
Fair Lakes Box Set
Boy Trouble
Home To You, a second chance novella
Beneath the Fallen Stars
Royal – Writing as Rebel Shaw

Lacey Black

Acknowledgments

When I finished Wild Side, I thought I was done. I had only planned for four books in this series, but after I sent it off to my editor and first proofreader, both felt there was more to tell. The seed was planted, and more book ideas grew. I have books six and seven in the works, and how many come after that, I don't know. I guess I'll know when the series is complete, right? So until that day, enjoy the Crüe.

My editing team – Kara Hildebrand, Sandra Shipman, Joanne Thompson, and Karen Hrdlicka. Thank you for all you do. I truly have the best of the best working on my books!!

The book team - Photographer, Wander Aguiar; Model, James Clippinger; Cover Designer, Melissa Gill; Graphics Designer, Gel with Tempting Illustrations; Formatting, Brenda with Formatting Done Wright; and Promotions by Give Me Books. Thank you for your professionalism and sharing your talent. You're all a dream to work with!!

Kaylee Ryan, Holly Collins, Lacey's Ladies, Chasidy Renee, and my ARC team, thank you for listening, for your encouragements, and for your constant support.

To my husband and kids, thank you for always standing by my side and forgiving me when I submerge myself into my book world. It's not easy, but we make it work together.

To all the bloggers and readers, thank you, thank you, thank you. I hope you enjoy this story as much as I loved writing it.

About the Author

USA Today Bestselling Author Lacey Black is a Midwestern girl with a passion for reading, writing, and shopping. She carries her e-reader with her everywhere she goes so she never misses an opportunity to read a few pages. Always looking for a happily ever after, Lacey is passionate about contemporary romance novels and enjoys it further when you mix in a little suspense. She resides in a small town in Illinois with her husband, two children, crazy cat, and three rowdy chickens.

Website: www.laceyblackbooks.com
Email: laceyblackwrites@gmail.com
Facebook: https://www.facebook.com/authorlaceyblack
Instagram: https://www.instagram.com/laceyblackwrites/
Bookbub: https://www.bookbub.com/authors/lacey-black
Amazon: https://www.amazon.com/Lacey-Black/e/B00MW2UGZI
Twitter: https://twitter.com/AuthLaceyBlack
Goodreads:
https://www.goodreads.com/author/show/8414783.Lacey_Black

Sign up for my newsletter so you don't miss a single sale, reveal, or release!
http://www.laceyblackbooks.com/newsletter

www.ingramcontent.com/pod-product-compliance
Lightning Source LLC
Chambersburg PA
CBHW060624260626
47161CB00008B/2795